Amanda Smyth is Irish-Trinida
Her first novel, *Black Rock* (Serpe
Roman Etranger 2010, and was se
in 2009. It was also chosen for Oprah's Summer Reads for 2009.
Amanda was awarded an Arts Council grant for *A Kind of Eden*. She
lives in Warwickshire with her husband and daughter.

Praise for *Black Rock*

'Amanda Smyth writes like a descendant of Jean Rhys. *Black Rock*
is a powerful cocktail of heat and beautiful coolness, written in a
heady, mesmerising yet translucent prose which marks Smyth out
as a born novelist' Ali Smith

'On the very first page the quality of the writing grabbed me, and
I spent the whole day reading it with the greatest pleasure. A novel
really does have to be the real thing to do that to me, and this is'
Diana Athill

'Her writing is as lushly beautiful as the landscape she describes—
it's the kind of novel that leaves your head filled with gorgeous
pictures' Kate Saunders, *The Times*

'Set in the intense heat and vibrant lushness of the Caribbean, this
compelling novel tells the story of Celia, an orphan with a prophecy
hanging over her . . . it sings with life, texture and verve' Victoria
Moore, *Daily Mail*

'There are hints of Jean Rhys's *Wide Sargasso Sea* throughout Smyth's
hypnotic, eerie novel . . . Smyth writes entrancingly on tropical heat
and light, indolence, vengeance and desire' Catherine Taylor, *Guardian*

'Certain novels are alive with colour. Written in lush, lyrical language evocative of its tropical setting . . . Smyth's debut is an absorbing and morally complex read with a bittersweet twist at the end' Melissa McClements, *Financial Times*

'In painterly images, Smyth evocatively shows more than she tells . . . There are echoes of the archetypal "mad woman", if not in an attic then in a marital room in the Caribbean . . . a vivid and compelling story, exploring the extent of our control over our destinies' Anita Sethi, *Independent*

'A damaged but irresistible heroine . . . Smyth's story is a powerful, authentic one and Celia is an appealing, earthy, yet spiritual heroine who grows, wounded and embattled, through the course of the book' Lesley McDowell, *Independent on Sunday*

'A captivating read' Aisling Foster, *Irish Times*

'This beautifully assured debut is rich with the sumptuous vistas, poetry and spirit of the Caribbean . . . Clashes of culture, temperament, loyalty and love jostle together, with the dramatic events and quandaries woven together with lyricism, tenderness and sensuality' *Easy Living*

'A lovely piece of storytelling' *Waterstone's Books Quarterly*

'A gripping story that transports you to rich, tropical climes . . . An impressive debut' Holly Kyte, *Sunday Telegraph*

A KIND OF EDEN

AMANDA SMYTH

A complete catalogue record for this book can
be obtained from the British Library on request

First published in 2013 by Serpent's Tail,
an imprint of Profile Books Ltd
3A Exmouth House
Pine Street
London ECIR OJH
website: www.serpentstail.com

ISBN 978 1 84668 813 3
eISBN 978 1 84765 804 3

Designed and typeset by Crow Books
Printed by Clays, Bungay, Suffolk

10 9 8 7 6 5 4 3 2 1

FOR MY MOTHER

Acknowledgements

Special thanks to: The Arts Council, Jill and Rupert Atkinson, Chris Cracknell, Ruth Petrie, Anna-Marie Fitzgerald and all the team at Serpent's Tail.

And to my sharp-eyed readers: Sharon Millar, Mez Packer, Andrew Palmer, Monique Roffey, Paul Smyth, Lee Thomas, Tindal Street Fiction Group.

Thank you Saskia Sutton for giving me a room to write in, and Mez and Orv for allowing me to camp out in their living room.

Thank you, Barrie Fernandez, for always encouraging me.

I am very grateful to my editor, Rebecca Gray, for her insight and clarity. And Lucy Luck, my agent, for her brilliant, tireless support and commitment.

Thank you, Wayne Brown, always.

Huge thanks to my mother for travelling the Atlantic three times in one year to take care of our daughter.

And finally, enormous thanks to my husband, Lee Thomas, for being there through it all. You're the best. Thank you.

ONE

They say it gets chilly here around December, almost like spring in England or in Canada. Although the days are hot, most evenings, right up until the end of February, it is cool enough to leave your butter out. Today he'd realised that wasn't true, and he told her as soon as she had arrived, presenting her with the oily glass butter dish which she always complained about. Look, his butter has melted. So what do you want, she said. A medal? At which point he didn't know whether to laugh or take offence. Then she tossed her handbag on the chair and kicked off her sandals—the flat tan girlish sandals she wore for work—and he knew she was okay; they would probably sleep together tonight.

Later, he looks up at the wooden rafters; there is just enough light from the passageway to see the shadows they make. Once, not long after they first met and they were lying naked, a cockroach fell and landed big and hard like a boiled egg. He shouted something, sprang from the bed and it scuttled over the sheet. Safiya laughed, and flipped up the sheet. Kill it, he said, kill it. But she lay there laughing, tears streaming down her cheeks. 'You're so English,' she said, when she found him sitting at the kitchen table. 'I had no idea I was going out with such a limey.'

He clicks on the small bedside lamp; she turns, and in one movement, tugs the sheet and rolls onto her side. He stares at the triangle of her brown back and the mess of her black hair on the pillow, the neck exposed. Her skin is shining and he knows she must be hot. She has never liked the air conditioner so when she stays he turns it off. But tonight he has forgotten to open the louvers, and the air is thick from their lovemaking. The last three weekends they had made sure to visit his favourite beach at Blanchisseuse. Although they kept in the shade of the trees and close to the rocks for most of the afternoon, they both came away burned. Now her skin is tanned to a delicious shade of tea. She pulls up her arm; her fingers curl against her full soft lips. When they first got together and he admired her lips, she told him, 'Yes, I have a *rude* mouth.' The gap between the nose and upper lip is short and it makes her look younger than she is. She looks quite different when her narrow, hooded eyes are shut.

A dog is barking now. It happens almost every night at this time. A gang of dogs gathers on the crossroads and when someone walks by they start and set one another off. He's been caught a few times, thinking the road is clear, walking down to Hi Lo grocery or Ali's pharmacy, and next thing they are rushing at him in a little pack. He is nervous of them: there is rabies here and a dog like that, the vicious little black one with slitty eyes like a pit bull, could rip your face right off. Some time ago, he saw a young man on the news lying in the street in a puddle of dark blood, his eye torn from its socket. 'How can they show these things on television?' he'd said to her. 'What about the man's privacy, his family?' 'Get used to it,' she said. 'This is Trinidad.'

* * *

It must be getting late. He wonders where they might eat tonight. Last week, he picked her up from outside her mother's house in Woodbrook and he didn't say where they were going. From her damp hair and sweet, soapy scent, he could tell that she was freshly bathed. On the radio, Supertramp's 'Logical Song' made him think of his youth, and he cruised steadily along the west coast feeling, for no apparent reason, lighter than he'd felt in days; feeling as if he'd had good news, which he hadn't. In many ways things couldn't have been much worse.

They passed the shopping complex with its Showcase cinema—he had seen two films there, *Shrek*, and *War of the Worlds*—and her favourite Ruby Tuesdays restaurant, which, despite her protestations, he had never liked. Not just the décor—the American old-fashioned posters and traditional wallpaper, but the food: he was certain they used additives in the strong sauces—barbeque, honey glaze, garlic cream, Thousand Island—and they made his head feel peculiar. 'It's all flavour-enhanced,' he'd said that last time, 'like fake food. No wonder it's tasty. It could only come from America.' When he told her this, she rolled her eyes and said he was getting old and miserable; you shouldn't have to worry about stuff like that at her age. 'There's nothing wrong with America,' she said. 'New York is a lot of fun. And nothing beats the shopping in Miami.' At one time, he might have mentioned a string of shops in London: Harvey Nichols, Harrods, the whole of the Kings Road, but he knew it wouldn't go down well.

After West Mall and the new Spanish-style condominiums, he slowed down. This was a wealthier part of town: you could look up at the soft dark hills and see the middle-class houses perched there, the glow of yellow lights. He had imagined everyone at home, taking a drink on the porch, getting ready for dinner, the evening news coming on; people with lives and aspirations. But then the road became narrow, dark, the houses more ramshackle and patched up. And as they drove through the shabby village before Chaguaramas, the village where only last week a man was shot twice in the back of his head while alone watching television in his living room, he wondered what Safiya was thinking about.

'Penny,' he said. She looked at him and he saw that she was sad. He pulled up at the far end of the car park. There weren't many people here, and he was glad. It was better that way; she wouldn't be in the mood to see anyone they knew. She was wearing a purple blouse, and dark tight jeans that he'd bought for her in Long Circular Mall. He liked that she dressed up like this when they went out. And he liked when she tied back her hair, wrapped it about her fingers and twisted it into a knot; it was like watching a magic trick. He took her hand, and she didn't resist as she sometimes did, and they walked slowly and without speaking down towards the seafood restaurant where little white lights hung along the wooden balcony of the upper level.

To the right, the water was black and silky. It was night, and yet patches of blue sky were still out there towards the horizon; stars punctured the dark world above them, and he wondered if the curved line he was looking at was actually the Plough. And then there was a white curl of moon. 'The moon's like a scythe,' he said, pointing, and he felt pleased that he'd thought of this. And he recognised how romantic this moment was, and

how unlike him, or at least the him that he was used to and had
known for forty-nine years.

They were shown to a table by the waterside, and from
there they looked out at the anchored boats which came
from all over the world. He had been here once in the day
when it was busy with young people, at the start of his trip,
and there was a boating regatta of some sort, loud music
pumping out from gigantic speakers on a truck. At first he
found it irritating, the pounding of the bass, the unfamil-
iar soca tunes. But then someone handed him a beer, and
he realised that the only way to fully enjoy the regatta was
to carry on drinking. He had never known people drink
and drive like Trinidadians. There was talk of bringing in
breathalysers from England. But the cells would be full in
no time. Here there were no health warnings, no mention of
units, and definitely no drink-driving laws.

'So how was he?'

'Tired. Scrawny.' Safiya shook her head and then looked
away at the water. 'He looks like a hundred years old.'

'He must've been glad to see you.'

She shrugged her shoulders, and he thought she might cry.
Safiya's father had been terminally ill for a while. The hospital
had sent him home that day with a small supply of morphine;
there was nothing more they could do. There would be no follow-
up care, no health visitor calls, no Macmillan nurses, no telephone helpline. Safiya's father had come home to die in the
room he'd shared with his wife for thirty-seven years, except
the bed had been moved and a new adjustable electric one was
in its place. There was talk of getting a night nurse, and he

had even offered to pay a contribution, but her mother was resistant—he wouldn't want a stranger in the room.

'It's mom I worry about. She's scared; I see it in her eyes. And she's anxious about money. This whole thing has eaten up their savings.'

The first time he met Marjorie Williams he arrived for dinner with a bottle of Californian Merlot; she was pleased: how did he know she liked red wine? She took him straight to the kitchen to taste the salt fish fritters she was frying. He told her, 'This is the most delicious thing I've eaten since I got here,' and he meant it.

'Thank you,' she said, and to Safiya, 'A sweet talker; he can definitely come again.'

At that point she didn't realise that he was sleeping with her daughter, taking her back to his apartment at the end of the day; sometimes in the middle of the day, if their schedules allowed it. No, to her mother, Safiya had simply described him as a lonely old English guy she had met through work, no more than that.

He was surprised by the old-fashioned feel of the house: the olive-green Formica cupboards and the white worktop, the narrow gas stove where the big coal pot rested, and the large fridge covered with paper scraps, postcards, mementos. Safiya was born in this house, and apparently nothing much had changed: the same wooden floors, the ceiling fan in the living room, the cabinet packed with crockery and her grandmother's cocktail glasses, the silver cocktail shaker. He'd noticed a line of blue glass bottles outside the swing door, and Marjorie said these were to keep away bad spirits.

Vagrants sometimes wandered into the yard and slept on the steps. Just a month ago, while going to lock up the gate, she almost tripped over a sleeping vagrant. He had long dreads—a headful of snakes—and no shirt on his sweaty chest; his trousers were held up with old rope. You could see his pubic hair sticking out. The vagrant cursed her for kicking him, and she told him she'd already called St Ann's, the madhouse, and a van was on its way. Since she'd put the blue bottles out, he'd stayed away. Black people were frightened of blue bottles; Safiya said they are both religious and superstitious. If someone robs you, start saying the Lord's Prayer and see how fast they run.

That night Marjorie cooked up a West Indian feast: rice with pumpkin and beef; she prepared a large salad with lettuce and tomatoes. There was garlic bread, cassava, fried plantain. They sat at the dining table, the oval mahogany table which she said her husband had made when they first got married in 1955. It was an easy night, and he managed to avoid discussing anything too personal about his life in England. They mostly talked about Trinidadian politics, the recent Miss Universe competition, and the appalling rising crime. He was always taken aback by how seriously Trinidadians thought about their ruling government; in England he could not imagine having a similar discussion about New Labour around the dinner table. When Safiya said goodbye at the door, he knew she was pleased; the evening had gone extremely well.

But a month later, when he went back to the house, Marjorie did not come to say hello; she stayed in her bedroom and watched *CSI Miami*. She had found a birthday card in Safiya's bedroom. There was a poor choice of cards in the mall and he'd settled for a soppy American Hallmark. On the front was a cute Labrador puppy with a red bow around its neck: *To the world, you may be one person. But to me, you are the world.* Marjorie confronted Safiya, who told her, yes, they are having a relationship, and yes, it is complicated, and no, she isn't worried about what she is getting herself into.

That night he waited to speak to her in the living room; Safiya made him a sandwich, brought him a cold beer. She wished that he would let it go, there was nothing more to say. But he waited, all the while listening to the American voices coming from her mother's room. Eventually, when he got up to leave, Marjorie appeared in the doorway.

'I don't want you in this house again,' she said, calmly. She looked as if she had been crying. 'My daughter is all I have.' Then, 'An old man like you, you should know better.'

He drove away into the night, around and around the Savannah, until eventually he pulled into the car park at the Hilton Hotel where he shut off the lights, pushed back his seat. It was shocking to him, at his age, to be reprimanded by someone's mother.

He steps quietly through his apartment, stopping to collect a beer from the fridge, to the back where his small veranda is in darkness. He unlocks the wrought-iron gates, and pushes them open. He dislikes the bars, but they are necessary. He has become less security-conscious in the last few weeks, and he knows that he needs to be careful. Just last month a woman in her fifties was found dead not too far from here. Someone had seen two men at her door, and she apparently let them in without struggle. She'd been renovating her house, extending her porch, and people were coming and going all day. No one noticed anything unusual. Later that evening her son stopped by and found his mother lying on the floor in the utility room tied up with a garden hose. Then he saw that one end had been forced down her throat into her stomach, and the pipe, like a giant green plastic noodle, was sticking out of her mouth.

Next door's security lights are on, and he can see the glow of their L-shaped swimming pool through the fence. The couple are often away. He has met them a few times—at their house, when they invited him to a pre-Christmas party, and occasionally over the fence. They seem pleasant enough.

He is certain that the wife, Jeanne, has had breast implants; she wears them boldly, with tight shirts and tube tops. She is friendly, but in a self-conscious way, often adjusting her straightened hair or her straps while complaining about the heat or the rain. He wonders if she ever plays away. He has discovered that it's possible, in a relationship, to present to the world a picture quite different from the truth. These days, when he meets other couples, he finds himself looking for signs; he contemplates, he speculates. Are they in love? Are they happy? Faithful to one another?

Yes, there is something about Jeanne that seems available, feckless. Satnam, her husband—immaculate, in long-sleeved shirts and slacks, works for the local airline. His senior position means they can fly wherever they wish, and that means mostly Miami, Florida, where she can shop, and where they own two houses.

It is curious to him—a steady, quiet person like Satnam,

caught up with a woman like Jeanne. He has seen it before, and it doesn't always go the way you think; time usually sorts things out. Yes, with time people reveal themselves. He'd put money on Jeanne trading in Satnam at some point down the road; cashing in the houses, the car, half of his annual income, which, by any standards, Trinidad or England, must be considerable. And swiftly marrying someone else; someone younger, more adventurous, better looking. Is this something Satnam ever worries about? Perhaps not.

The day they were leaving for Miami, he saw them in their black 4x4 Hyundai Tucson. Jeanne peeped over the blacked-out electric window, her long earrings dangling.

'Any requests from Uncle Sam?'

And he had felt embarrassed, and without thinking found himself blurting, 'I actually hate America.'

He knew by the way she looked at him that she was thrown.

'Just kidding,' he added. 'Have fun.' He seems to remember they are back on the weekend.

Ahead, he can make out the hills. It is incredible to him how quickly he has grown accustomed to sitting here in the veranda, on the ugly aluminum chairs with the plastic white straps. More than one of the straps has broken, and two of the chairs are more or less useless. Around the veranda is a little brick wall about three feet tall, and in the middle, a white plastic table. It is hardly luxurious. But he has grown to love these hills and the way they change colour; sometimes, particularly in the gentle morning light when he sits outside with his first cup of coffee, they are pale and blueish. By noon they are a hard yellow-green; and in late afternoon they are tinted with shades of violet and mauve. Now they are so very black.

He wanders into the yard. This tropical grass is thicker, tougher than the grass of his English lawn. The blades feel coarse and springy when you walk on them. Recently he has discovered something: he likes to feel his bare feet on the earth, particularly in the early morning when the ground is moist. In the rainy season it turns muddy, and the mud is reddish brown like clay. There is an old sink by the side of the apartment where he can wash his feet. He has to watch out for the tiny 'ti marie' that prick the skin. There are ants too, millions of tiny ants. According to Safiya there are twelve different types of ant in Trinidad. He has yet to see the gigantic leaf-cutting bachacs that live in the forests. One day, Safiya will take him there.

He looks out at the dark shapes, the shadowy trees, the small concrete shed, and he wonders about Fanta. Usually at this time, Fanta is sitting on the veranda wall, or sleeping in his wicker basket. He hasn't seen him all day. Maybe he has things to do: a cat is a lion in a jungle of small bushes. Three months ago, he found the stray kitten curled up in a shady corner outside the supermarket. Small enough to sit in the palm of his hand, his ribs protruded and when he stood he had no tail. But his orange coat was pretty and surprisingly soft. Without thinking too much, he put the cat in a brown paper bag, and placed him in the back of his car. At home, Fanta slept and ate milk and crushed water biscuits. Before long he was strong enough to run about. Now he is used to Brunswick tuna and IAMS biscuits imported from America, and Safiya says he is spoiling him. She doesn't like the name, either. He has explained to Safiya that Fanta is a fizzy English orange drink.

'I'm hungry,' Safiya says from the doorway, her voice a sleepy drawl. 'Are we going out to eat, or should we have something here?'

She is wearing a long yellow T-shirt. She sits, and draws her knees up to her chest. 'I could do Kentucky.'

In England he would never have dreamed of eating Kentucky Fried Chicken, but here everyone seems to like it. One evening, recently, on the way home from the beach, hungry, sandy and sunbeaten, and dressed only in their beach clothes, on Safiya's insistence they'd picked up a twelve-piece tub of hot and spicy chicken from the drive-by in Maraval, and parked under the huge Samaan tree; he was surprised at how delicious it tasted.

'I want to take you somewhere special.' He squats down on the floor beside her. 'Take your pick,' he says. 'Anywhere you want.'

There are a number of new restaurants on the long strip of road in the centre of the city. Since he arrived, Italian, Chinese and Mexican restaurants have all opened within a few weeks of each other. There is a bar that reminds him of a gastropub in England with its hanging lampshades and ambient music. Safiya likes it but he thinks it is pretentious, and a little young. It is also expensive. Everyone says the economy is booming; it occurs to him that Trinidad seems to be the only country in the world where this is so, where life is still 'sweet', as they say.

'A zinger,' she says, 'that's what I want.' Then, 'A zinger, fries and a large Coke.'

He understands why she doesn't want to go out. In some ways, making a big effort on their last night together makes the separation more poignant, and he doesn't want her to feel that this is in fact their last evening together. For two weeks, yes, but that's all. At the same time, an intimate dinner in an expensive restaurant might leave her with a better and more lasting memory; while he is away, he wants her to think of him at his best: supportive, loving, generous. Someone she can have a good time with; someone she can rely on.

He has noticed, since her father's decline, she is turning to him more and more. He has become a safe place to rest her troubled heart and he is pleased; he had hoped this would happen. The next two weeks will be critical.

Two

They have overslept. Someone is tapping hard on the bedroom window; he hauls himself from a deep sleep and staggers out into the passageway. He can see a dark shape through the frosted louvers, and he is disorientated. Then he remembers: it is not a workday; he is leaving for Tobago, and he has asked Sherry, his housekeeper, to come today instead of tomorrow. She has arrived early.

'Mr Rawlinson,' he hears her high call. 'Mr Rawlinson.'

She is holding up a plastic bag. 'I pick up some nice oranges on the highway, right there by the turning. I'll make a juice.' He lets her inside, and she goes to the spare bathroom, where she will change into a work dress and an apron. There is a place for her to hang her clothes, and a small shower. It is familiar to her, and he no longer has to instruct her—the way he likes things, the basics. He is not used to taking care of himself, so things are often left undone, unwashed, in a heap. He has to be conscious, make an effort. It doesn't come naturally.

He inherited Sherry with the apartment, and mostly he is grateful for her; to hear someone else making noises, the sound of the vacuum cleaner, the wringing of the mop in the big metal bucket, cupboards opening and closing, is reassuring.

It's only when she starts preaching that he finds himself feeling irritated. Like last week, when he dropped her off before heading to the beach. As she was getting out of the car, she told him she would pray for him at church on Sunday. 'It's too late for all that,' he'd said. He is sorry that she has come while Safiya is here—what had he been thinking—and in particular, on this last morning that they will be together for some time. He suspects that she does not approve of his relationship with Safiya. Apart from anything else, he is old enough to be her father.

'Sorry about the Kentucky boxes,' he says, and moves the empty drinks cartons, the napkins and little tubs of tomato sauce into the black bin liner.

Safiya says there is no time for breakfast, just coffee; she will put on make-up at the other end. She shouts, 'Morning,' to Sherry, who is now in the doorway, broom in hand. She grabs her bag, sandals, comb—and asks if he could open the gates, pronto. It is the one thing he wishes he had insisted on, electric gates. Unlocking the chunky padlock, opening and closing the stiff black gates, has become something of a pain.

Next thing Safiya is in her shiny white Mazda 626, and the engine is running and there is music blasting from the radio. She rolls down her window and turns down the sound.

'Don't drive like a madwoman, okay. Alert today, alive tomorrow.'

She gives him a look he is certain he will never forget: her eyebrows raised a little, a half smile. He leans in to kiss her, forgetting he is wearing only boxer shorts and there are other people around. She usually complains that English tourists never know how to behave in the sun, that they have no deco-rum. He tends to agree.

He can see that she has not quite dried herself, the top of her blouse is damp, and where her wet hair sits on her shoul-ders—it makes him want to pull her out of the car and take her back inside. If Sherry wasn't here he might consider it—to hell with the office, there are more important things. He had imagined them making love this morning, and he is annoyed that he slept so late.

'Miss me,' she says, like an order.

'I already miss you.' He kisses her again, aware of his coffee breath.

'Don't forget to wear plenty sunblock. You don't always feel the sun with a sea breeze.'

'That's a very wifely thing to say.'

She puts on her Ray-Ban shades, reverses swiftly up the drive, and with her arm stuck out of the window in a kind of salute, Safiya zooms away. He watches her car disappear around the corner of the cul-de-sac. And everything is quiet.

The morning sky is clear and light blue. Two emerald par-rots are sitting on the wire, silent; they must have escaped from the flock. They often fly in a crowd overhead and shriek like they are quarrelling. He can't think of any English birds that make a noise like that, geese, perhaps, turkeys. They are quiet when there are just two of them, it seems. Safiya said parrots are like swans, they mate for life: a very rare species indeed.

From the old-fashioned American mailbox attached to the gate, he takes in today's rolled-up newspaper, and wanders barefoot back into the yard. The ground is already feeling warm. At one time, he would have worn flip-flops to walk on the concrete because his feet were so soft; his entire life spent in shoes, boots, slippers and socks. But in the last year they have hardened, the soles have a layer of thickened yellowish skin, particularly on the heels, and he is pleased. Perhaps he is finally adapting to his environment.

Everything looks dry, and he knows that he should water the pots around the front area before he leaves. They are mostly ferns, and a couple of larger pots with anthurium lilies; their strange pink flowers look like ears, which he particularly likes.

Safiya has told him it will only get more dry as the coming months arrive. By June the yard will be begging for rain and all the plants and trees stooped like old people.

He finds it hard to keep up with the seasons. Safiya says there is only a dry season and a wet season, but it is apparently more complicated than this. What about the petit carême, a second spell of dry weather in the middle of the wet season? And then there is the hurricane season. Where does that fit in? In England the arrival of seasons is very clear, although they are less obvious than they used to be. It is one of the only things he misses.

Once a week, Vishnu, his gardener, cuts the lawn, clips the trees; there is a small mango tree and an orange tree, and the hedge with blue flowers that reminds him of forget- me-nots. In truth, Vishnu has transformed the garden; he has planted cassava near the fence, banana trees near the water tank, and it is Vishnu who has brought the lilies. Martin has told him he is making more work for himself. The place now needs a certain amount of attention. 'Not so,' Vishnu says. 'Come dry season, it will need watering, but that's all. You'll see. I will grow you a little paradise.'

He is glad of Vishnu. He lives in Curepe with Shanti, an older, alcoholic woman who, apparently, makes his life difficult. Sherry says Shanti stays home all day and drinks rum. If Vishnu comes back late, she beats him with whatever she can lay her hands on: a broom, a saucepan, a piece of pipe.

Sometimes, Shanti shows up at the apartment. Once, while he cut the lawn, she lay in the shade of the avocado tree, her arms behind her head, her skinny legs stretched out. After an hour, she made a peculiar noise like a cat, and they disappeared into the shed, where, according to Sherry, they 'copulate'.

Sherry was angry.

'How they could do that while I right here in the house? It is disrespectful. Disrespectful to me and to you.'

'Life is long, Sherry; the average person lives seventy years. Too long to go without fun. Surely Vishnu deserves a little bit of fun.'

Two years ago, he would have given Vishnu a proper ticking-off, but not now. As his mother used to say, Judge not yet ye be judged.

Sherry is stripping his bed, and throwing the sheets on the floor. Her arms are strong and thick; she has a paunch belly and small breasts. Today her black hair looks oily, and it is scraped back. He stands in the doorway and sips his freshly squeezed juice; it is delicious.

'You're looking forward to Tobago, Mr Rawlinson? Tobago nice and peaceful. They say it good for newlyweds or nearly

deads. You won't want to come back to this crazy place.
Trinidad is a mess.'

Fanta slips in through the open door, his nose up and sniff-
ing the air. This is a very good sign—a sign that the cat is
taking ownership. Sherry is unaware and starts to gather up the
sheets. The cat stops and looks at her, then turns and strolls
out again, brushing his long orange body against the cool white
wall.

'Port of Spain is like Miami now without the police. All
these high-rise buildings. Everybody keeps talking about first
world, but there is nothing first world about our country. We
should be ashamed.'

'Everywhere, Sherry,' he tells her. 'It's not just Trinidad.
Things don't always work smoothly in England, you know.
There are bureaucrats everywhere and it's impossible to get
things done. It's the same the whole world over.'

'But in England you don't have kidnapping like here. When
police say they come, they come.' She rearranges her arms to
hold the white mass. It occurs to him how close her face is to
their sheets. 'I hope you teach the police here something.'

He doesn't know what to say; Sherry has a point. The situation in Trinidad is not about to change anytime soon, if anything, it has got worse. The level of complacency, the resistance
to any ideas for improvement have, at times, bewildered him.
How often has he heard: That's all very well, Mr Rawlinson,
but it's not how we do it in our country. They are at least forty
years behind. But what can he do? It is what it is. When he first
arrived he was determined to make a difference; he continues
to do his best.

They stand there looking at one another for a moment, and he realizes that he is still wearing only his boxer shorts.

'Trinidad has a lot of money, Sherry. You have oil, natural gas. You're much better off than some of the other islands with only banana or nutmeg trees. Think of Grenada.'

'Yes, but what are we doing with the money? Building mansions for the prime minister, buying private planes. Putting up skyscrapers. Plenty people don't have water or a house to live in. And don't talk to me about schools.'

The telephone rings, and he is relieved. It is Safiya reminding him that she will be in Mayaro for the next couple of days, and probably without a phone signal, should he decide to text.

'Why aren't you ready to leave?' she says. 'You don't have long.'

'Where are you?' he asks, trying to conjure her.

'In the corridor outside the office.'

He remembers the passageway lined with photographs of Trinidad Carnival Kings and Queens taken over the years.

'They should have a photo of you up there. My Carnival Queen.'

Before he leaves for the airport, he rings the office. He assumes that Juliet has either left for an early lunch, or she is in the toilet. He tries again; the telephone rings and rings. The truth is, it doesn't really matter if he speaks to her before he goes. But this is something that frustrates him about Trinidad; it is one thing to be laid back in your own time but not during working hours. Juliet should have put on her voicemail. A simple thing. He wants to remind her, when his renewal contract is drafted and ready, to send it out immediately.

He has grown fond of Juliet. She clonks around the office in old-fashioned lace-up shoes and thick nylon stockings as if she has all the time in the world. And yet somehow she manages to get the work done. It is not part of her job to organise his holiday villa, but Juliet did it without turning a hair—the villa (a friend of a friend at an excellent rate), a driver to collect them from the airport and a hire car delivered to their address. What more could he ask for. Occasionally she will bring him treats—homemade coconut cake, brownies, mauby. Last week, when he asked about extending his visa, she made a face.

'Don't worry, Mr Rawlinson,' she said, 'no one is throwing you out of Trinidad just yet. We need you here. You're keeping our country safe. Even Raymond say so.'

He was flattered, especially the part about Raymond. He knew that Raymond was resistant to the UK recruits; Raymond thought Trinidad should sort out its own mess. It had taken a long time for Martin to feel accepted. Now, to his amazement, they are friends.

On his first day in the job, as part of his induction, Raymond took him to a lively pub in St James. They sat at the bar and watched the place fill while huge speakers thumped out a fast soca beat; the beer rushed quickly to his head—he hadn't eaten, and he wasn't yet used to the heat. He was soon feeling lightheaded. For the first time it hit him: he was in Trinidad; home of calypso and Carnival, according to the guide books, the melting pot of the Caribbean.

'Take a good look,' Raymond said, 'these are the people we deal with. There are some in here who've killed eight or ten people. They not frightened of the law or anybody.'

Young men, couples playing dominoes, women in shorts, flimsy dresses, tight jeans, some of them already drunk, shimmying around a pool table. It was all going on. Everyone seemed to be having a good time, including the two of them.

'You want to know why we have so much trouble? Drugs. Drugs are shipped all over the world—to the USA and the UK, Europe. Transshipment from Columbia to Trinidad is six hours. We've had cases where large ships were supposedly being refurbished in Trinidad, and then intercepted in Spain with a billion dollars of cocaine.'

Martin had heard about this.

'Two months ago, we pick up a boat from Columbia. It was thirty-five foot long. Five engines on board, each one 150h.p. They all stacked in the back, and to the front of the boat is all the big parcels of coke and marijuana. The men are heavily armed, eight or ten guns, including machine guns. They come here, drop off the drugs and fly back from Piarco, leaving their guns behind. So now there is a proliferation of guns.'

Raymond was on a roll.

'In June 1999, we hang nine people in the state prison gallows. You know how many murders there were that month? None. You know why?' He thumped his hand on the bar: 'Trinidadians don't like hanging.'

Martin said, with a half smile. 'Well, it's a little barbaric, don't you think?'

Raymond shook his head. 'Barbaric? You know what's barbaric? Kidnapping someone from their home, and when the ransom money come, shooting them in the face. Two young women bashed and beaten like piñata dolls in front of their children in West Moorings; a baby playing in her grandparents' blood. A child found in a cane field, raped so bad she split like a piece of bamboo. That is barbaric. This kind of thing is happening far too often. Like it's normal. Murders are up thirty-eight per cent. And we are letting it happen.'

He steamed on. 'Tell me, what do the Privy Council understand about this country? They don't live here; they don't know the mentality of the people or the history of the islands. So how can they tell us how to punish our criminals? They should mind their own business and let us hang those who need to be hanged.'

Martin wanted to say that capital punishment is a sign of a backward society and could never, in his mind, be justified. *An eye for an eye leaves everybody blind.* Yes, he could rant about this for hours. But he kept quiet and drank his beer.

'Just last week a woman up near St Joseph went to a salon in Tunapuna. There were three other women having their hair styled. Two guys burst in and raped all of them. In the middle of the day. You hear what I say,' Raymond wagged his finger, 'in the middle of the day. While raping one of them, the woman cried, "Why you do this? Why you do this to us?" The man look her in the eye and say, "I need a reason?"'

That same day, Martin was allocated a 9mm Glock pistol. Then he was sent on a two-week course where he learned how to use it; apparently superbly functional, compact; less recoil and blowback than others. He learned about stance, 'nose over toes', and for rapid fire how the shoulders must come forwards: grip as tightly as you can, until you feel a tremor in your hands. He learned about perceptual distortion; how, under pressure, you might take half a dozen shots and have no idea of the number you've fired. Working with firearms had never appealed to him. He preferred the world of policy, strategy, performance, governance.

But he was better than he'd thought; the instructor told him, another few weeks and he could decorate a target with clover leaves all day long. To begin with the pistol made him feel nervous. Though he's never had reason to use it, he is accustomed to it now, carrying the little case on his hip, the two-stage lock. He cannot deny it gives him a sense of empowerment, confidence. And he understands why in Trinidad it is necessary. As a young trainee officer in Warwickshire, he was given the best piece of advice of his career—get in, get it done, get out. Thirty years on, it still applies.

His instincts are finely tuned; he has always stood by them. Mistakes might as well be his own, rather than someone else's. It was, in fact, his instinct that led to his first success in Trinidad, and won over Raymond.

Soon after he arrived, the eleven-year-old son of a wealthy Indian family was snatched on his way home from school. There were a couple of phone calls, a ransom was mentioned. Before talking to the police, the distressed father of the boy dropped off half a million dollars to a cane field in southern Trinidad. Then everything went quiet. Days passed. Police cordoned off the area around the drop-off point, started searching the field, interviewing family members, colleagues. They exhausted every lead. Raymond was stumped. Martin was invited to sit in on the interviews, oversee the forensic part of the investigation process; see if there was anything they'd missed.

He pointed to the father's brother and business partner; likeable enough, there was something about him that didn't *feel* right. When they spoke to the man, he put his hands up to his face and wept. He loved the boy, he said. He would never hurt him. Martin suggested they seal off the uncle's house for a major forensic search. Raymond was unsure—it was costly, time-consuming; no one else thought the man was guilty. The house was big, seven or eight rooms; in the back room overlooking the large manicured garden was an eight-foot snooker table imported from San Diego. The green felt top appeared unmarked, clean, like new. It was Martin who hovered around the table, and suggested they strip it down, dismantle it. At first there was nothing, but then they checked the pockets and they were full of blood. The boy's blood. An angle saw was found buried under an orange tree in the garden. They had, in fact, cut him up on the snooker table.

The highway is congested, and he wonders if there has been an accident up at the crossroads by the Kay Donna Drive-In cinema. The traffic lights are often broken. It is not uncommon for drivers to assume the lights aren't working and accelerate straight through. Fatalities are on the rise, which is no surprise; Trinidad has one of the highest rates of road deaths in the Caribbean.

Cars crash in a way that makes it almost impossible to survive: high-speed collisions; passengers and drivers are often without seat belts and ejected through the windscreen. Most crashes take place during the early hours of the morning, between midnight and 6 a.m. along the three main highways, many along this same highway where he is now driving with his air conditioner notched up high, his small Antler suitcase on the back seat, the midday sun bouncing off the shiny bonnet.

This is the season for fires. And, in fact, a fire has started in a field on the left: black smoke curls upwards, and he wonders if this particular fire is deliberate, if farmers are burning cane to kill pests: spiders, rats, scorpions and snakes. Snakes can be a common hazard, especially in houses near the hills. Vishnu has warned him, a nip between the toes from a coral snake will have you dead in hours.

A local radio station is playing a Gloria Estefan song that he remembers from his twenties, 'Don't Wanna Lose You'.

It is a fact, in bars, clubs, restaurants, in hotels or on the radio, Trinidadians play the most unashamedly sentimental songs—American west coast wet, as he used to call them. To his surprise, these days this kind of music does not irritate him. Safiya says, songs like these make you feel things in a more powerful way: sadness, loss, longing. And today he is feeling a mixture of these emotions. He is feeling, for the first time in weeks, alerted to the reality and facts of his life; the many tiny decisions that have brought him to this place, to where he is right now. Two years ago, if someone had warned him, he would not have believed it. And yet he is not unhappy. His world is much too alive for him to be unhappy. How did this happen? How did he get here?

It was Safiya who once told him that decisions are discovered, not made. A strange thing to tell someone so early on, and he often wonders if, that first afternoon, she had some

kind of insight into their encounter. He was in the bar of
the Hyatt Regency Hotel, where he was staying when he first
arrived in Trinidad. The rain was clattering outside, and she
had appeared with a Trinidad Guardian Life umbrella, her
feet wet inside her sandals, the bottom of her blue jeans,
dirty and soaked. He was sitting near the entrance, waiting
for the rain to stop, and she plonked her bag, a leather carry-
all, on the next seat. She was looking around the busy lobby.
A young football team had gathered at reception, and their
luggage was strewn over the floor. Some visitors had taken
shelter from the blowy terrace, and there were delegates arriving for an international AIDS conference. He had never seen
the Hyatt so busy.

'Oh boy,' she said. 'Piccadilly Circus.'

He asked if she was looking for someone in particular. She
told him that she was there to interview a local musician but it
looked as if the musician hadn't turned up.

'Trinis won't come out in the rain if they can help it.'

He offered to watch her bag while she checked inside.
Outside the rain was getting heavier, a grey veil, and he could
hear the dark sky growling. She looked out at the entrance to
the lobby where cars were lining up. Then she came back and
slumped down in the seat opposite.

'We've been waiting for rain for so long and then the rainy
season arrives and it comes like a monsoon.'

Her green eyes were slightly hooded, small, and intense. She
could be Spanish, or Italian, but she was probably a Trinidadian
mix. African, Indian and maybe a little Chinese thrown in.

'It's still hot even with the rain.'

'Yes, it only ever gets cool here around Christmas. Then every-one starts putting on socks and sweaters.'

'Be glad it's just once a year.' He sipped his coffee.

'Are you on holiday?'

'No, I'm here working for your government.'

'Lucky you.' Then she said, 'What made you want to come here?'

'I'd had enough of English summers.'

'There's plenty islands in the Caribbean, why Trinidad?'

'I suppose I just made a decision.'

'Decisions are usually discovered and not made.'

She smiled wide and revealed her straight white teeth, and he thought how different she looked—bright, lit.

'Well, okay. It's exotic; it's very different from where I come from.' He suddenly felt awkward. 'Have you ever been to England?'

'No,' she said, 'I've been to New York a couple of times. I love the States, but I love here more.'

She told him that she worked for the *Trinidad Express*, although these days she was also involved in some television reporting, which she found more interesting. She had thought about going away to America, or even Canada. She had a good friend in Vancouver. But there seems to be enough work here to keep her going.

'You'd be surprised. There's a lot happening here.'

Her mobile phone rang, and she got up and walked towards the lobby. From behind, she was curvy, wide-hipped, and yet proportional to her narrow waist. She could be in her late twenties. He had always been good at guessing people's ages but she had him foxed. Something about her confidence made him wonder if she was older. She turned and saw him staring at her; he felt embarrassed.

'I'm going to make a run for it. The rain is slowing down.'

He hadn't noticed that the rain had, in fact, almost stopped. She tucked her phone in the pocket of her jeans, zipped up her bag.

'Do you mind me asking how old you are?' he said, getting up.

She grinned. 'Old enough to be your daughter.'

Five years ago, his friend, Nigel Rush, a Chief Officer in Shrewsbury, left a wife and two young children for his twenty-two-year-old secretary, Marilyn. Everybody was shocked. By chance, Martin had bumped into them while shopping for lamps in John Lewis. She was blonde and voluptuous, if a little cheap-looking. It was an awkward moment, and Nigel was red-faced. But they shook hands, and he told the lady it was nice to meet her, which it was. A part of him thought, good for you, Nigel, but at the same time, the whole thing seemed to him ridiculous, tragic, and as far as he could tell, completely avoidable. What would Nigel say to him now?

Ahead, cars are finally moving slowly. He passes an old truck full of gas canisters; it appears to have broken down. Two men are standing beside it smoking cigarettes; they are laughing and joking about something. He imagines that this broken-down truck was the cause of the delay. Safiya says that if you break down in Trinidad, hope that it happens in daylight.

The airport is not as busy as he expected. He parks the car

underneath an Air Canada advertisement and wheels his suitcase
to the terminal building. It is a large, attractive building. Sunlight
is streaming onto the shiny white tiles. It is cool, and spacious,
and he easily finds the check-in counter for Tobago where three
or four people are lined up. The attendant takes her time, slowed
by her long fake nails. She presses the computer keys with the
flat pads of her fingers. He cannot imagine how she manages to
do basic things—wash dishes, dress, or put on her make-up. Her
hair is tightly braided and bleached a coppery brown. She gives
him a boarding pass. They look at each other for a moment, her
dark eyes expressionless and staring, and he realises her job is
done and he must now make his way through security.

He is hungry. No doubt they will be eating dinner early
tonight, but he is not sure he can last that long. There is a
coffee shop, which reminds him of Starbucks. Muffins, sandwiches, croissants and quiches. Everything looks too yellow
and dry. He decides on a biscuit, a kind of savoury scone, one
of Safiya's favourites, and a cup of coffee. If she was here,
she would order a Mocha Chiller, a tower of frothy chocolate-
flavoured coffee, topped with whipped cream, sucked noisily
through a straw like a kid.

The table where he sits is greasy and he half-heartedly wipes
it with his napkin. Lately, he has realised that when something
big happens, small things mostly stop bothering him, at least
for a while. Yesterday, he saw a poster in the mall. 'Don't sweat
the small stuff'. And written underneath, 'It's all small stuff.' A
pocket-size book of affirmations by an American psychologist.
Is the situation he finds himself in small? How can it possibly
be small?

The departure lounge is quiet with fifteen people or so scattered on the bright plastic chairs. A mounted television is showing CNN and thankfully it is muted. George Bush is speaking from the White House, his chimp face close to camera, smirking as if he is telling a joke.

He finds a seat near the doors, where he can see the small Caribbean Airways airplane waiting on the tarmac. There is something romantic and old-fashioned about a plane with propellers. He does not particularly like flying, but a small flight like this can be thrilling.

Last year the wheels of one of these planes refused to come down and it was forced to land on its belly in a field. Passengers were mostly made up of a gospel choir who sang hymns as the plane crash-landed. On the evening news, people were seen stumbling from the aircraft, wailing and crying and praising God. It was a miracle, Safiya said. No one was hurt. But then Safiya believes in miracles. Asking for a miracle is as simple as ordering from a restaurant menu.

'And how do you pay for your miracle?'

'With your faith.'

A young woman sits opposite him with a small baby. She is overweight and her breasts look enormous in her pink T-shirt, which is marked with a number 19. She has been staring at him for a while, and he wonders what she has seen in him that holds her interest. He assumes there is nothing peculiar about his appearance, and he smoothes his greying hair. He is wearing a khaki cotton shirt and Levi jeans and dark leather sandals. Safiya has always said that the sandals are a giveaway, and with a tan he could almost pass for a Trinidadian. But he doesn't really have a tan, it's just that his freckles seem to have multiplied and given him a brown look. On his face there are hundreds of freckles, and thousands more on his legs and feet. He has never liked them. Safiya says his skin is unusually smooth. Sometimes when he is drying off after a shower, or searching his cupboard for something to wear, he catches her watching him intensely.

Once when she was drunk, she told him that he is physically fascinating to her in a way that no one else has ever been.

'In what way?' he'd said. 'Is it because I'm old?'

'Maybe,' she said and laughed.

He'd huffed outside to the veranda to smoke a cigarette. He had never been moody until he met her. In the early days, he behaved like a lovesick teenager.

The baby starts to cry. The woman shifts the blue bundle closer to her face and rocks a little. He imagines that her breasts must be a great comfort, the softness and warmth in this air-conditioned room. Cradling, she leans over and from her plastic leather bag plucks out a bottle which she eases into the baby's mouth. The crying stops at once and he is relieved. But then the glass doors open with a blast of hot air and everyone starts to get up. The airline clerk announces the departure of the flight into Crown Point, Tobago. In the distance, he can see an American Airways jet taking off, a silver finger penetrating the deep blue sky. He offers his boarding pass, and steps outside into the glare of the sun. It is fierce now. In the hot wind, he quickly walks across the tarmac to the small aircraft. What will they make of this heat?

As the plane accelerates and lifts, the propeller's sound

whirrs and intensifies, and he looks down at the land below as it rushes away—the waving coconut trees, the tiny cars on roads no more than fine lines, the clusters of houses with roofs like scraps of tin foil. The patchwork land becomes vast and sprawling and it is flat and scorched in parts. Rain needs to come soon; this is what everyone is talking about, the agriculturalists, the politicians, and the workers. To the left he can see the Northern Range, and the hills are darker now because of the position of the sun as the plane moves north and east.

He stares down into these hills; the forest looks benign: soft and edible as vegetables. Yet if the plane should crash here none of the survivors would ever find their way out of such dense bush. At one time this thought would have bothered him greatly. But today he does not feel bothered. He has lived his life; he has had his family and a career. Even if he died now, at forty-nine, he has seen and lived enough to constitute a full life. It is only with hindsight that we see our lives and the curious trails we have made. And in the last year he has been more than blessed. For the second time in his life he has found love. What more could he ask? Some people spend their whole lives searching for this kind of love and never find it. Safiya is too young to know how rare it is. He understands only this: there is no remedy for love but to love more; let it take him where it will. He closes his eyes and he is glad of the blackness.

THREE

The plane comes in to land; he can see the chop of the waves, the surf on their tips. Black rocks rise up and the pale yellow sand seems almost close enough to touch. The aircraft slowly drops and gently bounces on the airstrip: a hotel, houses, airport terminal whoosh by, then the tall palm trees and the brown green grass, and more grass and a field of coconut trees until the far end of the runway where there is another bay of blue Caribbean water.

He collects his suitcase and walks outside to a line of taxi drivers. On the right, the terminal is open and a breeze blows right through its large rectangular space. Mixed with familiar airport fumes, he can smell fast food, and he notices two large black birds picking at a little heap of stale French fries on the ground. There is a long row of desks and a few people are queuing up for domestic flights. As far as he can tell there is no one at the British Airways counter. He approaches a couple waiting near the desk; he asks if the BA London flight is on time.

The young man is tall and he is wearing a T-shirt and shorts. His blonde girlfriend is so sunburned the whites of her eyes are almost glowing in her red face. 'Yes, as far as we know.

The rep was here earlier and said it was on time.' Her accent is Scottish—Edinburgh, perhaps. She glances up at her boyfriend. 'We don't care if it never turns up. We've had such a brilliant holiday.' Then, 'Are you BA or Virgin?'

'Neither, I'm meeting people. I live here.' He can see the woman trying to work him out. 'I live in Trinidad.'

'Lucky you,' she says.

He wishes them a safe trip and crosses the road to the airport restaurant. Inside it's cool and dark; there are small groups of people sitting around plastic tables. Some of them look English, no doubt also waiting for the London flight. He orders a beer, a half packet of Du Maurier cigarettes and sits on a stool at the bar.

He is sorry that he has started smoking again. Yet everyone in Trinidad seems to smoke; the cigarettes are short and burn down quickly. They are cheap, too. Smoking abroad has always seemed okay; the warm air carries smoke quickly away. It doesn't stay on your clothes like in England, or stick to your hair, your fingers. At Las Cuevas, he'd seen surfers come straight out of the sea and reach for a cigarette. He had even done it himself after years of not smoking. And it had felt good: lying with his head propped on Safiya's stomach, he'd puffed on a Du Maurier while staring at the brilliant sky, listening to the crash of the sea. Why is it that everything that feels good is bad for you?

He doesn't see the plane, but he hears the roar of the 747 engines as the pilot pulls back the throttle, and almost at once the restaurant starts to empty. He finishes his beer, pays his bill and makes his way to the upstairs viewing gallery. Next door, passengers in transit are going through security. They will sit and wait in the hot little International departure lounge with the passengers in transit from Grenada while the aircraft is cleaned and restocked. The last time he took this flight he was stuck for three hours and swore he would never do it again. It occurs to him that in two weeks he will be back here at this exact same spot, waving goodbye, seeing them off.

He cannot imagine how that will be, and how they will all feel. He is almost certain that it will be appalling. Now he leans on the railings, glad of the breeze, and he watches the enormous aircraft turn and begin its slow approach to the terminal. With its swirling blue and red tail, and long, gleaming body, it is quite magnificent.

It is almost impossible to see the passengers disembarking at the rear, but he can pretty much see those at the front steps. Streams of people with their bags, hold-alls and carriers of duty-free, squinting in the bright light, coats over their shoulders, wearing boots, jumpers, jeans, jackets, pour onto the tarmac. Children clutch their toys while trying to hold onto the rail of the big metal steps. A small party of girls have already changed into their summer tops and shorts, their white stomachs and milk legs on show; they are excited, awkward. The English abroad. He feels embarrassed for them.

Everyone is walking quickly, keen to get through immigration. More spill out from the rear. He still cannot pick them out, and for a moment he wonders if they are on the flight after all. But then—there, he sees her, Miriam, his wife Miriam. She is walking under the enormous wing, and close to her is Georgia, taller than he recalls, taller now than her mother. How has this happened? His daughter is a giant! They have not seen him; they are talking, and he finds himself waving, trying to get their attention. He calls out, but the hiss of the plane's engine is too loud; they disappear underneath the balcony and into the immigration building.

Georgia is out first. She looks different. Her fair hair is wavy and longer, and she looks, to him, now, much older than fourteen. She is like her mother; the same oval face and slanted blue eyes. He is somewhat shocked by her clothes—low-cut jeans, a skimpy hooded top, dangling earrings. Her skin is startlingly pale. When he hugs her, he feels her thin back, the small breasts. He smells her gorgeous alpine hair. 'Where's my baby gone?'

'I'm still me,' she says, 'I'm still Georgia.'

Over her shoulder, Miriam cocks her head. 'Do I get one of those?'

There is something different about her clothes too, a more casual look and the white pumps. He hasn't seen her wear pumps in years, not since college. She has lost weight and it makes her look older. Her hair is darker; she has dyed it. She puts out her arms, and he goes to his wife. He kisses her lightly, loosely embraces her. But Miriam is having none of it; she wraps her arms around him tightly, pressing her bony body into him.

'You look great,' he says, reaching for her suitcase. 'How was the flight?'

'Oh, you know, long.'

He realises that they're blocking the way for other passengers coming through. He ushers them along the ramp and wheels the trolley further up where he can check for their driver. Georgia fans herself with a rolled-up magazine. He says, 'It's cool right now. You should feel it in the summer. How was the weather when you left?'

Miriam says, 'It's like St Petersburg. Do you remember when we were so bundled with scarves and hats all you could see were our eyes? Like that. I could hardly see on the M25. I'm surprised they didn't cancel the flight.'

Then she points at the cigarettes in his top pocket. 'You're smoking again.'

The driver, a well-built man in his sixties, leads them to a maroon Chevrolet Caprice. They load up the car; Martin sits in the front. A CD dangles from the mirror, light licks about the car. Slowly, they pull out on to the road.

'First time in Tobago?'

'I've been working in Trinidad for two years.'

'And now your wife has come to take you home.' He chuckles, a clicky sound in the back of his mouth.

'You could say that.'

'Very wise,' says the driver, checking Miriam in the rear-view mirror. 'A lady should never leave a man too long or he'll fall into mischief.'

The thought of Miriam flying across the Atlantic to drag him home is ludicrous, and yet it is also true.

When he accepted the job in Trinidad—it had happened so fast—they agreed they would not be apart for more than two months at a time. Absence, his mother always said, makes the heart grow fonder—for someone else. They decided, during school holidays Miriam and Georgia would fly to Trinidad, and whenever he could, he would return home to England.

But after a brief spell in the Hyatt hotel, he was given an apartment near the airport. Security was atrocious; the rear of the apartment backed on to a cul-de-sac of shabby government housing. He eventually relocated and the new apartment was a thirty-minute drive from the capital. Around that time, a gang of criminals took to highjacking cars with young babies and putting them by the side of the road. When a driver stopped, typically a woman driver, they robbed her, stole her car, and sometimes, for good measure, she was raped. He decided that it probably wasn't safe enough for his wife and daughter. So he returned to England whenever he could, a week here and there. It was always hurried, unsatisfactory. And then, of course, he met Safiya.

When Miriam telephoned to ask if the dates were okay, he sensed there was no way around it. The plan was always that she would come for a holiday at Easter, just before his contract ended. After his brief and rather painful visit at Christmas (more painful for her than him, he imagines), during which they barely spoke because Miriam was angry that he was home for only five days, she had decided on a last-minute whim to take advantage of Georgia's half term and escape 'the bleakest February I can remember'.

He checked his diary. Yes, he told her, he could manage ten days. But it was probably better if they flew directly to Tobago. It's quieter, he told Miriam, more of a holiday destination.

'Either will do. It's the Caribbean, and I need blue sky,' she said, her voice strained. 'I've had enough of these overseas phone calls.' Then more lightheartedly, 'Georgia wants to see where you've been working. She thinks you might be making it all up.'

'What about Easter?'

'I can't wait until Easter. I don't know about you. I keep thinking about Beth. It's her birthday soon.'

They had always made a point of celebrating Beth's birthday.

'If things get sticky at work, I might have to fly back briefly to Trinidad. I'm just warning you, okay.'

'That's fine. We can come with you.'

In truth, it didn't make much difference to his plans if Miriam came now or at Easter; this visit was always going to be extremely difficult. And the thought of seeing Georgia, showing her the island that he has come to love, made it feel worthwhile. He has missed her terribly.

As they cruise through the village, the taxi driver gives them a list of places they must visit: Buccoo reef, Pigeon Point, Sunday School, Lovers Retreat, Scarborough market, Blue Waters. His voice is soothing, soporific; he is clearly proud of his homeland. And why wouldn't he be? Outside, the light is infusing everything with gold and the sky is a delicate, pale yellow.

They have arrived at a perfect time of day when the island is cooling down. At this hour, everything becomes saturated with colour, the grass, the wooden houses, and the advertising billboards: Du Maurier cigarettes, Stag Beer—the man's choice! When they pull up at the lights, he can hear the sounds of crickets chirring. He hears a whoop, whoop, from a frog. Big and ugly like stones, he will find one to show Georgia. Along the left side of the road are fields filled with coconut trees, their tall heads barely blowing in the light breeze, their long branches like hair. These are the trees of paradise, the insignia of the Caribbean.

He says, 'Aren't the trees wonderful?' Georgia is looking out at the fields, too.

'They're amazing,' she says, and reaches for her mother's hand. 'Don't you think so, Mum?'

'Yes, yes. They're very pretty.'

According to Juliet, the holiday villa is not far from the airport. No more than twenty minutes. He wants to arrive while there is still light, get his bearings and look around the place. At this time of year, the sun disappears early. In England, of course, it would be pitch black at four thirty. This is something he has never missed, arriving home from work in the dark, leaving in the morning when it is still dark.

And while they drive along the Milford Road, he remembers a strange incident: driving to work early one morning in Warwickshire, along a strip of country road he had always liked, he was seized by an overwhelming sense of panic, as if everything was closing in. He pulled over, his heart hammering, his throat tight. He took a couple of deep breaths and looked around. Everything was the same as usual, the wild hedges, the little rowan tree he had always noticed in silhouette, the pointy church spire on the far left, the village lights ahead. He'd told himself everything was fine. It was dawn and the world was waking up. This darkness will pass. After a few moments, he started the engine and drove away. Later, his doctor told him it was a panic attack, and it was more than likely linked to Beth's death; panic attacks, disorders, and phobias are commonplace in the aftermath of sudden loss. How odd that he should remember this now.

The car turns into a narrow and bumpy road. Three or four goats are tied to a mango tree; they are bunched up and tugging, stretching their long ropes as far as they can.

'Look at the babies!' Georgia stretches her arm out of the window. The goats carry on eating as if they are not there. They are white and scrawny. It is something he has noticed here: cattle and goats are often malnourished, their stomachs distended, bloated. Like Africa.

On either side, there is a golf course, smooth shaved green mounds and a green plateau. There are two or three houses on the right, and up on the left is a large, low-roofed bungalow surrounded by land. They pull up outside and the driver gets out and rings a bell. Within moments, electric gates open and the long maroon American car swings into the gravelled driveway, past the dark lawn and a row of pots filled with brightly coloured bougainvillea.

The house is impressive. Dark beams reach high above the living room, which opens onto a large veranda. There are large comfortable white chairs and a hammock. More importantly, Terence shows him, there is a sea view. The water is dark now, and he can see it shifting and moving beyond the trees. Terence, the caretaker, has lived here for almost ten years. 'If you have a problem you come to me,' he says, and taps his chest. He has a pleasant face, probably in his early forties, or perhaps older, though it is sometimes hard to tell with dark skin. Safiya says black don't crack, and he has found this to be mostly true. Terence is short, and in his Adidas vest top and denim shorts he looks wiry, strong. Just the kind of man you might want looking after your property.

The house has been empty for weeks. Today the lady who cleans brought bread, milk, and basic provisions for them. She picked oranges from the tree and put them there.

'She knew you'd arrive when the stores are shut. They open again tomorrow at eight.'

Georgia has already found her room. It is at the end of a corridor, separated from the main living area by a glass door, which they can slide back and forth. He is glad to see it is also lockable, an extra security feature. There are twin beds, and a large bathroom with shutters; from the window you can see the driveway, the long garden. She has pulled her suitcase inside the room and started to open it up. There is a walk-in closet, how about that! She will come and see the rest of the house in a minute, Georgia says. For now she will lounge in her own quarters. Like a celebrity.

On the other side of the living room is another passageway, the left wing, and here are two good-sized bedrooms, and a cosy American den with plaid sofas and a television.

'You have cable and DVDs, whatever you wish.'

Terence opens the door to the master bedroom. It is a dark room and, without doubt, the most appealing. It has a four-poster bed, and an old-fashioned dressing table. Miriam, who he had almost forgotten about, says, 'Wonderful!' And she skips to the centre of the room and, holding out her shirttails, twirls girlishly around.

'Somebody's pleased,' he says, and follows Terence into the en suite. The bathroom is dated, a '70s beige, but it is big enough. While Miriam opens cupboards and checks for space, he walks with Terence back along the passageway to the kitchen, the big brown, earthy kitchen with its shining silver stove. Like something from a magazine.

Juliet told him, the owners, Steven and Jennifer Dial, work in textiles; they have property both in Florida and London. Jennifer liked the idea of an English family staying in their Tobago villa—these days it is rarely used—and offered a lower, family rate. Perhaps, as a small favour, he would check on their security. Yes, he could do that, no problem.

'Here is the telephone and emergency numbers,' and Terence holds up a slim rectangular box, like a television remote control. 'The gate opener: always remember to take it with you, without it you can't get back in unless someone opens the gate from inside.' Then he shows him a single key—for the hire car parked around the back.

They walk to the edge of the garden and look through the trees at the ocean. Now he can really see the water breathing in and out.

'Watch out for these,' Terence stoops and picks up a tiny brown shape like a nut or a fir cone. 'They'll hurt your feet.' He points along the edge of the garden. 'They come from the casuarinas.' The trees are tall with broad branches; they look like a kind of pine.

There is a drop onto the beach, and steps lead down through the rocks. 'We have a couple of kayaks, surfboards and lilos, goggles and snorkels. There's a dingy too, which is a lot of fun. I'll show you tomorrow.'

[44]

Since living in Trinidad, he has come to love the ocean. The first time he swam at Maracas Bay it was a kind of baptism. Born anew, his soul washed free in the cool, lively water. He had never experienced anything quite like it. He made himself into a ball and somersaulted in the sea like when he was a child. He dived down and swam over the pale seabed. Yes, he had been to the Costa del Sol, but the sea there was completely different, some-how stale, greyish, like it was dead. Then Safiya gave him a small surfboard, a boogie board, and he learned how to ride the waves as they broke at Las Cuevas. You're a natural, she'd said. Who'd have thought? If he kept it up, she promised to buy him a full-sized surfboard. They could spend their weekends up in Sans Souci. She would like that. They would both like that.

Terence leads him around the side of the house to his stu-dio apartment.

'This is where I live. You can find me here most of the time apart from Sunday. Sunday, I go to church and then to my mother's in Buccoo.'

It always surprises him how church-going people are in these islands. Safiya says that Trinidadians are a people of great faith: Hindu, Catholic, Church of England, Shouter Baptist, and Obeah can all find a place here. This is what will save Trinidad, she says. 'Think of all the different religions existing simul-taneously and harmoniously on this island. Where else in the world do you find that level of tolerance?' Safiya has a point.

There are two chairs in front of the French doors and a tree that reminds him of a weeping willow. He can see a bed, and a kitchen beyond. From the top of an old television set, Terence takes up a framed photograph.

'My daughter,' he says, proudly. 'Chelsea. After my favourite football team.'

'Lucky it's not Tottenham.'

Terence grins.

'How old is she?'

'She just turned five. Her mother lives in Scarborough but she's from Sweden.'

The little girl is light-skinned, her eyes are a greenish brown.

'Sometimes she comes to stay; usually when my ex has a date and wants the place to herself.'

'She's beautiful. I hope we get to meet her. I'm sure Georgia would love to see her.'

It is hot in the room, and they step outside. There is a cool, soft breeze swishing the tree. This is not a bad life, he thinks: looking after a luxury property with your own private living quarters and the Caribbean Sea on your doorstep: all this beauty without expense. There are worse ways to earn a living. Could he do it? Maybe so. Although he'd rather not be alone.

'This is Conan,' Terence says. A three-legged Alsatian trots down the driveway towards them and barks loudly.

'Conan is our early-warning system. Anyone comes to the gate and he barks.' The dog's tail is wagging, and he seems friendly enough.

'What happened to his leg?'

'He was down in the village chasing chickens, and someone chop him with a cutlass. The cut get bad and the vet had to take it off.'

'That's pretty brutal.'

'The vet or the man who chop him?'

Terence smiles and he catches sight of a gold tooth.

'Let me tell you, sir, Tobago people can be savage.' Conan rolls down on the ground and tips back his head. Terence puts his foot on the dog's stomach.

'I need to show you how to work the metal shutters. They only put them in the living room; the rest of the place has bars.'

From the doorway, he watches Miriam unpacking her suitcase. She has turned on the overhead lights and it is bright. She is tired but determined, her dark hair pulled back from her thin face.

'There's plenty of space. If I put mine on this side, you can have the other,' she says, cheerfully. 'And there's lots of drawers too.'

He glances around the room, and in particular at the large four-poster bed; her folded nightdress is on top of the sheet along with a clean pair of underwear, no doubt for after her shower.

He says, 'Are you hungry? There's bread; I can rustle something up.'

Miriam nods. 'Georgia is probably starving; she hardly ate on the plane.' She steps towards him, cautiously. 'I'm really pleased we came.'

'Me too,' and he rubs her arm awkwardly. He can see that this confuses her slightly and he doesn't know what else to do. At one time he would have kissed her mouth, put his arms around her.

Glad of an excuse, he leaves the room and goes to the kitchen. He opens a bottle of cold beer and leans for a moment against the tiled worktop. There is a large stone arch, and through it he can see the living room, and a painting of a woman with her breasts bared. It is a strange and erotic painting to hang in a family holiday villa. The buttery-coloured woman is wearing a headscarf and her arm is back, above her head. She is boldly showing herself to someone, someone she must like very much. At one time Miriam might have shown herself to him like this. Not now. At least he hopes not now. How do feelings change? Is it a slow, ongoing metamorphosis or a quick and sudden thing?

When he first met Miriam, she had seemed somehow familiar. She was attractive; her features were too hawkish to be pretty. Her cousin, a colleague and friend, introduced them. She seemed carefree and plucky, opinionated; different from any other girls he knew. That summer, she was visiting from northern Spain where she taught English as a foreign language in a small school.

At the time, Miriam warned him that she had a boyfriend, José, who lived in Barcelona, and they had been together for almost a year. For two weeks, Martin pursued her as if his life depended on it. When he finally persuaded her to cut loose, she discovered that she was six weeks pregnant with José's baby. Miriam was inconsolable. She said her life was over. He reassured her; she could stay in England and decide about her future. He would support her.

They moved together into a tiny semi-detached house, in Roundhay, Leeds. He had finished his two-year induction, and was about to start working shifts. For a while Miriam played homemaker. She stripped and painted the walls. She dug up the tiny garden and planted shrubs; where there had once been gravel, grass soon grew. When the house was finished, Miriam enrolled on a teacher-training course. There was no use in wasting her language skills, she said; she would teach Spanish.

For a long time, they didn't talk about the abortion. Yet he felt, instinctively, that she was sometimes disappointed in the path she had chosen; that she regretted leaving Spain and all it had offered. Even then, he was aware of his desire to make it up to her, to prove to her that she had, in fact, picked well. This desire had no doubt made him more ambitious than he might otherwise have been. He has loved her well, he believes.

But are we are really meant, by nature, to be monogamous? These days, people live such long lives. Last week in *Time* magazine he'd read and memorised a quote describing exactly how he feels and has felt for the last two years: *The world is big and I want to have a good look at it before it gets dark.*

He checks the cupboards. There are several tins of Vienna sausages and a couple of onions. He can fry these up, and make a kind of hot dog: a Safiya special. The first time she made it, they had come home late, hungry. After a few minutes of scrabbling in the kitchen, suddenly, there it was: a delicious spicy sausage mix squished between two slices of bread. Safiya had a knack for making something from nothing.

Georgia is lying on her bed, the small bedside lamps throw a soft amber light. It is cool; clever girl, she has figured out how to use the air conditioner.

'Dinner in ten. Is that okay?'

'Sure!'

He notices that her bed is nearest the door and he wishes it wasn't. There is something about sleeping away from the door that offers more protection; like walking on the inside of the pavement. He would like to tell her but she will complain that he is being overprotective. It is curious to him how the need to safeguard his daughter never goes away. His mother had warned him, when you have children you will understand why I worry so. Georgia's delicate frame, her gentleness, has always made him feel overly protective. That, and, of course, the other more obvious reason, has turned him, where she is concerned, into something of a worrier.

He remembers one afternoon, her primary school teacher telephoned to say that Georgia had fallen in the playground and taken a 'nasty bump'. Martin left the station and drove there at once. When he saw her small face bloody and scuffed, her gaping chin, he'd actually cried. These last months he has felt her absence deeply like a limb lopped off. In her young hands she carries his heart. He has talked to Safiya about this. Georgia is the one thing that always stops him in his tracks— his red light.

And yet, if it wasn't for Georgia, he might not be in Trinidad. Three years ago, after thirty years of service, he'd retired. Using his chunky lump sum, they moved from their detached, modern estate house to a five-bedroom farmhouse with two acres, and a paddock—and enrolled Georgia in an excellent private school. He carried on working in the same post as a civilian; with a smaller salary and his pension, they could more than manage. The Home Office warned of cuts but it was still a surprise when redundancies were announced and, more so, when his post was axed, along with an entire department of Community Safety Officers.

Miriam returned to work full-time, but they soon found themselves struggling to pay the £15,000-a-year school fees. It was either sell the house, put Georgia into a local comprehensive, or he must find another job. He registered with recruitment agencies in Birmingham, Leicestershire, and Nottingham. He was beginning to despair when, out of the blue, Nigel Rush telephoned about opportunities for former army and police officers in Trinidad. Easy money, Nigel said. Tax-free; expenses covered, accommodation included, along with regular flights home. Apparently, he fitted the criteria, perfectly. *You could do this standing on your head with your eyes shut.* Martin wasn't sure exactly where Trinidad was.

Miriam calculated, if he worked for eighteen months, Georgia could carry on at the school; they could put money aside for university, and even allow themselves a holiday or two. Eighteen months wasn't long; time would fly by. He spoke with Raymond on Friday, and the following Thursday he was on a plane to Port of Spain. At first he was unsettled by the tropical landscape, the intense heat, the chaos of Trinidad. He was lonely; he felt like an outsider. He called Miriam every day.

Then, slowly, he got used to being alone, and he began to realise that leaving England offered him a kind of relief. Since losing Beth, they'd existed in a permanent state of grief, as if the colour had gone from their lives. Trinidad gave him an escape; no one need know about his past, of his enormous loss. Here he was a free man, and this sense of freedom made him more confident, somehow; unfettered, alive. He rediscovered his sense of humour; people found him quick-witted, dynamic, a can-do man. After the incident of the eleven-year-old boy, he'd felt different. He started to believe in himself again: *There is nothing you cannot do.* This is the side he showed to Safiya. He never expected to fall in love.

He sets the kitchen table and fills a jug of water; he presses a button on the fridge and ice tumbles out. This Electrolux fridge would be perfect for his kitchen in Trinidad. He will ask Safiya where he might be able to pick one up. She'd be pleased to know that he is thinking of buying a fridge. He checks his mobile phone. There is a message from Juliet telling him that she will send the new contract, and to enjoy his family holiday. Good, he is glad. Juliet read his mind.

He notices how quiet it is, much quieter than Trinidad. In his apartment, he can often hear the television next door, or people talking, the dull thrum of traffic from the highway. Here, they seem far from anywhere and anyone, which is exactly what he'd wanted. In a hotel, there'd be no escaping Miriam. No room to think. He had told Juliet he wanted a villa with at least three bedrooms and preferably a sea view; a taste of authentic Tobago life.

From the window, he can see beyond the pool of soft kitchen light, the vast lawn, and tall security lamps at the end of the garden where the high chickenwire fence begins. Yes, he thinks, this will more than do.

Miriam and Georgia drift into the kitchen, pale and tired and still in their travelling clothes. They sit on the high chairs and start on the sandwiches.

'I'm dying for some tropical fruit,' Miriam says, picking through the sauce, and he knows she doesn't approve of tinned sausages. 'Is there anything particular in season right now? I remember when you first arrived mangoes were coming out of your ears. You were eating two or three a day.'

'I'm sure we'll be able to pick up fruit. Bananas, oranges, they're all year round.'

In England, every morning, Miriam made his sandwiches and in a small Tupperware box came an assortment of fruit, the total of which would amount to his five a day. If he came home with leftovers, she complained. It is on the tip of his tongue to tell her about the high rates of diabetes, heart disease and cancer in Trinidad. Most people hardly eat fruit; vegetables are often heavily seasoned with pepper and cooked in oil. There is no five a day.

He would also like to tell Miriam how much he has grown to like hot and spicy Kentucky Fried Chicken and French fries. And how he enjoys the Hawaiian cheeseburgers from Burger Bar on Maraval Road.

They clear the table and he can see they are exhausted. 'It's three o'clock in the morning for us now,' says Georgia. She kisses him on his cheek and goes off to her room. He tells Miriam that he will wash up, and lock up. There are electric metal shutters in the living room which he must remember to draw down every night. Terence has shown him how to operate them. He will see her in a minute.

By the time he comes to bed, Miriam is asleep, her bedside light still on, her mouth slightly open, and she is breathing deeply. He moves silently around the room, taking off his clothes and placing them quietly on the chair. He does not bother to shower, or brush his teeth. He slides in next to her, noticing how her in-breath catches on the back of her throat making a familiar ka sound. Thankfully, she does not stir.

His body is tired; it has been a long day; it is hard to believe that only a few hours ago, he was in Trinidad with Safiya sleeping deeply beside him. He misses her smell, her cinnamon skin; the sound of her sleeping is pleasing to him. And yet he often finds himself unable to sleep when she is there, tossing and turning until the early hours of the morning. Does his guilt keep him awake? Is it possible? In truth, he probably sleeps better with Miriam, or alone. If she knew, Safiya would be dismayed.

He knows this much: he has never been a good liar. During these past months, he hid his growing feelings for Safiya behind a heavy work schedule. He told Miriam he was up against the wire. When they spoke, especially in the early days, he often sounded exhausted. Miriam understood. She didn't complain about being alone; she handled it all without him— taking care of Georgia, running their comfortable new family home, project-managing the installation of a new Shaker-look Magnet kitchen, and all the while continuing to teach Spanish part-time at a further education college. She has been patient. A rock. But rocks can crack, and Miriam is here now because she needs him. There will come a point, tomorrow or the next day or the day after, when she will expect him to come to her, to want sex. She will want sex too. The thought of this fills him with terrific anxiety.

FOUR

They are up early. It's the time difference, Miriam says. For them it is already almost midday; half the day is gone! They are in their swimsuits and colourful wraps, flip-flops on, ready to potter down to the beach. Miriam rubs sun cream into Georgia's shoulders. Her hair is bushy in the heat and sits at the bottom of her neck. He always preferred her hair long, not this middle-aged midway length. It is neither one thing nor the other.

'Breakfast? Coffee?' His eyes are tired.

'All done,' Miriam says, and points to the little stack of washed dishes. 'Georgia had toast and juice.'

Georgia rubs her tummy and smiles at him. 'Good afternoon, Dad,' she says, and checks her watch. She pecks him on the cheek. She is going to look for towels and some goggles. Terence has shown her where they're kept.

He slept quite well, considering. It was a relief to hear the door close when Miriam got up, to stretch out in the bed. His waking thoughts were of Safiya, and he wonders if she woke in her Mayaro beach house thinking of him, too. He guesses not, or at least, not for long. She seemed determined to have a good weekend with her young friends. And so she should.

He makes a cup of instant coffee and follows them outside. He is fond of the local instant coffee. In fact, when he last went back to England he took a jar of Nescafé with him. Miriam said, 'You've been in Trinidad too long, you've lost your epicurean taste.' Yes, Miriam prefers her Krups capsule coffee maker with its milk steamer and adjustable stainless steel drip tray.

Through the casuarina trees, the sea is a bright turquoise. He stands for a moment and watches its rippling skin, and he is wondering if the tide is high. From here it looks calm enough, and in a moment he will follow them down to the sandy beach and make sure everything is okay.

Miriam and Georgia are walking quickly down the path, towels slung over their shoulders. Miriam waves, and then Georgia waves too. From here, Georgia is lanky and striking; her fair hair is flaxen in this light. Otherworldly. He has already warned Miriam that she must be mindful of the sun even when it is overcast.

'Be careful,' he shouts. 'I'll be down in a minute.'

In the yard, he can see Terence walking with a hose; Conan follows on behind him. Terence is spraying the small palms; their smooth trunks are red and bright, like blood. The large garden must take a lot of maintenance. An acre and a half, at least. What would young Vishnu make of it? It would certainly keep him busy. There are three or four coconut trees, and a large mango tree. There is a landscaped section to the right of the veranda with an enormous cactus and small boulders, and when he looks more closely he is surprised to see a camouflaged hot tub. It would take four people quite comfortably. Georgia will love it. He will find out from Terence how it works.

Above the hot tub is a lattice with a vine of some kind; pale purple flowers and grassy shrubs surround the steps. He wanders around the other side of the house where there is a bony white tree with long branches. Its leaves are deep green and it has bright pink flowers; they are scattered all over the ground. He picks one up and the sweet scent is almost overwhelming. Frangipani. He picks up more flowers for Georgia and Miriam. What an abundance of colour; what a wealth of beauty. This place is a kind of Eden.

'Good morning, sir,' Terence turns off the hose, he makes his way over. 'Did you sleep well?'

'Yes, thank you; I slept like a fool.'

This is an expression he has learned from Safiya and it has always amused him. Thinking of her, he feels a sudden longing, a lurch of the heart.

'And you, Terence?'

'I usually sleep good; the house next door has parties sometimes, and the music gets real loud. But nobody there right now. Tobago dead. You came at a good time. Come Ash Wednesday the island will be heaving with people.' Terence looks up at the clear sky, 'Plenty sunshine.'

'Excellent. That means the beaches won't be too full. Are there any particular beaches you'd recommend?'

'Well, you could go to Mount Irvine; the sea is nice but you're kind of close to the road. Or there's the beach by plantation villas. Turtle Beach, about fifteen minutes up the road. Back Bay is on the other side of this beach here.' He points to the right. 'It's my favourite. But better to go in a crowd.'

'Where do you go?'

'I bathe right here sometimes, or down by Buccoo. I like to take a sea bath at least once a week; it cleans the soul.'

He is curious, does Terence need to clean his soul, too?

Miriam has her towel stretched out below the clump of rocks and she is sitting up, watching Georgia in the sea. She is wearing a striped bikini. He has never seen it before. He notices that her stomach is surprisingly flat, almost hollow; her weight loss is obvious now. He has not seen her this skinny since they met. She looks as if she has already caught the sun. Her pale skin is turning pink.

Pelicans dive near Georgia, plunging the water for fish, and she thinks this is hilarious. 'I'm going to get abducted by a pelican!' Georgia shouts. 'Help me, Dad!' She is bobbing up and down, holding on to the purple foam noodle she must have picked up from the storeroom. He stands at the edge where the sand is grainy; the warm water licks around his ankles. It feels good.

'Help me!' Georgia feigns distress. Pelicans are large, prehistoric-looking creatures. He has never seen one quite so close up, like this, right there, circling in the middle of the bay—and then, crash! The enormous bird plummets like an aircraft into the sea; then it reappears, its big beak clacking with a wriggling fish.

'Amazing,' he says. 'Isn't that something else?'

Miriam is inspecting her toenails.

'Are you going in?'

'Not yet, I don't want to get all sandy.'

He had forgotten that about her, her aversion to sand. When they had not long met, they drove to Crosby Beach. They ran down to the sea, took off their shoes and socks and paddled in the water. It was cold, and rain was coming. Once her feet were wet, Miriam refused to walk back; at first he thought she was joking, but then he realised that she was serious. She insisted that he carry her over the sand to the car, which he did. He remembers thinking it strange.

On holidays abroad, she always preferred a swimming pool, its easy concrete surround, especially for sunbathing on loungers. But surely, this could be an exception—this white Caribbean sand.

'It's a good spot, isn't it? The house, the beach?'

'Yes,' she says. Then, 'Could you put some cream on my back?' She flops onto her stomach, and adjusts her bikini bottoms.

He stoops over her, squeezes the orange tube, and the cream plops onto his hand. He quickly smears it onto her shoulders, and down over her back. Her legs are short, and her veins stand out like electric blue lines. For as long as he has known her, she has hated her legs. If he is honest, he has never much liked them either. Her ankles are thick and her thighs are soft like luncheon meat.

Her upper body was always her best asset: her neat back, round breasts, and cinched waist. His mother used to say: you're either an apple or a pear. And Miriam is most definitely a pear. Safiya is also a pear, but she is taller, more streamlined. If Miriam is a Comice, then Safiya is a Conference, although entirely more exotic.

'You can bring a towel and lie here, too, if you want.'

But he doesn't want.

* * *

The water is deliciously cool and he swims fiercely towards his daughter as if he is trying to save her from something. He ducks under, swims quickly through her legs, and lifts her up and over his shoulders. Georgia screams, and, at once, topples backwards and splashes hard into the water. Now she reaches onto his back, and clings there. He can feel her breath on his neck. 'Come on, Dad, I'm tired. Take us back to shore.'

He flips her off and there is a lot of shrieking and squealing. He can see Miriam sitting up watching, her hand a visor in the sun. Georgia waves at her mother. 'Save me!'

They swim further along, keeping close to the land, and paddle around the curve of the bay. On the other side of the rocks, it is difficult to see what lies ahead. The water feels cooler here, and it is a darker blue. In the distance he can see a couple of rickety wooden houses perched on the hillside. That must be the start of the village. They swim a little further, to where the beach seems to rise into a sandy bank. He can see sea grape trees but not much else. He calls behind to Georgia, 'Shall we?'

They climb out of the water and walk slowly up the slope. Between a cluster of rocks is a pool of turquoise water, like a pond. There are tiny white crabs crawling here in the crevices. Georgia sticks her foot in the water. 'It's warm,' she says, her eyes wide. She wants to jump in but he says they should carry on and see what's ahead. They pass around the side of a large rock to where there is a clearing. Above, and to the right, in the shadowy light, he can see a broken set of steps, and the branches of the tall trees marked with a cross. He knows what this cross means: they are manchineel trees; the sap is like acid. He tells Georgia to stay clear. There is a tangle of bushes here, and some long grass. They step through the bush and out into the light.

The beach is long and curved and coconut trees stretch along the edge of the pale yellow sand. The sea is restless; big waves are exploding onto the shore. There is a strong and warm breeze.

'This is amazing!' Georgia says, and her blonde hair is blowing back from her face. Better than Blanchisseuse, he thinks. How can that be? He wishes Safiya was with them. Has she been to this beach? He will bring her someday. They stare in silence. He thinks: we are nothing. Those waves could pick us up and hurl us against the rocks like matchsticks. And yet we are not separate from nature; we are not without power. Safiya would say that we have that same power, the force of the waves within. She would call it God. He is not so sure.

'Mum would love this,' Georgia says. 'We've got to show her. I wonder if there's a way to get here without swimming.'

Ahead, about halfway down, he can make out a line of figures; a few are wading in the water. It looks as if they are pulling a net. He has seen this kind of fishing before with Safiya at sunset on Store Bay. He'd made a joke about giving up his job for a simple life as a fisherman. Safiya said, 'There's nothing simple about these fishermen. Like you, they work hard to feed their families. Just because they're poor, it doesn't mean they're simple.'

And he remembers feeling embarrassed, irritated, and fixing his eyes on the busy scene, the young men packing fish into Styrofoam boxes, and carrying them on their heads to the road. They didn't speak until after they got back to the hotel and he told her he was sorry. He knew Safiya was right; it was easy to make assumptions.

Martin and Georgia start down the beach and the wind is blowing through their hair. The sun is now high overhead. They walk on the wet sand, and Georgia flings little pieces of stone into the waves—chip, chip, chip as they skim the surface of the water. He shouts: *Tic, tac, toe, my first throw, three jolly butcher boys all in a row.* And, to his surprise, she joins in, her voice shrill and young: *Stick one up, stick one down, stick one on the old man's crown.* The white foam rushes at their ankles; it feels cool, and the smell of the sea is strong.

The men seem to be deliberating over how far they can pull the fishing net up the beach. They look fit, especially the front man who is calling the shots; his black, lean body gleams with sweat. Behind him are three younger men, and then an older man in his seventies, perhaps; his legs are bowed, his skin hangs like a suit. A Rasta man with waist-length locks fools around in the middle of the line, cocking his leg out to the side. He is singing something familiar. Martin gives a friendly wave and offers a hand.

Georgia watches as he takes grip of the rope. There is a rhythm of sorts—reach, pull and hold. Reach, pull and hold. Reach, pull and hold. And so it goes. Part of the net is exposed on the wet sand, a kind of horseshoe shape in the bay. Bobbing out in the sea is a pirogue, and he is guessing that the owner of the net owns this boat. Is it the pirogue that drops the net out there? Who knows how long it will take to haul the thing in. A couple of dogs are lying on the other side of the fishing line. One has long dark teats hanging from its bloated stomach. The other, prettier dog seems more alert, ears up, nose held high. The two pick themselves up and move with the men along the beach.

'Hold,' says the front man. Then again, 'Hold!'

A couple of younger men, more like boys, watch from the side. Then one of them steps in front of Martin and takes up the rope. The other smokes a cigarette and sits by the rocks.

The rope is heavier than he'd thought and unwieldy, and the beach seems to rise, a gradual slope. If he did this every day, his hands would get rough—his soft, English hands. Gentleman's hands, Safiya says. Like his feet, they need to toughen up.

'Pull,' the front man shouts, and suddenly there is the entire net and he can see the caught, trapped fish, the glittery splattering bits of silver as they jump on top of one another. Their job is done. The sand here is soft and powdery like hot flour. Martin hops to where it is cooler; the front man thanks him with a high five. 'Nice work,' he says, to Martin. And Martin feels good; he feels alive. This is how we are meant to feel all the time; he is certain of it. Go with the flow, the young people say. And why not! He must seize the moment. *Carpe diem!* There is only one life; there is no room for compromise.

Georgia comes closer for a better look. Hundreds of silver fish are jerking and flipping on top of one another, gasping, dying. Thin long fish with sharp long noses, big broad fish with thick lips. Tiny baby fish, no bigger than a finger. Grey and white fish with meaty bellies. Georgia pulls a face. Above the wind, Martin says, 'My daughter doesn't approve. She'll eat the fish, but she doesn't want to know how they got onto her plate.'

'Dad,' Georgia says, embarrassed. Everyone is gathering

around the catch, and he realises they ought to head back; it will take ten or fifteen minutes; by now Miriam will be starting to fret.

They say goodbye, and set off along the beach, feeling invigorated and excited about their adventure.

Miriam is indeed anxious, standing under the casuarinas, her towel folded up, her beach bag packed. He sees her relief when she spots them swimming around the rocks. She waves and then sits down on the steps. She watches them climb out of the sea.

'I was worried,' she says, handing him his towel. 'I imagined calling the police to say you'd gone missing.'

They eat lunch at a small pizzeria in Crown Point. They sit near the window overlooking the paved garden in the air-conditioned restaurant. After the heat it is a relief.

For some reason, their rental car—a silver Nissan Tiida—has no air conditioner. It will not be comfortable or big enough for long drives. He wonders why Juliet chose such a small vehicle. There are no seat belts in the rear; no stereo. Tomorrow morning he will drive to Scarborough and change it for something more suitable.

This part of the island feels busier. Last time he was here, the place was swarming. It was Divali, and at the end of the trip, Safiya came to meet him for the weekend. She took him to a well-known tourist beach. The first time he saw the bay with its jetty, little cabanas, and clear green water—he thought it was paradise. 'My God,' he said, 'look at this.' Safiya held his hand and they walked along the white sand. He'd felt proud to be seen with her. This beauty was with *him*; she had chosen *him*. The water was warm and shallow; they walked out for thirty metres or so and it still only reached his waist. He'd wanted to hold her close, to kiss her, but Safiya said no. 'One day you will leave and I will be left with my reputation to think about.'

Yes, he will take Miriam and Georgia there; perhaps they can spend the day. There are restaurants and beach hut facilities. They can even take a cooler. He has decided that it is best to keep busy.

They drive home via the supermarket, and pick up basics to add to their provisions. While Georgia scans the aisles for local sweets, Miriam is disappointed by the lack of choice, and after a while, she gives up. There are few fresh vegetables, and what fruits there are look bruised, wrinkled. The bread, she says, reminds her of Nimble, a low-calorie bread she used to buy in the '80s. It's like eating air. There must be a decent bakery somewhere; he will ask Terence.

On the way to the villa, he misses the turning to the private road. He finds himself driving along the edge of the golf course where the coconut trees stand tall on the rolling stretches of clipped grass. They pass Mount Irvine bay, and it is flat and blue and shimmering. Up on the right is a low-rise house. He would like to wake up to a view like that! Perhaps one day he will. There are cars parked along the side of the wall where the beach starts, and people are cooking, smoke is rising, a make-do barbecue. They look like they are enjoying themselves.

No one seems to have noticed that they have come too far. He turns off to the left, into a village where the houses are old, wooden and patched up. Is this where Conan lost his leg? There is a concrete church on the right, a Centre for Worship, and behind it, a ramshackle old church on stilts. The grass is growing tall; the road is narrower now. People are standing on the side of the road—waiting for someone or something—and they stare into the car. Safiya once told him, Tobago people are a rare breed; they can sit and watch the world passing all day long and never get bored.

He spots a breadfruit tree; bright green balls hang amongst its leaves. 'Breadfruit,' he says, and points upwards. 'Can you see them, Georgia?'

She looks up through the rear car window.

'We'll try and get one for you to try. It's delicious, fried.'

'Where are we?' Miriam says, 'I don't remember coming this way yesterday. Are we lost?'

Underneath a wooden house, hens are running and a small child is shooing them. Martin slows down.

'Look at that little boy,' Georgia says. 'So cute.'

The boy turns and looks at the car. Georgia waves at him. He continues to stare, his eyes wide. Miriam says, 'It's hard to imagine people actually live here.'

'It's no different to poor housing in England. At least they have sun, they don't have to think about heating.'

They pass a kiosk selling cigarettes and snacks. An old man is wearing a pork-pie hat. He waves at them and Martin waves back. It is still hot, the sun burning down on the asphalt. Safiya often complains that the heat at this time of the day is murderous.

'Maybe they're happier than we are.'

'Just because they're poor and black, it doesn't mean they're happy. That's like saying all fat people are happy.'

'I didn't mean it like that. Sometimes I think we have way too many choices.'

He says, 'If they don't have choices, they don't have freedom. Give me choice any day.'

Miriam is looking at him, and he suddenly realises that he is getting himself into a tight spot.

Miriam says, and she is frowning, 'Choice of what?'

'Look,' he says, lightheartedly, 'it doesn't really matter. Who knows what these people feel about their lives. How can we tell? I imagine they are proud; proud of their heritage, their island. They have every right to be. Maybe that's something we've lost in England.'

'The fact is, Martin, the British came here like pirates and took whatever they wanted. They exploited these islands and their people. I don't think that's anything to be proud of. Colonialism has a lot to answer for.'

He is reminded of Miriam's ability to skilfully argue a point. Verbal sparring used to be a part of their foreplay. It was something he enjoyed.

He drives up what appears to be the centre of the village, and he's back out onto the main road. He notices Georgia is quiet, her head hangs out of the window, feeling the breeze.

'Be careful,' he says. 'Cars can fly along here.'

Later, Terence offers to pick coconuts from the trees in the yard. He climbs the shorter tree: his feet grip the sides of the slender trunk, his arms make a loop like a rope, and he hoists himself up the trunk. He makes it look easy, natural. The green and yellow nuts hang in clusters. He cuts down seven or eight nuts, and drops them on the ground. They each land with a dull, heavy thud. Miriam sits on the step watching, transfixed. Martin and Georgia perch on the veranda wall.

'If a coconut falls on your head, would you die?' Georgia says.

'Not necessarily. It would depend where it hit you. It could catch you on your body as you pass, and do no more than give you a scrape. The fronds are as likely to fall.'

Georgia says, 'You'd have to be pretty unlucky for it to hit you on your head.'

'Exactly,' says Martin. 'How often do you hear about it?'

'But if it did fall on your head, it would kill you?'

'If it hit the top of your head at full force from a height, especially a green coconut, which is probably around four kilos, then yes, chances are it would kill you—a subdural haematoma.'

'How?'

'If it hit an artery it might cause bleeding or swelling in the skull.'

'Like what happened to Beth?'

'Not really. Beth had an aneurysm, which caused bleeding in her brain. But, yes, sometimes a blow to the head can cause an aneurysm too.'

'An aneurysm can be hereditary, right?'

'Rarely.' He gets up and puts his hand on Georgia's head. 'I don't want you to worry about that, okay. Just don't sit under the coconut trees.'

He is sorry this conversation got started; he noticed on his last visit to England that Georgia talked often about death. On her bedside table he found a rather depressing non-fiction book about terminal illness called *How We Die*. It had bothered him. The counsellor told Miriam, when death arrives like an unwanted guest in a family, life is never the same again. It was normal and inevitable that, as she got older, Georgia would start asking more questions. It worries him that he will not be there to answer them. How will they communicate? By email? Skype? Will she want to talk to him? Or will Georgia align herself with Miriam and cut him off entirely? It is possible. The thought of this makes him feel anxious.

Right now Miriam seems okay; she is up and watching Terence who is putting the nuts into a pile. He is glad that she hasn't been paying attention to their conversation.

Martin says, 'Come, let's go see how he does it.'

'Don't get this on your clothes,' Terence says, 'you'll never get the stain out.'

They gather around for a better look. Terence holds the nut in his left hand and, using his cutlass, chops the end until he makes a sharp point and then he slashes the top and the coconut water squirts out. Georgia's eyes are wide; the speed and precision of his hand as he rotates the nut, combined with the controlled slicing of the long silver blade, is impressive.

'That's quite a skill,' Miriam says.

'Can I hold it?' Georgia asks. Terence tells her to be careful; the blade is as sharp as a sword. He offers the cutlass with both hands. It is heavier than she thought; she lets it dangle, then she swings it like a cricket bat. 'No,' he says, 'like this.' He wraps his hands around hers. Together, they lift the cutlass.

'You always lead with the elbow and cut down at an angle,' he tells her. 'Flick with the wrist at the last moment.'

Georgia gives Martin a look. 'This feels scary,' she says. Terence brings the cutlass down into the earth. Whap!

'My goodness,' Georgia says, her face lit.

The juice is a perfect lukewarm temperature. Coconut water can heal, Terence says. It will rehydrate, and it is full of protein. 'It's good for wrinkles.'

'So, do I pour it on or drink it?' says Miriam, patting her thin face.

He was always intrigued by Miriam's long ritual of face cleaning at the end of a day: the Alice band, the cotton pads, the lotions and creams. Has it paid off? Perhaps. Without it her skin might look older than it does now. Safiya mostly uses soap and water, and occasionally a little cold cream, which she keeps in his fridge. He likes the old-fashioned smell.

When they have finished, Terence lays the nuts on the grass.

'They look like people's heads,' Georgia says.

He raises the cutlass high in the air, and hacks through the middle of each coconut.

'Ouch!' shouts Georgia, then 'ouch!' again.

He rips the two halves apart. The inside is pale like wood, and when splayed, offers two bowls of white jelly. Using a flap from the chippings, they scoop out the white flesh. 'Isn't this incredible,' Martin says, and he swills the jelly around his mouth. Miriam isn't sure about the slimy texture, but she likes the juice very much.

It is almost dark when they help clear away the husks into a wheelbarrow; Terence will take them to a pile on the other side of the fence. Now and then when there is enough to burn, he makes a small bonfire.

After dinner, Georgia and Miriam play scrabble on the coffee table while Martin watches the local news. The expressive face of the newsreader strikes Miriam as she reports on a Trinidadian kidnapping.

'She acts as if it was her mother snatched from the family home. Look at all that emotion.' Miriam finds this amusing. 'Can you imagine if this was Moira Stewart or Trevor McDonald?'

'Trevor McDonald was actually born in Trinidad. A little place called Claxton Bay.'

'Well, he clearly wasn't trained here.'

There are images of a large concrete house on stilts, and a residential street. This might be Arima; it looks like somewhere in the east. The footage is shot with a cheap video camera. A young man in shirt and slacks is talking to camera. Martin has met him at various media events: a bright, bilingual graduate, slightly effeminate, who has worked with Safiya as part of the news team. Once when he was leaving a party at the American embassy, the man helped him with a flat tyre. Martin seems to remember that he sings in a professional choir.

Miriam says, 'The anchorman is the same. He looks as if he's about to cry.'

'Trinidad is small; he might know this woman. He could have gone to school with her. Anything.'

'How long has she been missing?'

'Ten days,' he says. 'She's probably already dead but the kidnappers want the cash so we have to keep negotiating. These kinds of operation cost them a lot of money. You have no idea how organised these criminals are. They have more forensic know-how than the police.'

When he first arrived in Trinidad, he worked with Raymond on several kidnapping cases. He was surprised by the expertise of the kidnappers. They often maintained anonymity by bandaging their victims' heads with gaffer tape. If victims caught sight of the perpetrators, they shot them. He knew of a fourteen-year-old boy who, after seventeen days, was about to be released to his mother and father. During the removal of tape from his face, one of the kidnappers accidentally tugged his eye open. They shot him dead, tossed his body on the shoulder of the highway.

'These people show no mercy.'

Georgia says, 'But what happens if they don't deliver the body?'

'It's too late—the money has gone. It's a risk they take. It happens pretty often.'

'That's awful,' says Georgia. 'So either way you lose.'

Miriam is half lying down; her legs are resting on the leather pouf. Where her tie-dye dress falls away, he can see the top of her white thigh.

Miriam says, 'What would you pay for me?'

He should have seen this coming; he carries on looking at the television.

'Yes, what would you pay for Mum?' Georgia is now sitting up straight.

'It depends what they were asking.' He gets up and goes to the shelf to look at the DVDs. He scans the titles.

'Well?' says Miriam.

'No one would take you; I'm not wealthy enough.'

'But what if they did take her?' Georgia wants an answer.

'Then I'd sell everything I have and give it to them.'

By nine they are exhausted. They are still on UK time, and it is some unearthly hour in the morning. Georgia has fallen asleep watching *Forrest Gump*. Forrest has started running, out of his yard, into the street. He is bearded, scruffy, and running all the way to Alabama. Martin imagines what it would be like to do exactly this—to get up now from this sofa and run outside, to keep on running until he reaches Port of Spain and the door to Safiya's Woodbrook house.

Miriam loudly yawns and stretches her arms above her head. 'Sorry to be such a wet rag.' She gets up, pecks him lightly on his lips and shuffles to the door. 'Maybe if you can come to bed a little earlier, we'll get on the same time zone quicker.'

While Georgia dozes on the sofa, he stays until the end of the film. He'd forgotten how sad and unashamedly pro-America it is. And that famous line: *Life is like a box of chocolates: You never know what you're gonna get.* What they don't say is that you can exchange the chocolates for something else. There is a returns policy, even if it's complicated and costly.

Curiously, with all his plans to leave Miriam, money isn't something he has thought too much about. If he can find a way to stay in Trinidad, he will let her keep the house in Warwickshire. He will pay maintenance for Georgia, school fees. He does not want Miriam to struggle financially if he can help it. He can rent for a while, perhaps even stay where he is. But it has occurred to him he will need a base in England, too—a small flat or a terraced house: a home for Georgia to visit.

He checks the gate at the end of the passageway and draws down the electric metal shutters. He must remember to tell Juliet that the Dials have done a good job. The place certainly feels secure. He wakes Georgia and sees her to her room. She walks as if she is still sleeping and when they reach the sliding door, too tired to kiss him, she rubs her eyes and nudges her cheek against his. From the passageway, he can hear music; it must be Terence. His room is right there.

FIVE

Island Car Rentals is on the other side of the highway, near the main turning into Scarborough. He pulls up outside a small concrete purpose-built block decorated with red, white and black bunting, the national colours of Trinidad and Tobago. There is a line of cars on one side of the building identical to the one he is driving. In the air-conditioned room, a young woman sits behind a desk reading the *National Enquirer* magazine.

He tells her that the car is not right for them; there is no air conditioner and it is too small for a family. Is it possible to exchange it for something else, something bigger? Without getting up, the young woman opens a door behind her and calls out to someone.

After a few moments, a tall black man, in his fifties or so, wearing a baseball cap embroidered with NYC, steps into the office. He is sweating, overweight. He looks like a man under pressure. He explains that all the cars outside are actually booked. They have been running a special deal with Virgin Holidays and they have no more cars left.

'Two flights coming in this afternoon from London. We have the Virgin flight and BA arriving. Next week is Monarch.

And then we have the Scandinavian flights too.'

He can believe it; and, of course, Carnival is coming; migration to Tobago is part of the Carnival recovery process.

So, they are short of cars. And he has already paid for this. What to do? He takes out his wallet.

'My wife and daughter have come to Tobago for the first time. I want to show them your beautiful island. But as I've just explained to the lady, that car won't get us very far.'

He flashes a wad of $100 notes.

The man takes off his cap and rubs his shiny head. He is thinking hard. 'I really can't help you. Everything booked. Everything.'

Then his expression changes; he has an idea.

He says, 'I could rent you my second vehicle. My personal car. It'll cost you another $3,000. It's yours if you want it. I can't do it for anything cheaper than that.'

The woman whistles. 'He love that car like it his baby.'

They walk outside and around the back of the building to a black four-wheel-drive car. A Hyundai Tucson. It has dark windows and it looks like a security vehicle. It is exactly like his neighbour's car in Trinidad. How about that? This could be fun, he thinks. And the interior looks almost new, the seats are well-upholstered. There is a cardboard box in the back, which the man removes. It is full of papers, cigarettes, office junk.

'I'll take it,' he says, counting his cash before the man changes his mind.

'It has everything—air con, stereo, central locking, big trunk. And it's automatic.'

'Great. I'll feel like Patrick Manning.'

The man rolls his eyes. 'That scamp.'

'Well, they say people get the government they deserve. We've got Gordon Brown, you have Patrick Manning.'

'Look,' he says, 'there's a new stamp of Patrick Manning's face here in Tobago. No matter how they try, they can't get the stamp to stick. You know why? People spitting on the wrong side of the stamp.'

He laughs, and shakes the man's hand. He must remember to tell Safiya.

Over the next two days, in their new black Hyundai Tucson, he takes Miriam and Georgia on a tour around the island. Georgia hooks her iPod up to the stereo; these are songs he hasn't heard before. Young people's pop music, he supposes, tunes Safiya must know. Georgia sings along, loudly at times. Miriam gazes out at the lush, passing green land, the little houses on thin stilts, the blue, glittery sea, the wild, thick bush. Yes, he thinks, Miriam has always been happiest in the sun.

They cruise along the Milford Road to Englishman's Bay, to a restaurant he has read about in the guidebook. It is empty; they are the only customers. The waitress, a young black woman, is shy or a little unfriendly, he cannot be sure. Safiya says Tobago people can be sour. The girl brings menus and a complimentary jug of lime juice. The lobster was caught right here in the bay early this morning.

It is quiet here like a dream. Overlooking the water, they eat the curried lobster, sweet corn fritters, sweet potato pie, cassava.

'Swiss Family Robinson,' Miriam says.

He realises that they have little *normal* time left together, and he wonders how Miriam will cope when he tells her about Safiya.

They walk along the beach; the sand here is pale like unrefined sugar. Georgia wants to swim—the sea is clear as glass—but there are jellyfish floating like little sails in the water, pale mauve sacs. He recognises the Portuguese man-of-war. He tells them about the time he was swimming and this same type of jellyfish stung a young boy paddling near the shore. The boy began to scream. His mother tried to pull him away, but its long tentacle attached itself to her neck, and then looped onto her face. It was only by going deeper into the sea that she could free herself.

'Yuck!' Georgia says. 'This happened in Trinidad or on another island?'

'At Mayaro beach in Trinidad. But there are other places to swim which you'd love. Like off the mainland, there are all these little islands: a leper island called Chacachacare; the island where the nuns lived; there are dolphins there sometimes. It's like *Pirates of the Caribbean.* The water's not like this, it's green.'

'How do you get there?'

'If you're lucky, someone's kind enough to take you on their boat.'

'Who did you go with?' Georgia ties back her hair; her long neck is pale like soap.

'There was a group of us from the office.'

He catches Miriam's look.

'One day we'll go there and you can see for yourself.'

* * *

There is something remote about this part of Tobago, something that feels uninhabited, untamed. And yet, he knows of villas tucked away in these small, pretty hills: luxury villas with infinity swimming pools and armed security guards. When he suggested to Juliet that they might stay here, or further up by Parlatuvier, she reminded him of a brutal attack some years ago, on the wife of an Italian diplomat. During a dinner party for her female friends, four masked men broke into the house and subjected the women to all manner of humiliations. One of the women, a UK national, was spared because she was menstruating.

He drives into Scarborough, an old-fashioned town with colonial style buildings and a fort overlooking Rockly Bay. He shows them the old police station, a tatty white and blue wooden structure, where, for two weeks, at the start of his trip, he worked hard with a small core team advising on interview and interrogation techniques.

He was shocked to learn that there were no audio recordings, just notes made in longhand and A4 notebooks. A superintendent might ask an officer to go and speak to a suspect, then tell him what he said. Often, there is nothing written down.

Like Chinese whispers, the information is easily misinterpreted or forgotten. Before an interview, there is no preparation, no research on the person or the crime he's connected with. In England this simply would not do. When he explained how procedures worked elsewhere, the younger officers were surprised and amused. One or two seemed keen and made notes. At the end of the training, the human resources manager told him his techniques would only create more work.

'This might suit your country, Mr Rawlinson, where you have plenty resilience and resources. But Tobago police are extremely busy; they don't have time for all this.'

He points out the Blue Crab restaurant where he ate lunch every day. Usually alone, although sometimes he was joined by Stephen Josephs, a senior officer, a macho individual, who seemed, to him, to enjoy nothing more than hobnobbing with foreigners.

'We could go there for lunch one day,' he says. 'They do a delicious soup with cow heel and dumplings. Their rum punch is pretty good, too.'

'Cow heel? Like cow feet?' Georgia makes a face. 'Ewwww.'

Miriam stares at the frontage as if she is piecing together something in her mind. Then she says, 'Do police here drink while they're working? Is it allowed?'

'No, but it happens. More than it does in England.'

In fact, when he went on patrol with Stephen, he spent most of his time in rum shops. That night, Stephen drank four or five beers. Conversations with locals were chummy, familiar and often inappropriate. Everyone was 'uncle', or 'breds', or 'sweetheart'.

'You have to ask yourself,' Stephen told a barman, 'if your wife keeps coming out of the kitchen to nag at you, what have you done wrong? I'll tell you—you've made her chain too long.'

And later, to a group of young men, 'What do you say to a woman with two black eyes? Nothing, she's been told twice already.' Martin felt awkward, embarrassed. What was the man thinking?

When the shift was over, Stephen drove him back to his hotel, taking the long scenic route over the old road parallel to the coastline. He drove slowly with one hand on the wheel, the other hung out of the window. The sea was lit by the moon; there were small rolling waves. He told Martin this was where he swam as a child, and where he now took his own children, aged two and five; it was his favourite spot on earth. He lost his father when he was a boy. But this loss had made him more determined than ever to succeed. What doesn't kill you must make you stronger, he said. He is living proof.

As he got out of the car, Martin thanked him. Then he said, and it was clumsy, 'You know, in England, Stephen, drinking on duty is a serious criminal offence, not to mention drinking while you're driving. Tonight you'd probably have lost your job.'

Stephen's face changed; the friendly openness was gone, and immediately he wished he could take back what he'd said.

'Mixing with locals is how we gather intelligence, sir. It might not be how it's done in your country. But it's how things are done in my country.'

In the morning Martin spoke to Raymond. He was wondering if he should report Stephen. 'What kind of example is he setting for the younger officers?'

Raymond laughed, and told him not to bother. He probably wouldn't have to deal with them again. Tobago police are a law unto themselves.

'But the man is a bigot, an idiot.'

'He may well be; he also has friends in high places.'

No, he was not a popular guest. He suspects they thought him pompous and arrogant, which he probably was. He is sorry about this. In truth, if he were in the same situation now, he would handle it differently. He has learned a thing or two about island life since then.

They head up the hill, and beyond, where the winding road twists and turns into the hillside, along the coast towards Roxborough and Charlotteville. It is glorious here, the sea sparkles a brilliant blue and the land juts out like the huge paw of an animal. They drive for an hour or so; the road is rough and full of potholes and he must swerve to avoid them. At one point, Georgia feels queasy. They stop at an old wooden church and stretch their legs; the warm breeze is gentle, and it carries the smell of the sea.

He shows them a bush of black and red berries, right there, near the side of the road. Jumbie beads, he tells Georgia; go ahead and fill your pockets. They are good for warding off evil spirits. So say the black people. *So says the young and beautiful Safiya Williams!*

Eventually, they come to an old hotel on the beach. They wander into reception where, apart from a few sugar birds perched on the backs of the chairs, it feels empty, abandoned. Miriam says it could do with a makeover. He disagrees; it has a certain charm, an authenticity. He likes the bamboo furniture with its sun-bleached flowery cushions; there is something of the '70s about it.

It's retro,' he says. 'I like it.'

'Your father's standards are slipping,' Miriam says to Georgia. 'A worrying sign.'

'Perhaps they are,' he says. 'Which means I'm probably growing more tolerant with age. You should be pleased.'

Miriam does not look pleased; she looks irritated.

'Come on,' he says, looking at the sea view. 'It doesn't get much better than this.'

They have lunch on the terrace under a canopy of coconut branches; it takes a long time to come and Georgia complains that she is starving. But they are on holiday, he tells them, and this is the Caribbean. Nothing happens quickly.

As they sip their delicious fruit punch and look out at the island of Little Tobago—the Bird of Paradise Island—he imagines they must appear like any other normal British family on holiday. And it troubles him that he is able to play a part in this charade. It seems heartless, cruel. But what are his options: to announce his plans, to tell Miriam about Safiya now? As far as he can tell he has no choice but to carry on. For now let it be so.

'I like this place,' Georgia says, when they are driving home along the ocean front with the windows down, the salty sea breeze wafting in. 'No wonder you love it, Dad. Can't we just sell up and move here?'

'And what about school?' Miriam says. 'And all your friends.'

'There must be schools in Tobago.'

'Actually,' he says, 'the standard of education in Trinidad is very good. They take their studies seriously.'

Then Georgia says, 'Is Trinidad like this?'

'Not really, Trinidad is more industrial, a bustling, hectic place.'

'Can we go there before we leave for England? Just for a day?'

It would be possible to do exactly that; they could leave on the first flight out and return on the last flight back. He would love to show Georgia the Northern Range Mountains, the coastline up to Toco. She would love Las Cuevas, the Marianne River at Blanchisseusse. But not this trip. It would make for complications. And Trinidad is small; Safiya would hear about it soon enough. Why make things more difficult. There will be other opportunities further down the road.

He says, 'Next time.'

'But you're coming home at Easter.'

'We can always visit for a holiday; I don't have to be working here.'

'There are lots of places in the world to see,' Miriam pipes up. 'You promised to take me to Vietnam one day.'

This is true, he had promised. But that was then.

'And Venice.'

'Venice is infested with rats and the canals smell awful, especially in the summer.'

"We could go in February for the carnival?'

'If you want Carnival, then Trinidad is the place.' To Georgia, 'Do you know how many people take to the streets and party? Thousands and thousands. They come from all over the world. The children's carnival is incredible.'

Miriam looks out of the window. 'Well, that settles it then. We'll just have to move to Trinidad.'

And as they drive along the final stretch of the Windward Road and head towards the capital, he wonders for a moment what it would be like if Miriam was serious, if she wanted to live here. He had never actually considered it.

✳ ✳ ✳

For the moment, Miriam is avoiding any difficult conversations, and he is relieved. He doesn't blame her. It was something his mother used to say—don't look for trouble, it will find you soon enough.

In her own way, he can see she is trying. He notices her new clothes; every day she models something different. To protect her hair, this dark new shade he does not like, she has taken to wearing a cowboy hat, and it looks, he thinks, ridiculous. She applies lip gloss, and checks herself in a white plastic mirror. A new habit. But there is something about the way she is holding herself together, her effort, that makes him pity her, and he doesn't want to pity her.

The fact is: Miriam has lost her moisture. She carries a dry quality like bread when it is old. She is only forty-six, and yet a part of her seems to have given up; she has relinquished a fundamental part of herself. He has met many mature Trinidadian women who, despite their years and personal struggles, hold on to something: a love of life, an easiness with themselves and the world around them, a certain *joie de vivre*. Yes, Miriam has had a difficult time, but she needs, now, to learn to kick back, to let go. At twenty-five, Safiya is dripping with moisture; and she will still have her moisture when she is Miriam's age; of that he is certain. He wants to be there to see it.

Six

It is Tuesday afternoon. They have returned from the beach and everyone is cooling off inside. He sits in the veranda flicking through a local guide to the island when Miriam suddenly appears; he can see at once that she is agitated.

'Can you show me how to turn down the air conditioner?'

'Sure,' he says, and follows her to their room.

She is wearing a long T-shirt with a slogan on the front, it says: Go Girl! He wonders why she has bought a T-shirt like this and if it perhaps belongs to Georgia.

'It's freezing,' she says, 'like England.'

'When you've been in the sun all day the air con feels cold. I know that feeling.'

He adjusts the temperature and shows her how to work the digital control system. It is similar to the one in his apartment in Trinidad and easy enough to operate. He is about to leave when she sits heavily down on the bed.

'Please, come. Just talk with me for a minute. It feels weird. Everything feels weird. I don't know what we're doing. Here we are in paradise, but you're out there looking at maps and I'm in here alone.'

Her voice is shaky, and he suddenly feels sorry for her. And yet at the same time, he is irritated. He doesn't want things to get heavy yet. There will be time for that later on. But this is so typical of Miriam; he should have known. He sits on the edge of the bed. Her hair is towel-dried and her face looks scrubbed. A clean slate.

'I just feel as if we're not communicating with one another. I feel like a stranger, and you're a tourist guide.'

She cries a little, and wipes her eyes with the back of her hand. 'We've come a long way to see you. I want things to be okay. Things were so weird at Christmas. I keep thinking that maybe you don't want to come back. You want to stay here and live in Trinidad.'

'Whoa,' he hears himself say, 'steady on, Miriam. You haven't been here a week and you're assuming all kinds of stuff.' He talks with a surprising confidence. 'I want more than anything for you both to have a good time. There's so much to see and do in this place. It's a great opportunity for Georgia.'

He runs his fingers through his sticky sea hair. 'We've both had a lot on. Just try to relax and enjoy the sun. Stop worrying.'

She smiles weakly and says, 'I'm okay when I think we're okay.'

'I know.' He looks down at the doves embroidered on the pillowcase. Hand-stitched birds of peace.

'So, are we okay?'

'Yes, we're okay.'

He pats the top of her leg, and for a moment, he hates himself.

Deceit, the cruel enemy of love.

Miriam says, 'There's something else: last night I dreamt of Beth.'

A hook in the heart—he is caught.

'She was right there like she was in the room. She was wearing her purple nightshirt.'

He remembers well her Bart Simpson nightie, the cheeky caption read, 'And your point is?' When she died, Miriam took to wearing it daily under her clothes like another layer of skin.

'Did she seem all right?'

'She said she keeps trying to telephone us but we don't answer.'

'Was she anxious?'

'No, not anxious.'

'Well?'

'She was a bit agitated; as if we were ignoring her. She seemed to want my attention.'

Miriam is relieved to be able to talk to him about this. Her face twists with pain. He has no choice but to allow her to come closer to him. She shuffles over the bed; he puts his arms around her thin, stiff back.

'Breathe,' he says, softly.

This was something they learned in counselling; by taking deep breaths it is possible to release pain more quickly and effectively. Holding the breath can block the release of uncomfortable feelings. In the long term it can create chronic illness. He is not sure about this. But the part about releasing he knows to be true. He feels Miriam shudder with her crying; she sobs softly into his chest. They stay like this for a few moments.

'You know, there was a girl on the plane sitting right behind us. She reminded me so much of her. She might have been eleven or twelve. I almost said something to Georgia but I thought it wasn't fair. Then when we were coming through immigration, Georgia said, did you see that girl, didn't she look like Beth?'

Miriam wipes her nose. 'It's ages since I dreamt of her. In the early days, it was all the time. Do you remember?'

It was true; back then Miriam used to look forward to going to bed. Her dreams were vivid and alive. At the time he was envious. The only problem, she said, was waking up.

'I wonder if she's trying to tell us something.'

'Like what?'

'I don't know. It's strange to dream of her now.'

'Maybe it's being in another place; a part of your mind is more open.'

'I don't think so.'

'Or maybe it's because it's her birthday in a few days.'

'Maybe.'

Miriam's eyes are watery. 'I feel a bit fragile at the moment. I don't know what's wrong with me. I think such bleak thoughts. I'm hoping the holiday will help, all of us being together as a family.'

It is obvious to him, she wants him to reassure her. But he cannot. Cannot or will not?

'Something needs to change. I feel like we need to get our lives back on track. It's hard to do that when we're in separate countries.'

He doesn't know what to say. A phrase comes to him: *The truth will set you free.*

Georgia calls loudly from the passageway and he is saved.

'Whatever you're doing you can stop it now.'

Miriam smoothes her hair and pulls her T-shirt down over her thighs. Georgia slowly opens the door, peeks through the gap.

'So you *are* in bed!'

He says, 'What did you expect at siesta time?'

'I'm starving. I'm doing all I can not to bite my arm off. Can we go out for some food?'

They eat dinner at a popular four-star hotel. The dining tables are set around a stage and a steel band is playing. The night air is cool, coming off the sea; the small coconut trees at the edge of the terrace are lit by fairy lights. The silky water, the dark sky, the sentimental tinkling music, make him think of Safiya.

The waitress keeps topping up his glass with rum punch— and Georgia thinks this is funny. He is soon feeling light-headed.

'Dad, do you remember when we went on holiday to Majorca and Mum collapsed with food poisoning in the restaurant?'

'And the paramedics almost knocked me out with a canister of oxygen which they dropped right by my head.' Miriam makes an unattractive, ghoulish face.

'I remember your mother throwing up on the floor of the restaurant. The other guests started getting up to leave.'

Georgia says, 'You were jealous because the doctor looked like George Clooney.'

'Jealous?'

He had forgotten this part. He can't remember anything about it. 'In the hospital?'

'Yes,' says Miriam, 'and he came to see me the next day at

our hotel; at the time you thought it a bit over-zealous, beyond the call of duty.'

Georgia adds, 'You insisted on staying in the room while he examined her.'

Perhaps he has erased the memory. Simple as that. He has no recollection of a handsome doctor.

'The point is,' he replies, 'your mother always liked dark men—Italian, Spanish, Latinos. God knows what she ever saw in me.'

'Awww, Dad,' Georgia puts a protective arm around his shoulder. 'I'm sure she fancied you like mad.'

Miriam smiles; she is enjoying this.

After dinner, tables are cleared away. Miriam asks him if they can dance—she has always enjoyed dancing, and they do, in an awkward but familiar way to Lionel Ritchie's 'All Night Long'.

Miriam insists on driving home. He explains that there is no such thing as 'over the limit' here, but she won't hear it.

He looks out at the passing fields of darkness, and he wonders how long she will accept his excuses and lies. It is a fact: people do not believe lies because they have to, but because they want to.

He leaves Georgia watching television and flops down on the bed. He might fall asleep before Miriam finishes in the bathroom; he hears the rush of the shower and feels himself drifting off.

'Don't crash out just yet,' Miriam says, looming over him. She is wearing a different nightdress. She looks too thin, he thinks; her bony chest pokes through the peachy lace. A cadaver.

She stands back so he can see the whole effect. It is short and the lace makes a V to the waist. Her breasts are partially exposed. It was probably expensive. French.

'Do you like it?'

'It's pretty,' he says, and he sees she needs more. 'Very nice. Very you.'

She looks pleased; her eyes are steady as she climbs on the bed, and he wonders for a moment what he should do. He tries not to think too much; it is easier to go with it. He reaches for the light switch.

'Are you sure you want the light off?'

'Yes,' he mumbles, and now he feels Miriam's mouth, the soft hole of her mouth with its strong tongue. She runs her hand over his trousers and opens the zip. She tugs his trousers away, and he feels exposed. She lies beside him now, stroking and rubbing. Her wet hand starts to work him gently. She was always good at this part, getting it just right. Can he get away with this, with just this? She will want more.

He feels below where she is naked, and, at once, she opens herself up. Before he knows what he is doing, he has wrestled Miriam so that she is underneath him and he is penetrating her. She holds on to his back; she lifts her head to press her face into his neck. It is familiar. Old terrain. He moves in a steady and slow rhythm. Miriam lets out breathy little coos. He had forgotten—she has always made this simpering, urgent sound. Now he can feel the sweat on his stomach as he slides over her.

But it is difficult for him to come. She says, 'Let me, let me.' And she pushes him a little so that he lifts and rolls to his side, and onto his back. Miriam climbs on top of him and he can see her now, a greyish shadowy shape, and suddenly the room is brighter—a mobile phone going off, perhaps, provides light. Could that be Safiya? And her hair is in his face, brushing against him, and then she is burrowing down in his neck. She feels hot; there is no air. He lets Miriam do the work now—rising up and down, her hands above his shoulders. She is working hard. Finally he comes, a sudden rise and a fast cascade into a sweet and minor release. There is none of the explosion he feels with Safiya, the rush from root to crown of pure pleasure. And yet it is familiar and he is satisfied.

Miriam is not ready for him to finish, but she doesn't seem to mind. It has always been difficult, getting the timing right. Miriam wants him to be fulfilled first.

She lies down beside him, her head on the pillow. There is enough light for him to see her eyes are open and she is looking at him.

The room seems to spin a little, and he wonders if he might be sick. An old song pops into his head: *If you can't be with the one you love, honey, love the one you're with.* He doesn't want to think about this. He shifts onto his side; he can no longer feel Miriam's breath on his face. Before he has a chance to think about anything else, he falls asleep.

SEVEN

Safiya complained about the man-made reef prohibit-
ing the natural ebb and flow of the tide. She said the
water is not as fresh as it used to be. But for Miriam
and Georgia, with its leaning coconut trees and wooden jetty,
Pigeon Point beach is a holiday dream. A paradise.

They put their towels and cooler in a large cabana and look
for loungers. He drags a couple from further up; he had forgotten about chairs. He seems to remember they are expensive;
last time he was here Safiya refused to pay tourist prices and lay
on a towel. In a while, no doubt, a man will come looking for
money. Georgia starts to cream up.

'Use plenty of sunblock, please, Georgia,' he says. 'Don't be
fooled by the breeze, the sun is extremely hot.'

Miriam is wearing a different bathing suit, a whole piece
with no straps. It is more elegant than her bikinis. If only she
would ditch the cowboy hat. He pulls off his T-shirt and tosses
it behind him.

'I'm going in,' he says, and makes for the shore.

'Wait for me!'

Miriam trots after him and they wade into the warm water
together.

'Ah,' she says, 'this is wonderful. Like stepping into a bath.'

He dives underneath and swims quickly along the bottom of the pale seabed. It is clear and calm. He wishes he had brought goggles and snorkels. There are hundreds of tiny fish swimming around the bottom, darting about, synchronised. How do they know to swim like that? Like birds in a flock. Safiya would say this is God. He calls it nature. He wriggles up and breaks through the surface of the water.

From the corner of his eye, he sees Miriam swimming towards him, and he starts, slowly, with a gentle breaststroke, to swim in the opposite direction; away from the shore and cabanas, towards the jetty, the open sea. He swims and swims until he feels his legs begin to tire.

Out here, some way from the beach, the shallow water reaches his chest. He can see Georgia lying on her sunbed reading, Miriam's head bobbing. He is aware of a heaviness around his heart, a sadness. It was there first thing this morning when he woke, along with a headache from last night. He wishes he felt differently; that he could slot back into the way he used to be. He has thrived within his family—with Miriam, Beth, Georgia, and he has never felt alone. They have accepted and loved him without question; he has belonged to them. He knows this is not a small thing.

There was a time when he and Miriam were deeply in love. He'd arrive home in the evening, keen to speak to her and share the events of his day. Miriam had a way of getting to the heart of the matter, articulating his feelings when he wasn't able to. Miriam understood him. Yes, she understood his inner workings. Curiously, this is what Safiya says about him: unlike the young men she meets, he *understands* her. Has Miriam's role become redundant? Has he become too self-sufficient? Has he outgrown her? Can it ever change again? Or is it too late? He suspects it is too late.

Today Miriam is more relaxed, more like her old self, which is mostly a good thing, although this troubles him too. Apart from feeling guilty, he doesn't want to raise her hopes, for her to think that everything between them is fine. Yet he cannot protect her forever. The truth is, if he hadn't slept with Miriam last night, it would happen today or tomorrow or the next day. It is likely that it will happen again. It was naïve of him to think otherwise. Regardless, Miriam is still his wife.

It would help if he could speak to Safiya. But escaping to make a phone call has been difficult. The signal at the house is poor. He has sent text messages. Last night she sent a message telling him that she misses him. She asked if they could speak at some point soon. He wonders about her father.

While Georgia reads, and Miriam lies in the shade, he takes a walk around the other side of the beach where a strong breeze is blowing. The water on this side is less calm, almost choppy, and it is more turquoise than green. Two windsurfers skim the horizon, their bright sails small from here. He finds a place to sit and lights a Du Maurier—his first cigarette since they arrived. It tastes good, and he feels a rush. Part of the pleasure of smoking is that it allows him time to think. How can that be a bad thing? He checks his phone; there is no signal.

Safiya told him that she came here as a child; she hunted for shells and coral chunks. She found all kinds: music shells, bubble shells, magpie shells. Fan coral was collected and put in the sun to bleach. The beach was littered with treasure. But now there is almost nothing. Where has all the treasure gone?

The day they came, they almost made it to the far end of the bay, but the tide was too high. For the first time, she told him about her ex-boyfriend, Pete Blanc, a French-Canadian vet working at the university. They were together for over two years. When his tenure finished, he had asked her to join him in Vancouver.

'Were you in love with him?'

'Yes.'

'So why didn't you go?'

'People abandon Trinidad all the time. Parents send their children abroad. They study to become lawyers, dentists, doctors. No one wants to live here. But then they keep coming back because they miss their homeland and they miss the sun. They want their doubles, their Caribs, their carnival. I'm not going to do that to my country. Or my children. I'm not going anywhere.'

She was looking out to sea, her hands resting on her waist.

'So you'd rather be alone?'

'In case you hadn't noticed there's half a million men bursting with testosterone in Trinidad and Tobago.' She grinned, a mischievous look.

'Do you still hear from him?'

'At first he wrote every day. But then he stopped.'

'He could've stayed here.'

'It never seemed to be an option. When he wasn't working, he spent most of his time picking up stray dogs. He was obsessed; then he started to hate Trinidad. His life was in Vancouver.'

Dreamy with longing, Martin put his arms around her neck; he kissed her salty skin. 'Well, I think he definitely made the right choice, and so did you.'

'My mom said I should've gone, just to see what it was like. Everybody said so.'

'Just because they all thought you should go, it doesn't mean it was the right thing to do.'

'Exactly.'

He caught a look of sadness. Safiya didn't strike him as someone who looked back too often but he wondered if she ever regretted it.

He said, 'One day I'd like to take you to England. There's so much to see: not just London; there's the Cotswolds, the Lake District. We could drive up to Scotland and see the islands. It's beautiful.'

'And freezing cold.'

'We'll get you a coat; you'll be warm as toast.'

'I'll need more than a coat.'

'You'll have me,' he said.

That day he realised, in her own way, Safiya was letting him know that she would never leave Trinidad for anyone. Not for Pete Blanc, not for him. If he wanted to be with her, he would have to find a way to stay.

'Where've you been?' Miriam asks. 'We almost sent out a search party.'

'There's a windsurfing hut. I wondered if Georgia might like to try it. There's jet skis, paragliding. It looks like fun.'

'She's gone down to the shacks to look for postcards.'

He pulls a lounger underneath the tree beside Miriam. He spreads his towel and lies down. Above he can see snippets of sky through the branches, the almonds between the leaves. He lets out a long sigh; the breeze has gone, the air is hot and still.

'What do you miss most about England?' Miriam says. 'Apart from us, of course.'

He looks out at the line of birds flying over the sea and wonders how honest he can be. The question feels like a trap.

'Not the cold or the dark mornings. I miss the garden.'

Miriam turns on her side. 'But you don't like gardening. I can never get you to do any gardening.'

'Well that's not the same as the garden; they're two different things. I always liked the beds, the roses. I miss the woods at the back of the house.'

She looks at him quizzically, as if she is learning something new. 'Do you miss the food? Sunday roasts.'

'Sometimes. I like the food here. You haven't tasted shark and bake. Or rotis.'

'Rotis?'

'Chapati filled with curry. Curried prawns, curried pumpkin with green beans.'

She makes a face.

'Look,' he says, 'Trinis enjoy their food. In England no one seems to like eating anymore. There's no pleasure left in it. Everything's bad for you.' On his fingers, he counts, 'Coffee, red meat, white bread, dairy, alcohol, sugar, fats. It's all forbidden. Where's the fun in that?'

'Is eating about fun, or about nutrition? I just don't believe eating greasy, sugary foods is good for you on a long-term basis. You have to think about your health; you have to try to be moderate.'

The point is, and he would like to say this to her, Miriam is not moderate, Miriam is obsessed with healthy eating, and he is tired of it. He'd like to remind her of their sickly vegetarian neighbour in Roundhay. The woman lived on raw vegetables. Her nose was red with broken veins; she was thin and grey as a phantom. It was something they used to joke about. Right now, he can't be bothered to argue.

Then she says, cheerily, and he can see that it is hard for her, 'Do you get lonely?'

'Of course,' and he brushes away the sand on the backs of his hands, his forearms. 'We always knew it wouldn't be easy. Mostly I'm too busy to really miss anything.'

He wonders if Miriam suspects something. It is possible, he thinks, but unlikely. Thankfully, she has never been sexually jealous or suspicious.

Later at the villa, the water in the hot tub is pleasantly warm and the jets are strong enough to feel like they are massaging his back. He is surprised and relieved that Miriam doesn't want to join them. She is feeling tired from the sun, she says, and goes to their room to lie down. He senses that she wants him to follow her, but he doesn't. Instead he climbs in beside Georgia. He rests his head on the lip of the tub. He feels relaxed, calm; the dark cloud has lifted. The water is warm, just right. Above, a lizard is green and stiff like a plastic model; it flicks its tail, and quickly vanishes amongst the vine leaves.

'So, tell me how you're doing at school,' he says. 'Exams are this summer, right?'

Georgia rolls her eyes. 'I'm supposed to be on holiday.' She dips her head under the water and her hair slicks back from her face.

'You are on holiday, but I can still ask the question, right?'

'Yeah, exams are this summer.' She quickly reels off her chosen subjects: 'French, German, Maths, English, Biology, Chemistry, Drama, Art and Media. That's it.'

'Good,' he says. 'Are you okay with them?'

'Sort of.' Then Georgia says, 'Did you always know what you wanted to be?'

'Pretty much. Well, I knew that I wanted to work within the law somehow.'

This wasn't true. When he was young, he had no idea what he wanted to do, and the police offered a way of life, unlike university, that could pay him while he learned. At the time, they were recruiting in large numbers with the slogan 'Police: Dull it isn't!' It seemed like a way out.

'Have you got any ideas?'

She shrugs and looks up at the flowers.

'Come on,' he says.

'I want to get married and have a family, and live in a nice house.'

'But you used to want to be a zoologist, do you remember? Or a photographer? You can have a career and a family; lots of people do that these days.'

'It doesn't always work, though, does it?'

'Who says so?' He splashes water on his shoulders.

'Everyone. Not many of my friends have parents who stay together. Maybe it's because they're all working. No one's keeping an eye on the family. Harriet's one of the only ones, and even she says her parents argue a lot.' She smiles and taps him with her foot. 'Sorry, Dad, but you know what I mean.'

'I do know what you mean. It's never that simple, is it? And if I wasn't here, I'd be at home getting under everyone's feet and your mother would be fed up. You'd both be complaining about me.'

Georgia gives him a look. She reminds him of Miriam now, her head cocked to one side. She is prettier than her mother. 'Yeah,' she says, 'you're probably right.'

'And just think, if I hadn't been working here, you wouldn't have had the chance to come to the Caribbean.'

He holds up his hands, to the villa and its glorious garden.

From the vine, Georgia picks a purple flower and looks at the centre, like paper, a work of origami.

She says, 'I'll be glad when you come back, though. Even if you do get on my nerves. It's not the same without you.'

Although Georgia is smiling, there is a look of sadness in her eyes, as if she knows something is looming.

He feels his gut twist, an uncomfortable sensation.

She plucks at the delicate petals.

Martin says, 'Well, let's not think about all that, because you're here right now. Let's stay in the present moment. Okay?'

She makes a funny face. 'That's a bit deep for a Wednesday afternoon.'

'Cheeky,' he says, and he climbs out of the hot tub, his

heart heavy like marble; he gently rests his hand on Georgia's head.

Is it possible that she could come to accept Safiya? Could she benefit by seeing her father find happiness? Or is he deluding himself? Perhaps a child doesn't care if her parents are happy or fulfilled—so long as they stay together.

He leaves her lolling in the warm bubbling water.

Eight

From the veranda, the sea is pure liquid silver, and the tall trees are dark, their branches long and feathery. There are no other houses in sight, just this stretch of tended land and sea. The sky is pale, dim, and soon it will be dark. Georgia is painting her fingernails with black nail polish, her long fingers splayed on the wide arm of a planter's chair. He has always liked these chairs, the easy pull-out arm with a footrest; they are practical and yet handsome. He would like chairs like this in his veranda in Trinidad. Georgia is concentrating. He wonders why on earth she has chosen to paint her nails black.

'Is this a vampire look?' he asks. 'Black varnish?'

Georgia rolls her eyes. Miriam doubts she can see in this light. 'There's no point in ruining your young eyes,' and switches on the side lamps; they brighten up the space at once. She flops on the chair next to Georgia and looks out at the sea. Then she picks up a thick, glossy magazine she bought in the airport and flicks through it.

Martin wanders off into the kitchen to find a cold beer. He hasn't seen Terence; he is probably watching television in his room. He would offer him a beer. He checks his mobile, but there is nothing.

He brings Georgia a Coca-Cola he'd put in the freezer earlier, now deliciously cold. Another Safiya trick: bottled Cokes in the icebox. Once a forgotten bottle exploded and splattered in his freezer. While he cleaned up the brown frozen mess, Safiya lay on the sofa watching *The Young and the Restless*. It amazes him that she likes to watch this trashy American soap with its flimsy sets and hammy actors.

He lights a mosquito burner and places it by Georgia's feet. The mosquitoes here are more aggressive than in Trinidad. These days he rarely gets bitten; he likes to think this is further evidence that he is adapting to his environment.

It is Miriam who spots the boy: a tall black figure running out of the darkness. He comes from the direction of the sea, and Miriam says, 'Martin.' He gets up, and Georgia stops what she is doing and looks out. Martin calmly tells her to go inside, now.

The boy is skinny with broad shoulders; his features are hard to see in this half-light of the veranda. He is Afro-Caribbean, seventeen or so, bare-chested, and wearing shorts; his hair sticks out in short dreads, tubes of thick black.

'Goodnight,' he says, and he puts his hands on his knees and drops his head; he seems to be out of breath. 'We get caught in the current and jus' manage to get in. My brother on the beach, the boat break down out there.' He points at the sea, which is now a dark, moving mass.

Martin feels a rush of heat. It is not fear, exactly, but it is some new feeling: he is on alert. He tells himself the boy is in trouble, he is asking for his help. There is nothing to be concerned about.

'Okay,' he says. 'What do you need? Do you need to come through the house and go out? You can get out from here to the main road.'

The boy points down to the beach. 'The boat still there. We pull it on to the sand. My brother hurt his foot.'

There is enough light to see the path to the steps. Martin calls out to Miriam and she comes at once. Suddenly Conan is there, barking loudly. The boy shuffles backwards, away from the dog, towards the bush; his arm a shield.

'Conan,' Martin goes to the animal, and for a moment he wonders if the dog might attack him too. But Conan seems reassured, and he allows him to take hold of his collar. He is still snarling as if he wants to hurt the boy.

'Miriam, turn on the security lights so I can see the grounds. We need the light by the steps.'

He notices Terence's room is in darkness; he must be out for the evening.

Miriam stands by the entrance where there are all manner of switches. Switches for the burglar shutters, switches for the outside lights, the main light in the lounge, the veranda lights. So many switches.

'How long were you out there?'

'All day,' the boy says. 'We drift for three, four hours in my uncle's boat. We start to paddle but the sea strong; the current carry us here. We see the lights.'

'Where do you live?' Martin is now standing on the top of the three steps that lead up to the raised veranda.

The boy points behind him. 'Not far.' He looks agitated; he wants to go back down to the beach. 'You come with me?'

There's no way Martin is going to walk down there in the dark.

'Let's just make sure we can see. Let's get some light first.'

The garden is suddenly flooded with bright security beams. Well done, Miriam. He can see the boy better now. He is slightly bug-eyed with high cheekbones, a snub nose. Martin is almost certain he is one of the boys they saw fishing that first day.

'Go down to the beach while I tie the dog. I'll see you there in a minute.' He watches him take off over the grass.

Miriam says, 'Is everything okay?' She looks surprisingly calm.

'Tell Georgia to stay inside. He seems all right. I'll see what I can do to help.' Martin leads Conan around the corner to Terence's porch, and quickly ties him to the tree. Then he heads back towards the steps.

The boy is squatting beside the boat, and, yes, he can see the brother now. Also bare-chested and younger, he is obviously in pain. He pulls his brother's arm around his neck and then lifts him up. Martin watches him help his limping brother over the sand; one of his feet drags underneath him.

'What happened?'

'He's stood on a sea egg.'

They have wrapped a T-shirt around his foot. It is difficult to see if there is blood.

Martin takes the other side, and they make their way up the beach towards the steps. The wounded one is younger; he grips onto the wooden rail, and, holding onto his brother, slowly hoists himself up. The stairway is narrow and there is a clump of plants along the edge with barbed long tongues that seem to get in the way. They make their way along the path; the brother's face is pouring with sweat.

Miriam and Georgia are waiting in the veranda. He is sorry Georgia is there, but it is too late now. Martin explains quickly what has happened. Miriam says, 'We should go inside to the bathroom where the light is brighter.' Then, 'I'll get a bucket of water.'

They follow Martin through the main doors of the veranda. They both smell bad, a rich and sour sweaty smell. He leads them through the living room, which is now much brighter with the ceiling lights on. The huge Turkish rug feels luxurious underfoot. He catches sight of the wounded boy's pained reflection in the mirrored mahogany cabinet where there is a display of Swarovski crystal ornaments.

They reach the double bathroom attached to his and Miriam's bedroom. It is a peculiar function in this house that there is not a separate guest bathroom. Each bathroom is attached to one of the rooms. He could have used the spare room, but it's too late now. He throws open the door and turns on the bathroom lights. Miriam has left her underwear on the floor and he quickly picks it up. The young one sits on the toilet lid and puts up his foot. The heel of his foot is dark with spikes, some of them are broken, and they are embedded in his skin.

Miriam brings a bucket of warm water. She goes to her wash bag and pulls out her tweezers, blue-handled tweezers she's had since they got married. She lays the hand towel on the floor. Martin stands near the door; in the mirror he watches the other boy who keeps looking around.

'How is it, Miriam?'

'Maybe we should call a doctor. I can get some of them out, but it's not easy to see.'

Martin realises, if he were to call the emergencies, he is unsure of their exact address. They are, of course, somewhere near the golf course. He remembers the road had a simple name, something like Back Road, or Lower Road? And the house belongs to the Dials. That's all he knows. How can he describe the house? It is probably the only house on the golf course with lights. He wishes Terence was here. It is unfortunate that this should happen while he is out.

Suddenly the brother gets up. He feels sick. He stands and leans over the basin, a fountain of pale yellow liquid pours out of his mouth. He groans.

'Come, come,' the boy says. 'Let's go.'

Georgia is perched on the sofa. She looks concerned, worried. Martin is sorry this has happened.

'All okay,' he says, cheerily. 'We've got it under control.'

The two boys make their way through the living room. The older brother stares at Georgia. She smiles at him but he doesn't smile back.

She says, 'Are you going to the hospital?'

'No, I'm dropping them home. They'll go to their doctor.'

She opens the front door, allowing them to pass through.

'Do you want me to come with you?'

'Stay here with your mother. Why don't you both watch a DVD or something. Make sure and lock up the house when we leave.'

'Okay,' she says. 'I love you, Dad.'

Outside the yard is dark, and he hears the electronic double beep as Miriam opens the car doors. They can put him in the back, she says. They shuffle along the gravelled path and the brother is sweating profusely; he is making a peculiar groaning sound. In the last few minutes his condition has deteriorated. Miriam lays a towel on the back seat and Martin moves out of the way, letting the older one tip his brother sideways into the back of the vehicle. He can still sit up; and his head is back on the headrest, his eyes are half closed.

'I'll drive you home but you'll have to show me where it is.'

'I will show you,' the boy says. 'It's not far.'

Miriam says, 'I'll wait here with Georgia. Don't worry. Call me, okay, tell me what's happening.' She gives him the gate opener.

Martin tells the boy to put on his seat belt, and he does. He reverses up the drive, through the gates and out on to the track. He tucks the gate opener on a shelf under the radio. The road is dark; there are no streetlights here.

He puts his foot down. In the rear mirror, the brother is propped up against the window; his eyes are now closed. Martin hopes he doesn't vomit again.

The boy runs his hand over the dashboard.

'This car cost plenty money.' He strokes the leather seat. 'I would like a car like this. How much it cost?'

'About $150,000. Maybe more.'

He could explain to the boy that the vehicle is rented, but he doesn't.

The boy fiddles with the buttons on the door and his window slides down. He does it again. Up, down.

'Easy on the buttons. We have the air con on.'

Martin turns on the radio; he finds the easy-listening station and gets Madonna's 'True Blue'. Somehow it does not seem appropriate and he turns it off. He is glad of the power of the vehicle; no doubt he is going over the speed limit. He remembers from his last trip: Tobago police rarely patrol the smaller roads.

'Were you fishing out there today?'

'They have no fish.'

'So what were you doing?'

'We look for lobster, crayfish. They didn't have anything. We have to go up on the north coast. Too many people fishing these days—it's like they empty the sea.'

He drives down along the dark road. He has never been here before, although it looks vaguely familiar and he wonders if this is the road to Englishman's Bay. They carry on, the sea is to the left; he can see the light from the moon playing on its surface. There is a hotel.

'They go here to watch the turtles, is that right?'

The boy nods. He is looking out, enjoying the journey.

'Is it somewhere here?'

'Yes,' he says.

The road begins to curve and twist. He feels as if they are climbing, and he opens the window to let the breeze in. There are no lights, no sign of life. He wishes he had cigarettes; perhaps he will pick up a packet on his way home. On either side of the road there is tall grass; and the view of the sea has gone. The sky is black and vast. It is hard to tell the difference between the land and the sky. Where are they?

'I hope I can find my way back.'

'Yeah, man, you'll find your way.'

Houses start to appear. They pass a church, a school next door. This is a big village, he thinks, more like a town. On the main street there are a couple of bars, a small supermarket, still open. The boy tells him to slow down. On the right the road forks. A couple of small houses sit at the top of an incline. He thinks how poor it is, the patched-up houses, the tatty curtains, the old falling-down steps.

'Here is good,' the boy says.

On the side of the road is a life-size Spiderman figure, sitting crouched, looking up at the sky.

He says, 'What's with the Spiderman?"

'Somebody steal it from the cinema and put it here. They never come for it.'

'How long ago?'

The boy shrugs; he doesn't know.

Together they help the brother out of the back of the vehicle. He is still in pain, but he looks better, and, at least, he can rest his bandaged foot on the ground. Good old Miriam.

'Will he go to the doctor?'

'Maybe,' the boy says.

There are chickens running around, pecking at the ground. One rushes underfoot, the boy kicks it hard; it lands like a small pillow in the drain.

Martin says, 'Your brother must see a doctor; he could get a serious infection. He'll need a tetanus, maybe antibiotics.'

'Yes,' the boy says.

Martin turns the car around. In the rear-view mirror, he sees them staring after the vechicle as he drives away. What are they waiting for? He follows the road back through the village and down the hill towards the crossroads. It seems shorter heading back, and soon he is on the main road leading to the house. He feels relieved. When he reaches the house, Miriam opens the gates. He parks up near Terence's room. The lights there are still not on. Perhaps Terence has a lady he visits at night. The mother of his child. Unfinished business. Who knows. It is not his concern.

Miriam calls, 'You okay?'

He locks the vehicle. 'Yes,' he says, 'coming now.'

Above, stars glimmer like broken, scattered crystal. The black sky is enormous. Martin feels tiny, a pinprick of consciousness looking out at itself. Is everything part of him? Is he part of everything? The stars, the planets, this island? Buddhists would say so. Buddhists would say, all that we are is the result of what we have thought; we are all one. He does not know; he can accept this as a theory. But he doesn't actually feel it. He has never felt it. Perhaps we are nothing more than crabs scrabbling in the bottom of a barrel.

From the pathway, he can see inside the house, the orange light of the kitchen. Through the burglar-proofing, Miriam is talking to Georgia. They look surprisingly cheery, especially Georgia who is laughing, her head back. They are having a good time without him. He is not a part of their lives; he hasn't been part of their lives for some time. He is disconnected from their world, unplugged. It is not a pleasant thought; in fact, it makes him feel strange. And standing outside looking in, he wonders for a moment if this is how it feels when you die, when you leave your body, and witness your loved ones carrying on without you. He goes inside.

Nine

He doesn't sleep well. At 5.30 he goes outside to the yard where it is just beginning to grow light; the sky is a smoky blue, the air is cool. It occurs to him, they have been here exactly a week; it feels more like two. Time, as they say, is relative. It has always been a mystery to him. The curious fact: a clock on the top of a mountain moves differently from a clock positioned at sea level. Tall people age differently from short people. Why does time seem to rush towards us when we are older? And why does our youth seem easier to recollect than later years. There is mind time, and there is real time. Lately, his sense that time is running out has been real and acute.

He wanders over to the storeroom where Terence is sorting through a large bag of snorkels and goggles and armbands. Conan sits at his feet, his stump on show. Chelsea, Terence's daughter, is arriving this afternoon; he knows she will want to swim. Terence is surprised to hear of last night's drama. In all his time here he has never heard of trespassers.

'People know this is private land; they never use the beach.'

'Well, to be fair, I don't think they came here intentionally. They got washed up when their boat conked out.'

'Did Conan bark?'

'Yes, he didn't like them much, did you, Conan? What does that tell us, eh?' Martin pats Conan's dark head. 'Look, the boys were okay, we just didn't expect to see them and they caught us offguard. I'm sure they meant no harm.'

They walk to the end of the lawn and look down at the beach. The pirogue leans against the bank; a rope ties it to the tree that reaches beyond the rocks. It is a tatty-looking boat with the word *Princess* painted on its side. There is a net slung in the back, a couple of empty Coca-Cola bottles, cigarette butts. The engine looks pretty new. Terence thinks it belongs to a fisherman in the village known as Tin Man.

'Why do they call him Tin Man?'

'Tin, like thin.' He holds up his little finger, and grins. 'He likes to smoke weed. The boys are probably his nephews. I'm sure I'll have seen them around.'

Terence says he did a good deed; he might have saved the boy's life.

'I didn't really have much choice, he was in a lot of pain.'

'The first thing you should do with a sting like that is pee on the wound.'

He tries to imagine what would have happened if he had offered to pee on the boy's foot. Not a pleasant thought.

'If you'd been here, Terence, you could've done just that.'

They both laugh, imagining the scene.

Martin says, 'Why not bring Chelsea over to meet Georgia later? Miriam is making a cake.'

It is still only 6.45. Terence opens the gates and Martin drives away, leaving Miriam and Georgia sleeping. The road to the airport is clear. He drives steadily through Canaan and into Crown Point. Outside the hardware store haulage trucks are starting up. At the traffic lights, two brown dogs stand in the middle of the road, and they look as if they are stuck together. At first it appears as if there is something wrong, a kind of mutant double dog, an accident of some kind. But then he realizes that the dogs are fucking. As if they've been soldered together. One of the animals is trying to pull away and cross the road, but the other one is attached and heading in the opposite direction. He toots his horn, and the male gets his way, dragging the female to the grassy pavement. She looks terrified.

He is glad that Georgia is not with him; he would have to make a joke, and no doubt he would feel awkward. He has no idea what Georgia knows about sex; he hopes very little. There is something about her that seems remarkably innocent; perhaps because he would like to think her so. But then no one really loses their innocence; it is either taken or given away willingly. For now, Georgia seems to be intact. Long may it last.

He picks up coffee from a Vie De France café. It is surprisingly quiet; the world is still waking up. On the front of the *Express* newspaper, the headlines report on a family drowned at Toco. How does this happen? The photograph shows a young woman, the mother, kneeling and bawling in the road, and to one side four bodies covered with white sheets. Their feet stick out. A shocking and distressing image; it would never be allowed in an English paper.

He's heard about police officers using their mobile phones to photograph crime scenes and selling them on to the press.

It's a way of making extra money, of subsidising their low incomes. No doubt this is one of them.

The Internet café is open but there is no one inside. He waits for a few minutes, and eventually a woman comes in and, without speaking, points at one of the machines. He checks through his emails swiftly. Juliet has sent through a PDF copy of his new contract. He scans it briefly; apart from the date it looks almost identical to his last contract. He is surprised by how relieved he feels. Two more years in Trinidad—it will do for now.

There is nothing else that needs his urgent attention. Whatever is there can wait. He'd wondered if Safiya would write to him, knowing he'd check his emails, and he is disappointed.

He dials her number, and her voicemail kicks in. He tries again. If she gets this within the next half hour she can call him back. For now, he misses her *like the deserts miss the rain.*

He knows this is schmaltzy and later she will tease him, but it will also remind her of a happier time when they danced to the song in the platinum members' lounge, at Zen nightclub, Port of Spain, before he left for England.

They'd been drinking tequila shots, and it came on at the end of the night. When the song finished, he remembers kissing her deeply in a cloud of dry ice. A few people actually clapped. Later, Safiya was embarrassed and blamed the tequila. She never liked a public display of affection, and that night she'd given in. He'd told her, 'It's good to surrender; the greatness of a man's power is the measure of his surrender.'

He is glad to be out; he feels like himself again. He likes this car, its size and solidity. It attracts some attention at the school bus stop. He has noticed, rich or poor, children here are always sent to school looking immaculate. In their bright turquoise uniforms, the young girls stare; they think he is somebody important. Ha!

At Penny Savers there is new stock: oranges, pineapples, apples and bananas. Miriam will be pleased. He finds eggs, Milo, a powdery chocolate drink that Safiya loves. He is sure that Georgia will like it too. He picks up flour, cocoa, sugar, butter. Later, Miriam will bake a cake for Beth's birthday. It is what they do. It is what they have always done.

'You must celebrate her life,' the bereavement counsellor told them. 'Celebrate all that you loved about her.'

At the time, the idea of celebrating anything was incomprehensible, and he'd felt angry with the counsellor. But anger, she said, is an important part of the healing process; beneath anger is sadness.

'You have to mourn losing, not just your daughter, but the person you were before she died.'

He remembers thinking, will I recognise the person I am going to become?

Meanwhile, Miriam was drowning in her grief; she was prepared to hold onto anything. At times she found it difficult to breathe, as if, she said, concrete blocks were pressing on her lungs. That day she lay on Beth's bed, her face red and swollen from crying. She said, 'How is it that God could need her more than me?'

He was astonished. 'God?'

Back then, he'd wanted to protect her from the outside world, the looks of pity, sad glances. It was bewildering to him how clumsy others could be.

A work colleague told him she could understand exactly how he was feeling; she had lost her beloved horse the same week that Beth died. A horse! And then there was Audrey Hanson, who worked part-time in the post office, and had come to know Beth over the years. Breezily she said, 'After a storm the birds will sing again. Thank goodness you have Georgia.'

Would it have been easier if there'd been a sign or a warning? If they had known of a blood vessel growing big like a berry inside her young brain.

That Tuesday night when he got home late, Georgia was asleep, and Beth was watching an old episode of *Cheers* with Miriam. The room had recently been painted and the smell lingered in the house. She was wearing her Bart Simpson nightdress, and making popcorn on the stove in an old aluminium pan. He was irritated by the noise.

'Sorry, Dad,' she said, and pulled a sad face. 'It can't be helped; this is a matter of extreme urgency and importance.'

'Are you being cheeky?' he said, pouring himself a whisky.

'Maybe. You're working too hard. You know what they say, all work and no play makes Dad a dull boy.'

Miriam said, 'I'm with you, Beth. Tell your dad to lighten up.'

'The problem is, I have to earn enough money to keep my family in the luxury to which they have become accustomed. Some of us have expensive hobbies.'

Beth tipped the popcorn into a big plastic bowl, melted a tablespoon of butter and trickled it on top. She was excited; she was going horse-riding in the morning.

'I hope it doesn't rain. I hate when it rains. I don't like riding in the rain.'

She sat on the velvet sofa between the two of them, feet on the coffee table, the bowl of popcorn on her lap. Then—and for no apparent reason—she said, 'I love you both. We should tell each other more often. We should make it a house rule.'

Martin felt both embarrassed and awed by her confidence, her willingness to express her feelings. It was something he had never done easily. When they said goodnight at the top of the stairs, he told Beth that he was proud of her. And, yes, he thought this new house rule was an excellent idea.

At 5.30 she came to their bedroom and said her head was hurting; she started to cry. Miriam got up and followed her into the bathroom, where she was sick. She lay on the bathroom floor, sobbing and holding her head.

Georgia wandered in to see what was wrong; she had seen the light on the landing. Miriam ushered her back to bed. 'It's okay, George, go back to sleep. There's nothing to worry about.'

After a few minutes, Miriam came to him, her face long and pale. 'Actually, I think it's serious. The doctors' surgery doesn't open for another hour. We should get her to hospital.'

They were going to leave Georgia with a neighbour, but she didn't want to be left. She started to cry. 'I don't want Beth to die.' Until that point it had never occurred to him that she might.

Miriam quickly packed an overnight bag. By this time Beth had a high fever and was mostly incoherent. It was freezing; in the darkness he scraped ice off the windscreen. He lifted Beth and carried her out to the car. The roads were hazardous and he had to drive slowly. The sun came up; the world was white with frost.

It was two hours before a young paediatrician consultant arrived. After a CT scan, they rushed Beth by ambulance to another hospital in Birmingham for emergency neurosurgery. She was bleeding into her brain, they said. Georgia and Martin followed Miriam in the ambulance. He telephoned his mother and asked her to meet them there.

In the private waiting room, the consultant said it was unlikely she would survive; Beth had suffered a cerebral aneurysm. She was brain-stem dead. Martin looked at the small, balding stranger with glasses, the bearer of this catastrophic news; he felt as if he was dreaming, his insides were cold.

'It is extremely rare,' the man said, and he put his hand on Martin's shoulder as if they were friends. 'You must know you did everything right.'

He remembers the organ transplant coordinator talking to them about donorship. Was Beth the kind of person who would want her organs used to save someone else's life?

'Yes,' he told the woman. 'Beth had talked about it only recently.' She'd asked her mother how to make a will. To the woman he said, 'Do you think she had some kind of premonition?'

The woman smiled, weakly. There were forms to sign, documents to take away with them.

His mother arrived. She looked at him with such sorrow and pity he has never forgotten it. She took Georgia back to her house; Miriam and Martin sat with Beth in the hospital room. Her head was bandaged, but she looked strangely well, as if she was sleeping. They held her cool hands; they took turns to talk to her. At one point, Miriam lay down next to her, and put her arms around her.

He had seen it over the years, particularly in the early days: murder, road traffic accidents, suicide. Like other parents, he had never expected this to happen to him. He was often the bearer of bad news, never the receiver.

The road back is clear. He stops off at Buck Buck Alley to pick up bread on Terence's recommendation. The bread is warm, heavy. Proper bread in a brown paper bag. Like the bread he buys from their local bakery on Saturday mornings in the village. He always arrived as the bread was coming out of the oven; he took it home to make bacon sandwiches for Miriam and the girls. And he realises—driving towards the crossroads, the field to his left where horses are grazing, dark and shiny like molasses, the vast blue open sky—he is slotting back into his role of husband and father.

Perhaps it will be easier for everyone if he carries on as normal. Why make things more difficult. Miriam is fragile, overwrought. In three days she will go back to England and he will have his life back. Does she need to know the details of that life. Does she need to know—right now—about Safiya? He has tried to visualise telling her that he is leaving her, that their life together is over, and he can't. Can't or won't? It doesn't matter. The truth is this: right now, his life with Miriam and Georgia in England is separate from his life in Trinidad; it is separate from his life with Safiya.

After breakfast, Miriam packs a cooler with drinks and fruit. Georgia wants to go to Store Bay.

'Chop-chop, Dad.' Georgia is dressed, her hair is loose and wavy. The sun has made it lighter.

'We want to get there before lunch. There's some great food huts. Where's your cozzie?' She kisses him lightly on his cheek. 'You okay?'

He is sometimes astonished by Georgia's brightness.

'You bet I am.'

'Did you see Conan? Terence was looking for him; he thought he might be out on the road.'

'No, not when I came in. I saw goats, horses. No dog.'

Georgia pulls back her hair and ties it into a knot.

'We're leaving in five, okay?'

'I'll be there or be square.'

'Dad,' Georgia says, 'that's such a naff thing to say. So incredibly uncool.'

'I am un-cool, darling. I'm your father.' He puts his arm around her waist. 'One thing you can be sure of, I will always embarrass you.'

'Mum's cool. She doesn't show me up.'

'You see,' he says, 'this is what happens when we're all together. You start ganging up on me. It's a form of persecution. That's why I have to live in Trinidad.'

'Not for much longer,' she says, over her shoulder.

With his coffee, he pads along the passageway to his room. He stops to watch hummingbirds feeding on the Antigua Heath. He has the same plant in his garden in England, only it is called Montbretia and the flowers are more orange than red. The tiny creatures stick their long bills into the mouths of the red bellflowers; their iridescent green feathers shimmer.

Safiya told him, the wings of a hummingbird beat sixty times a minute and their hearts a thousand. Or is it the other way around?

He checks with Terence to make sure he will he be there when they come back from the beach. He can't seem to find the gate opener.

Miriam brings the guidebook in the car. Birds, it seems, are the theme of the day.

'Did you know the Scarlet Ibis is the national bird of Trinidad and Tobago? And they're on a one-dollar note.'

He wants to say, yes, and with Safiya, I've seen huge flocks fly into the Caroni swamp as they come back from feeding grounds in Venezuela.

'And the orange-winged parrot, the most common parrot in Trinidad and Tobago, pairs for life.'

'Every morning I hear them flying over my apartment. They sound like geese.'

'Really, Dad, you have parrots in your garden?'

'Parrots, kiskadees, yellow birds, blue birds.'

For some reason there are more cars on the road, and he wonders if a flight came in yesterday from England. The car park at Penny Savers is packed. It is Ash Wednesday; if Terence is right Trinidadians will be starting to arrive from carnival.

At the turning, tourists walk along the sandy road. They must be English. Trinidadian women lean back when they walk, hips forward, easy. Not like these clompy-looking folk. What is it about the English?

He drifts away to Trinidad, and his apartment, and he

wonders if Sherry has watered the yard, and if young Vishnu has come. He had told Safiya, while he is away, she is welcome to use his apartment whenever she likes. She might enjoy the independence, a break from home. Has she been there? He doubts it, somehow; it depends on how much she misses him. And what about Fanta—is he eating? Without him there, Fanta might run away. Curiously, the cat has become an anchor. It would be a bad sign if he left. He must call Sherry and check that she has seen him about the place.

Store Bay is lively, with music booming out from a nearby sound system. He recognises some old favourites: Bob Marley and the Wailers, Jimmy Cliff, the Police. Everyone is in a good mood, even Miriam, and he is pleased. There is no mention of Beth, which is probably as it should be. They buy lunch from one of the local vendors, curried crab with dumplings. Miriam thinks the crabs are awful, the look of their blue grey claws in the curry sauce and the rubbery white dumplings. To his surprise, Georgia likes them and tucks into Miriam's leftovers.

He loves the sea here, the yellow sand; it is more like the beaches in Trinidad. There are some real waves, and both he and Georgia are caught in the surf a couple of times.

Later, from a handicraft booth on the roadside, Georgia buys a coral bracelet, and a beaded necklace for her mother. 'This will cheer her up when we get home,' she tells him.

'Is it that bad?'

'Of course, she hates you being here.'

'Yes, but she has people around.'

'It's always harder if you're on your own. They're all couples;

they have dinner parties for couples. Mum ends up feeling like a lemon. She drinks too much.'

They walk back down to the beach. An old woman is sitting on the steps selling sugar cake and chennets.

'What are those?' Georgia says, pointing at the fruit.

'They're like lychees. They're good.'

He buys a large bunch.

The sand is hot and powdery. They hurry to the water's edge and let the cool froth rush over their toes. It feels wonderful.

'What do you mean, she drinks too much? At home or when she goes out?'

'When she goes out, when she's at home. Same thing; she's miserable.'

It worries him that Georgia is mothering Miriam, or over-compensating. It is not her job to protect her mother. The counsellor warned them—after the loss of a sibling, all too often the remaining child steps into a parental role. Something to keep an eye on. And Miriam was never much of a drinker. Has Georgia got that part right?

The weather could not be better. There are no clouds, just a clear, perfect blue sky. It is one of the hottest days so far, the white sun blasting down on the island. Everything feels bleached out, dry and crisp; the grass, the trees, the bush; as if ready to crackle and burn.

And today there is no breeze. So much so, that by the time they get back to the villa, Georgia and Miriam are keen to retreat to their air-conditioned rooms to shower and rest. He rings the bell; from his room, Terence opens the gate. Chelsea must be here. Martin tells Miriam he will join her soon for a nap.

He wanders across the freshly cut grass, and through the casuarina trees to the steps. The tide is rising. He looks down on the beach; the pirogue has gone. The boys must have come for it while they were out. He is glad. There was something about last night that unsettled him. No doubt Terence will give him the details.

From here the sea is huge, indifferent and endless as a galaxy. It has no interest in him and his little difficulties. The sea does what it wants. Safiya says the cure for anything is salt water—tears, sweat or the sea. Perhaps, he thinks, when we look at the ocean, we are reminded of our true nature. But what really is his true nature? Is there such a thing?

In the last year he has discovered parts of himself that he never knew about, parts he would rather not admit to. He has discovered, for instance, that he is 'territorial', 'uncompromising', and 'moody'. He is also 'passionate' and 'liberal'. These are some of the words Safiya has used to describe him.

Maybe in Trinidad, he is finally waking up to his real self, to the real Martin Rawlinson. And looking out at the waves, the pristine, white rolling foam, it occurs to him that it is a marvellous, wondrous thing—to be more than halfway through your life and still making discoveries. He would never have thought it possible.

In the kitchen, Miriam touches his back as he passes. A Miriam gesture. She asks him to tell Georgia that the cake will be ready in about half an hour.

'Find out what she'd like to drink,' she says. 'No more cola.'

He says, 'It's not cola, it's Coke, and she is on holiday.'

'Have you ever seen what it does to a twopence piece? It strips it back to its original colour like a cleaning agent.'

"You won't stop her liking it. She'll think you're a killjoy.'

'I don't care what she thinks. Think what it does to our guts, what it's doing to your daughter's guts. One of the ingredients is anti-freeze. Would you let Georgia drink anti-freeze?'

Today Miriam looks better; she's finally turning a reddish brown; the green halter dress is feminine, more flattering. It covers her legs and fits well around her breasts. Yes, something is different, or is he simply getting used to her?

While her father prunes the small trees, Chelsea has come to play with Georgia in the verandah. She is shy, and at the same time completely mesmerised by Georgia. She leans against the veranda wall and stares at her. Her hair is braided in little fair plaits, held in place by small colourful beads. A Rasta child, no less.

Georgia has been setting up her camera to take night photographs as part of her media course. She is using film and an old Sony SLR of Miriam's. She tells him, there are only a few days each month where moonlight photography is actually possible.

'Do you know the moon is 250,000 times dimmer than the sun?.'

'Great. Let me know where you want me.'

'I don't want you in the photos, Dad. These are landscape pictures.' She looks at him incredulously.

She will set up near the casuarina trees, and try to capture the sea, the house from a distance. It could take a couple hours.

'I want to get a feeling like you're being watched.'

He likes Georgia's enthusiasm.

'Chelsea, come and sit with me. You can listen to my favourite ever song. Do you like Black Eyed Peas?' Georgia turns the sound up loud and it blasts through the tiny earphones.

'Come listen.'

Chelsea hides behind a chair; Georgia pretends to ignore her.

This seems to do the trick. In a few moments, Chelsea runs over to show off her big plastic doll and two dresses she has brought. She climbs onto Georgia's lap and, using a comb for her doll, tries to brush Georgia's hair.

'Gentle not mental,' Georgia says. 'Let me show you,' and she guides her eager hand. 'Like this.'

'Your mum wants to know what you'd like to drink,' he says.

'Coke!' Georgia says.

At the top of the drive, Terence is throwing dead branches onto a pile. He is hot, his T-shirt is soaked through. Terence works hard; but then, no man ever drowned in his own sweat. Terence asks about Chelsea; he will be done soon.

'If she's bothering Georgia, she can play here in the shade.'

'She's enjoying looking after her. She's very well behaved; you must be proud.'

'Chelsea has her moments.'

He wants to tell Terence about Beth, to be grateful for what he has, to enjoy every moment.

Terence says, 'I just want her to have the best chance she can.'

'Of course; we always want the best for our kids.'

Terence lobs a long branch on the growing pile. Martin asks, 'Did Conan come back?'

'No, sir, Conan has a wandering soul. I'm going to have to tie him in the day.'

He asks what time the boys came to collect the pirogue.

'They haven't come as yet. I'm sure they'll be here before nightfall.'

'The boat's gone.'

Terence looks surprised.

'I walked down to the beach around four o'clock and it was gone.'

Terence wipes his face.

'I was here the whole day. I went into the village before lunch to look for Conan, but I wasn't away long—half an hour at most. I would've seen them.'

'Maybe they came from the sea.'

'Why would they come by sea when they could walk up the road? I never heard the bell ring. They would've had to ring the bell.'

'Maybe they jumped the fence?'

They both look at the high fence; they look at the electric gates.

Miriam calls from the house. Tea is ready.

Cake cutting begins, a clattering of plates, cutlery, napkins. Chelsea takes first slice. Should they sit here or take their plates outside? Decisions, decisions. He is glad of the distraction—this place, the weather, Chelsea. He doesn't want the afternoon to be miserable. Last year, while en route to England for Beth's birthday, his flight was delayed with engine trouble in Barbados. When he called from Grantley Adams airport, Miriam was distraught.

'Please go back,' she said. 'I don't like the sound of engine trouble.'

He tried to reason with her but she was so insistent he gave in and caught a return flight to Trinidad that same night.

The following day, Safiya suggested they drive up to a Benedictine monastery nestled in the Northern Hills. The sun was slipping away, leaving strips of orange in the pale blue sky. In silence they walked in the grounds of the Spanish-style building; they looked down on the flat lands, out to Tunapuna, and all the way up to San Fernando. There was a quietness about the place that made him feel calm. In the chapel he lit a candle for Beth. Not bad for a non-believer.

Later he telephoned Miriam, 'You've got to stop catastrophising about everything. The plane didn't crash. I'm still here.'

'It could've done.'

'But it didn't, darling. And if you carry on like this, you'll be miserable. You'll make everyone miserable. I don't want Georgia to be afraid of things.'

He flops down on the sofa and browses through the pages of last week's *Sunday Times*. This is something else he misses, English newspapers; glancing through the stories of the week, the editorial pages, the magazine. He must tell Miriam. He looks up at his daughter happily eating cake with little Chelsea beside her.

All shall be well, and all shall be well, and all manner of things shall be well.

Around six Terence appears at the kitchen window, still wearing his work clothes. Usually at this time, he is showered and changed.

'Sir, do you have a minute?'

'Sure.'

He puts on flip-flops and follows him around the front of the house. Through the window he sees Chelsea watching television, her face fixed, entranced. They walk around the side of the apartment where, along the fence, banana leaves hang low and ginger lilies stick out their red tongues. He notices it is getting dark. Out on the lawn, Georgia is setting up the camera on a tripod. She doesn't see them.

'Just here, sir.'

Terence stops where the path bends and the trees start. At first he can't see anything, just the reddish tree trunk and the shadows of the branches. But then, underneath, he makes out a long dark shape and moves closer. The dog's mouth is open; there is vomit on the grass.

Terence squats down and puts his hand on Conan's head; he strokes the neck, the flat, lifeless ears. The dog is dead.

'Has he eaten something bad?'

'All by the fence is blood and diarrhoea.'

'Poison?'

Since working in Trinidad he has become familiar with gramaxone. Often used in suicides and murders, he has seen its devastating effects.

'For chasing chickens?'

Terence shrugs; he looks upset.

'How long has he been here?'

'Maybe all day. He missing since breakfast.'

He doesn't want the girls to know. Will Martin help lift the body to the back of the car port? At least it will be out of sight. He will get an old sheet from the storeroom and wrap the dog in it.

Tonight, before he takes Chelsea home, he will hose down the mess along the fence, and early tomorrow morning while everyone is sleeping, he will dig a hole and bury him.

TEN

There is a knock at the door just after 7 p.m. He assumes it is Terence or Chelsea; he thought he heard them leave earlier but perhaps not. It is neither Terence or Chelsea. No. There are three young men standing in the doorway, not where light falls, where a visitor would normally stand, but away from the light and where it is dark. He recognises the older boy from last night.

'Hi,' he says, 'I see you came for the boat.' And then he realises that something is quite wrong, something he cannot put his finger on.

'Yes, we got the boat,' and without invitation, the brother brushes past him and enters the house. The other two quickly follow.

Martin says, 'What's going on? Has something happened?'

A moment ago, Miriam was in the kitchen, now she stands in the corridor, her cotton dress floating around her.

'Everything all right?'

He tells her to go inside.

Here in the bright light of the living room, he gets a good look at them: the second one is tall and lanky, his green shorts hang low. His front teeth protrude giving him a dumb, goofy look. The third one is shorter, older and very black, with fine features; he wears his hair in thin, short dreads. In his left hand he holds a cutlass.

Martin says, stupidly, 'Is your brother okay?'

Miriam is still standing in the same spot. They exchange a look. Georgia, where is Georgia? Last time he saw her, she was going to take a shower.

They quickly come around him; he feels a tightening in his upper body, a weakness in his legs. There is a ripe scent of sweat. His heart pounds. He has been here before—he knows the signs: trouble has arrived.

'You can't just storm into someone's house like this.'

'We come for money,' the boy says, looking him straight in the eye. His face is hot, sweating. Then he shows his weapon— a fishing knife, used mainly for filleting.

He will give them what they want and then they will leave.

'I have cash. There's nothing else in the house.' He pulls out his wallet. 'This isn't our home; we're renting it for a few days—take what you want.'

The boy quickly removes the dollars, driving licence, bank cards. There is not, in fact, much cash; he meant to get more today but there wasn't time. Now he is glad he didn't. The other two stand by, their eyes flickering.

'Is this the thanks we get for helping you last night?'

The boy tells Miriam to fetch her purse; it is on the coffee table.

Miriam looks at Martin. She walks slowly as if on a precipice, as if her life depends on it.

'Move,' the boy says.

'Please don't shout at my wife.'

He checks the front door, car keys. His mobile phone is on the sideboard. There's no time. Georgia, where is Georgia.

The boy tips her handbag upside down and her life spills out: make-up, sunglasses, diary, keys. He quickly empties her purse of notes, coins and cards. He finds a picture of Beth, a Christmas photo they have always loved. He stares at it.

'Where she? Where the young meat?'

'Fuck you.'

The one with the cutlass slaps Martin hard in his mouth.

'Old man is rude, you being rude?'

Shocked, he presses his fingers to his lips; they sting; they are wet with blood.

'Please,' Miriam says, creakily, 'we can give you whatever you want. We don't want any trouble.'

He wants to reassure her but he's no longer feeling confident.

'Listen,' Martin says, and he sounds pathetic, 'I work for the police. If you stop now, things don't have to be so bad.'

'Tobago have no police.'

The boy looks around, scans the room, the veranda, the passageway. He is getting agitated.

Martin speaks calmly, slowly. 'The caretaker's due back any minute. You should take what you want and go.'

'Where the girl?'

'She went into Scarborough.'

The boy signals to the others, and takes off down the corridor to the left wing, towards the master bedroom, the kitchen, the den. It is familiar to him; only last night he was here accepting their help and hospitality.

The lanky one heads in the opposite direction, to the right wing, the storeroom, Georgia's room.

'Georgia!' Martin roars.

Too late. Sliding doors.

He tries to push the one with dreads aside; his fingers dig hard into the side of his face; they grapple and the cutlass clatters to the floor. The young man is stronger than him; his body is hard like a wall, and for a moment, they are locked together.

From the corridor, the crash of something, then a high-pitched scream. Georgia.

'Daaaad!'

'Georgia!'

Miriam is on her feet.

The boy is back; he is wearing Martin's shirt, the one Safiya gave him for Christmas, open like a jacket, collar up.

From Georgia's room, there is scuffling; a sharp cry.

'Please don't hurt my daughter,' Miriam says, her hands up in her face. 'Please.'

The boy pushes her out of the way and she stumbles back towards the sofa. Martin sees his opportunity and lurches for the sliding doors. But he is not quick enough; they wrestle him down, his legs crumple as if made of sand.

'Georgia!'

He feels a dull clump on the back of his head, and the floor, like a white sea, rushes up to meet him.

He wakes, disoriented. The lights are low; the tiles are hard and cool. How long has he been lying here? He can hear voices. He checks himself. The back of his head is sore and soggy. He tries to get up; the floor is slippery with blood. *His blood.*

Through the hatch he sees the boy's profile, his lumpy hair. There's laughter; the sound of bottles clinking, ice. They are helping themselves to whatever they want; they are having the time of their lives. Georgia, where is Georgia?

He looks at the front door. Did Terence come back? He must do something; he must get help. What time is it? Where is Georgia. God help us. Help us. He must get help.

Then in the half light, he catches sight of Miriam. She is lying on the sofa. A sound escapes from him, a kind of gasp. He crawls quietly towards her. *What have they done, what have they done.* They must not hear him. They must not see him. He whispers her name.

She opens her eyes.

'Georgia?'

She closes her eyes. There is blood around her lips. He adjusts her top where it has come away; his whole body is now shaking.

'Hey!'

The boy has seen him. He makes a clicking sound with his fingers. A black sound, Safiya says: click, click, as the fingers hit.

He makes for the door; they are on him like dogs. His bladder gives way, a warm, wet rush. They haul him up and push him through the front door and out into the darkness. The lanky one will stay behind with the girls. They will come for him in a while. Right now, they are taking the old man for a ride.

* * *

The yard is dark; Terence's apartment is in darkness. Everything is quiet. The one with the cutlass shoves him along the gravel path, while the boy lolls ahead, keen to get into the Tucson. Plink, plink, the sound of electronics, the doors unlock. To anyone outside, they might look like friends heading out for a night on the town.

He feels sick, and his head whirrs like a helicopter out of control.

'Where's my daughter?'

They reverse quickly up the drive and pull out on to the track. He must follow their route and pay attention so he can find his way back. Left onto Buccoo Road and they quickly reach the junction. He knows this road. They are avoiding the village; they head across the main road towards Carnbee. They are taking him to an ATM. He remembers a bank on the right. But how far along? There is nothing around this area; no bars or restaurants or hotels; houses are scattered. This is not a place for tourists.

From here, in the back of the car, he can see the boy's big feet. He plays with the radio; surfing through the local channels. He turns up the volume—a Safiya song. The bass throbs through the speakers.

After a few miles, they slow down and pull over onto the side of the road, away from the street lamps. The engine is running, handbrake up. The boy has Martin's wallet, his bank card. He wants the PIN number. He speaks calmly.

'Boss man, you know if you fuck up, somebody have to die. We will spin back and kill she.'

Martin's stomach lifts; he wants to vomit.

The driver leans in; his little pigtails are alive. 'We not afraid to cut she throat. You remember the number good, right?'

Their shadowy faces loom.

He reels off the numbers. Then he says, 'I want to sit up; I feel sick.'

The boy reaches over him; he smells foul; his rum breath, his strong, sour sweat. And he pulls Martin up so that he is slumped, half upright, looking out of the windscreen. He recognises the street; he knows where they are. The road is empty, a ghost town. The boy runs across the street to the bank. He uses one of the cards to slip through the security door and he is in, lit by the neon light of the ATM room. Scruffy and out of place; a barbarian.

A car approaches; its bright lights dim as it comes closer. The white Mitsubishi Lancer pulls over on the other side of the road. A young black woman gets out wearing high heels and a short dress. She is also going to the ATM machine. She glances over at the vehicle, and waits to let the boy out.

The boy comes running. 'Let's go.'

'Where?'

'There's an ATM in the mall. This one have no money left.'

They swerve out into the road and carry on along this same route, picking up speed as the road straightens out. The boy lights a cigarette, puts his feet on the dashboard. He is pleased with himself, puffed up; more man than boy.

They swing into the large empty car park. A security vehicle is parked near the entrance; there is no one sitting in it. Tall lamps are dotted around.

The boy jumps out and disappears into the darkness.

The driver turns the car around; he switches his lights on low and keeps the engine running. It is difficult to see. The ATM is built into a wall. The overhead light appears to be broken.

How long have they been gone—half an hour? Forty minutes? It seems as if hours have passed.

Georgia, Georgia.

The boy is back. 'Ride out!'

They head in the direction of the house. Trees rush by, the open field, where just this morning, he saw horses grazing. They turn right at the crossroads and drive down the strip that follows the beach along Mount Irvine. From here he can see the lights of the villa. His wife, his daughter? Where is Terence? Is he back yet? They drive past the turning to the private road.

'You've missed the turning. The house is back there.'

The Tucson zooms alongside the bay, up and over the hill as if heading towards Black Rock village. The car slows, he assumes they are turning around. On the left is an area of deserted land. He has seen signposts here with warnings about safety. It is dark; there are no streetlights.

They drive into this darkness. There is a kind of path. Bush scrapes against the side of the car as it bumps along. And then the path widens out, and ahead there is a patch of land, stripped back and without bush. They pull up and jump out. The boy opens the back door; they reach in for him and throw him on the ground. He can hear the sea; he rolls over, his head next to the wheel.

He says, knowing it is useless, 'I gave you money; this is not what we agreed.' He pulls himself up. 'Fuck you.'

The car lights give the boy a glow like there is a fire behind him. The boy kicks him hard in his side. 'Hush your mouth.'

He nods to his friend, and they both start to kick him with their big, bare feet. Their legs are strong, quick like animals. Martin rolls onto his front and curls himself up; he tries to protect his head. He groans into the dirt.

Silence.

Car doors slam. Lights on full. He hears the vehicle reversing, the twist of the wheels in the earth. He opens his eyes, and he can see only darkness. And within it, white specks float like broken lights. The world has disappeared. He can hear the sea; yes, the sea roars in his ears. A wave is coming; it wants to take him under. He will go with it; he will surrender. The greatness of a man's power lies in his willingness to surrender ...

Martin is light, floating. There is no pain; the pain has gone. He is aware of the night air, the stillness, and he can see the stars, clear points of light, and they are exquisitely beautiful, and the colours of the cosmos are purplish, like the colours of the hills at the end of the day at the back of his house, and he can see the bright light beyond them, and he knows this to be like the sun, only it is not the sun. The light grows brighter, and it is almost too bright for him to look at, and he looks down and sees the sea, the dark sea, and he wants to lie on it. He floats on the sea, and he is carried by its gentle, phosphorescent waves. And the waves become brighter with a strange moonlight.

Eleven

The sun wakes him. Soft, low rays cutting through the trees. He tastes the powdery earth smudged against his mouth and opens his eyes to a tangle of weeds. Through a canopy of bush he glimpses fragments of a pale, clear sky. Slowly, he raises himself up. Coconut trees reach high, their branches frayed and rotten, diseased. The grassy wasteland is covered with a sprawling vine. Barefoot, he makes his way.

Where the land seems to stop there are manchineel trees. A painted sign: *Be cautious, secluded area.* There is a sharp drop, a path of some kind. Below he can see rocks and sand. It looks familiar, this beach; the long stretch of pale sand. Yes, this is where he came with Georgia that first day, where they saw the fishermen, the dogs.

So they brought him here.

At the stripped-back place where the vehicle was parked, he looks for his sandals but they are not there. He finds other things: a condom, empty beer bottles, a KFC carton, dirty plastic cups. He gives up; his head is as light as a balloon. Georgia, Georgia. He hears a car; the road must be nearby. If he can just make it to the road. He follows the tyre tracks away from the deserted beach.

The empty road stretches out. He keeps to the right—*always walk on the edge of the road facing the traffic flow*—instinctively holding his left and bloody leg as he slowly limps. He cannot see the cut; there isn't time to stop.

A car is approaching, its lights on low. He stops and waves like a man drowning. The woman keeps driving, her face turned to him as she passes. He must walk, he thinks, keep walking.

Ahead there is a turning into a residential area. There will be a telephone; someone will help him. He rests on a low wall by the side of the road. It is here that a young mechanic finds him, lying by this wall, his head in the grass.

'Mister, you okay?' he says. He helps him into the pick-up truck, making room, shifting his cigarettes, tools, papers. He will take him to the hospital or wherever he wants to go.

Martin's voice is thick. 'Do you know the Dials' house, on the golf course?'

'I know it. Terence Monroe is watchman?'

'Yes,' he says, so grateful he could weep.

The world is still asleep. The land is as clipped and shaped as before; the track, as they turn on to it, is bumpy and rocky. The goat feeds under the mango tree, its rope stretched; the kids are lying in the shade. It is familiar. It is the same. All is as it was, and yet nothing is the same; everything is entirely different.

The electric gates are open. The Tucson is not there, only Terence's blue car. No ambulance, no police cars. What does this mean? What was he expecting?

The mechanic pulls up and Martin gets out. From his apartment, Terence appears, his chest bare. He runs outside to the driveway, his face stricken.

'Sir,' he says.

Martin makes his way up the pathway to the house. Inside the veranda doors are closed and the metal shutters are down; the sidelights are on. Order has been restored—it is clean, tidy, smelling of bleach. And yet the room has the thickness of a morgue. If he were arriving here for the first time, he would know something had happened. He thinks: if the police were doing their job it would be taped, untouched.

He shouts, 'Georgia,' and limps through the house, catching sight of his reflection in the mirrored cabinet. One side of his head is covered with blood—a ghoul from the grave. He notices the cabinet is empty; the Swarovski crystals are gone.

Terence says, 'I'll call an ambulance.'

There is noise from the end of the corridor.

'Georgia,' he calls. 'Miriam.'

A door is unlocked, Miriam appears and he sees that she is dressed in practical clothes—jeans, shirt and canvas shoes. Behind her is Georgia.

'Martin,' Miriam cries, and she throws her arms around him. 'Martin. Oh God. We thought you were gone; we thought you were dead.'

For a moment they hold one another and he smells her freshness; her wet hair is cold against his face.

God have mercy. If there is a God, have mercy.

'Come,' she says, and helps him into their room where clothes are scattered on the bed which has been stripped; suitcases are open on the floor. This room, too, feels different. He drops heavily on the mattress, shivering; she wraps a blanket around him.

Georgia's damp, tangled hair falls like a veil, and he pushes it back so he can see her properly; he searches her face as if it is a map to get somewhere. He scans for marks, bruises, discolouration. Her eyes are dark, her face is pale, somehow different, somehow younger. He knows he must look horrific, and he smells of piss, blood and sweat. He wants to tell her that he is so sorry for the way he looks—for frightening her.

He hears himself say, 'Did the police come?'

Miriam says, 'They're searching for you right now. They went out looking for the car. I couldn't remember the registration.'

'There's no tape. Did they talk to you both?'

Georgia looks at her mother.

'Yes,' Miriam says. Then she says, 'Are you in pain?'

'No,' but he is lying; his head is throbbing as if something has fallen out of the sky and landed on it.

'Where did they take you?'

'A beach, a wasteland.'

Miriam looks at him with horror. 'Why? Why would they do this to us?'

Outside an engine starts up. A lawnmower next door; guests must be arriving.

Life carries on.

He feels sick, and leans to one side and his stomach heaves. Onto the tiles, he coughs up a trickle of clear liquid.

Miriam says, 'I'll get you some water.'

'I'll go,' says Georgia, her voice flat.

He thinks: she wants to leave us alone so we can talk.

'Keep the door open, darling,' Miriam says, 'then we can hear you.'

Georgia's footsteps flip-flop slowly along the corridor.

They stare at one another. The air is still, as if the world had stopped.

He says, 'Miriam,' and a shiver passes through him. 'What did they do? Tell me.'

Miriam is unable to speak; she starts to cry. It is as he thought, he is sure of it. She puts her hands up to her face; her strong capable hands. Hands he knows well.

'Miriam.' Then he says, 'Georgia?'

She nods, crying.

His head is reeling, vhoom, vhoom, vhoom. He pushes his fingers in his eyes. It cannot be, he thinks, this cannot be true. No. No. No.

'Who? The young one, the boy who was here before?'

'Yes.'

He pictures the boy, his bug eyes, his lumpy hair. Barely out of school. An image flashes through his mind of the boy on the night of the boat incident, the way he'd looked at Georgia. Yes, Martin caught something in the boy's stare, and he'd dismissed it. Instead of feeling alarmed, he'd felt proud. His daughter was a beauty; why wouldn't the boy want to gawp at her? But he should have known. His instincts should have warned him. Or did they, in fact, warn him? Was his mind too preoccupied?

'Did she see a doctor?'

'Yes.'

'They took samples, swabs?'

'Yes.'

'Where?'

'A clinic near the station.'

They look at one another. They keep looking.

Miriam puts her head in her hands. He wants to know more; he is afraid.

"How bad was it?'

'It happened once. Just the boy.'

'The others?'

Miriam shakes her head.

'Did they give her medication? There's HIV.'

'The Medical Officer gave her tablets. She said they'll make her feel sick.'

'They can. But not always.'

Headaches, tiredness, dizziness, muscle ache. All these things and more. His beloved Georgia. His baby girl. He did not protect her. The room is moving around him as if he is on a carousel.

He says, 'When did Terence come back?'

'Around nine. We were in the den. We thought they'd all come back. He didn't expect to be so late; his ex cooked him dinner. He called the police but they took a while to come. Miriam shakes her head in disbelief. 'They told Terence to clean up the mess.'

'Clean up?'

If this was England, the room would be immediately taped, samples collected and sent for testing. He must phone Raymond. They must get on to it, now. The boys can't be far away. Tobago is small. They will find them.

'Did you both give statements?'

'Yes.' Then Miriam says, 'We have to get you to a hospital.'

The ambulance arrives, its siren whooping. Terence shows the paramedics into the bedroom; Miriam and Georgia stand back while they see to him. The two men are friendly enough. He is strapped onto a gurney and lifted through the house. Terence opens the doors.

They carry him outside into the bright sunlight; he looks up at the sky—a clear, cloudless sky, a perfect day for the beach. The crunch of gravel, the path where they dragged him last night, charged, thrilled with their luck. The doors of the ambulance flip open, and they step onto the ramp, and lower him down into position. It is swift, professional; he is grateful.

And he is glad, too, of the dark, the cool. His eyes are heavy, and he wants to slide down inside himself and sleep; for the blackness to come and take him. He can hear Miriam and Georgia; they are here in the back with him. Good, he thinks, they are with me. We are alive. They are putting on seatbelts. One of the seatbelts isn't working properly. 'You really shouldn't ride in here without it,' the man says. Miriam says it is fine. She will do without, as long as Georgia is safe. *As long as Georgia is safe.*

Terence will follow them to the hospital. He hears Miriam thank Terence. Then, to Georgia, 'Your dad's going to be okay. We're all going to be fine.' He is glad of the sound of the engine, the motion of the vehicle as they accelerate. He will fall asleep—there is nothing else to do.

He is carried into Emergency on a stretcher. There are forms to fill in. Miriam, where is Miriam? The place is in chaos: an old lady is sitting in a wheelchair and a large pool of urine has been left on the floor underneath her. Chickens run about near the open doorway. A security guard with a machine gun stands nearby. People are looking at them. A beaten-up white man. What has happened here? Miriam signs the relevant forms, and the nurse makes a joke about the number of people today. Busy like Friday's market. She tells them a doctor will come to the ward within the hour.

Beyond, into what feels like a labyrinth of endless yellow corridors, they carry him. He feels nauseous; they should wheel him on a trolley, not this jerking, jumping motion. He wants to know where his wife and daughter are? Are they following? How on earth will they find him? There is a breeze coming through the open windows and he is glad of it.

'They're right behind us,' the paramedic says.

'Can't you put me on a trolley.'

'They don't have trolleys. You want a wheelchair?'

No, he thinks, I just want to get where I am going.

He is taken to a small ward with five other beds. An air conditioner throws out cold air and it feels like bitter winter. Better this than heat. A curtain has come away and he asks Miriam to take it down, he will use it for a blanket. There are no sheets. They help him onto the bed.

Miriam has brought clean clothes and fresh towels. She says, 'I didn't think to bring sheets. What kind of hospital has no sheets? They need to get you washed, cleaned up.'

For the first time, he notices her left eye is bloody, and there is some swelling. How did this happen? 'Somebody should look at your eye, Miriam. Ask the nurse.'

Georgia looks around the ward. A man is lying on his side;

his trousers are missing and there is blood seeping through a make-do bandage wrapped around his thigh. Why don't they clean it up? The man looks weak as if he is dying. Opposite, an elderly man with a partly shaved head has a growth dark like a plum.

Miriam says, 'We need to go and find a hotel—apparently they're all full. Something to do with Carnival. If we go now, Terence thinks he can help.'

They are leaving? He doesn't want them to leave. What if no one comes? What if he can't find his way back to admissions?

'Isn't it better if we all stay together?'

'Once we find somewhere, we'll wait for you there. It's best that way. We can't stay at the villa.' She nods to Georgia who is expressionless.

He reaches for his daughter's hand and puts it to his lips, remembering too late that they are thick with bits of blood now hardening like scales.

He says, and his voice is weak, 'I'm sorry. I'm so sorry.'

Miriam puts her arm around Georgia's back and they shuffle closer to the bed where he is lying now. And for the first time, he sees, just below Georgia's jaw and at the top of her neck, a band of redness. What happened here? Is it from the boy? The grip of his hand at her throat? Did he hold her down? Filled with more horror, Martin wants to say something; he wants to ask her. But this is not the time. And his eyes fall to her chest, her sparkly belt; her childlike marrow hips. He wants to weep—for her, for Miriam, for himself.

From the corridor, a loud terrible yell. A man is shouting,

cursing at someone. Georgia looks at the swing doors. On it goes from the corridor—a vile diatribe—and then it sounds as if the man is shouting the word *cunt* over and over.

'It's okay,' Martin says, 'he's probably just drunk.'

He is still shouting but it sounds as though he is running and it is fading now. Yes, it is fading. Thank God. A madman, a drunk, that's all they need. Scarborough Hospital. He remembers Raymond saying, you go there to die. Miriam is right, it is better if they leave.

He says, 'Do you have money?'

'I have my Barclaycard. For some reason they missed it. I cancelled the rest of the cards. You'll need to talk to your bank here.'

She will call him later and tell him where to come. He will have to take a taxi. She gives him some cash—from her beach bag. Miriam is being efficient, holding it all together.

'Is my phone in the house? Did they take it?'

'No, I have it, but it's dead. I'll pick up your charger. If you need me, ring me from Georgia's phone.' She gives him Georgia's bright pink mobile phone.

'It suits you, Dad.'

'I thought you might say that.'

Her face is pale; all traces of sun and well-being have gone. She is paler than when she arrived.

Miriam says, 'I'll let you know where we are.'

He notices her hands, bare, ringless.

'They took your wedding ring?'

'And my mother's chain.'

He pictures the gold pendant: Saint Christopher, patron

saint of travellers. The figure with a staff, and inscribed on the back: *Si en San Cristóbal confías, de accidente no morirás. If you trust in St Christopher, you will not die in an accident.*

They leave him alone; he watches them disappear through the swing doors; he fixes his eyes on the nearby window and the bony tree outside with its mass of pink flowers. His whole body is trembling. In his mind's eye he sees—the villa at night, the boy, the flash of the cutlass, the little serrated knife, Miriam's look of shock. Georgia away in her room, oblivious—doing what? What was she doing before they got to her? His beloved Georgia. If there is a God, if there is a God, then help them now.

At three o'clock, an orderly wakes him. He must get up, the woman says. He is wheeled down a passageway. Christian posters line the walls with rainbows and lakes and eagles soaring over mountains—*A wounded spirit who can bear? A merry heart doeth good like a medicine.* Proverb after proverb.

The young doctor is on a placement from Nairobi. A tall man with thick glasses. He says, 'What war were you fighting in?' Martin tells him what happened, about Miriam and Georgia. The doctor asks about his injuries.

'Since I came here in 2005, I've seen a lot of this going on. The government should be doing more. It's getting like Nairobi. Nairobi's a bloody mess. These days they call it Nairobbery.'

Don't worry, he tells Martin, he is an excellent tailor. He checks him over. He is bruised, yes, but nothing seems to be broken. He may have some internal bruising, a cracked rib or two, but this will all heal in time with rest.

[153]

He removes a piece of glass from his thigh; a sharp curve of bottle. It is excruciatingly painful. Martin asks if he can look at it, and he is astonished by its weight, the bloody effect like marble. The doctor washes the cut, carefully patching the torn skin back together. He stitches it quickly, efficiently, and covers it with a large plaster. He examines his head, shaves carefully around the bloody area; cleans the wound, dabbing and wiping, dropping the cotton balls into a plastic dish. In ten minutes he is finished stitching and snips the black thread.

'You must have a CT scan,' he says; the machine in the hospital is not working. 'Go to Trinidad. Mount Hope medical centre will do it free of charge. If something is wrong usually there are signs—dizziness, vomiting, pain. Do you have any of these signs?'

'No.'

'It is not always obvious, so you must pay attention to anything different, unusual. It could kill you. Do you understand?'

'Yes,' he says.

'Have you spoken with the police? They need to get a handle on these tourist attacks.'

'I'm not a tourist. I work with the police in Trinidad.'

'But you look like a tourist. That's the point. They should be worried. The police do what they want. We had an attempted burglary last week, a policeman took an hour to come from the beach on a bicycle. It is a nonsense.'

The doctor tapes a large, thick bandage across the back of Martin's head. As a precaution, he should probably stay tonight in the hospital for observation. He washes his hands and calls for the nurse. She will give him a tetanus injection, cream for his wrists, antihistamine for his bites, Band-Aids for the small cuts on his face and feet. There are painkillers; they might knock him out, but he will be glad of them later.

He speaks with authority, 'You should go back to your country. This is not a place for people like you.'

After he has seen the nurse, Martin limps back slowly through the corridor—there's no time to waste—holding his leg as he walks. He checks Georgia's phone—a text has arrived. Miriam has sent details of the hotel. They are in room 302.

Miriam, his capable and competent wife.

Outside, music blasts from an old car and a crowd of young people stand around it, dressed for the beach; they eat from a cooking pot balanced on the bonnet. He thinks, This is a hospital, people are sick. Can't they turn it down? A security guard stands by chatting to a friend. Why doesn't he say something?

From the taxi, he telephones Raymond who is deeply sorry, as if this is somehow his fault. When news came in of a robbery, he'd tried to reach him. He'd been calling his mobile since this morning, but it was switched off, dead.

'Tobago never used to be like this. What is happening with these people?' He called Scarborough police station and spoke with an officer from last night. He understands that they want to keep the part about Georgia confidential, away from the press. Is there anything else he can do?

'I'm going to the station now to give a statement.'

Martin asks if he will ring Safiya and let her know that he is out of hospital.

'She probably knows something through the news desk; she might not realise it's you. We knew there was a robbery, but there were no names yet. There wasn't much information.'

'Better that way,' Martin says.

'I understand.'

He hears Raymond lighting a cigarette. 'Did you see them?'

'I saw them. Clear as fucking day.'

Sergeant Usaf Rochford and Police Constable Curtis Willoughby introduce themselves. They bring chairs and take him into the interview room. He remembers this airless room, its poky dimensions; the framed photograph of the Prime Minister on the wall. The officers look him over—his shorts, the Wimbledon Tennis 2000 T-shirt and his sandals. They rest their A4 notebooks on the table and sit down opposite him. Sergeant Rochford remembers Martin from his visit over a year ago.

They have good news, they say: they have found the Tucson burned out in a lay-by in Plymouth.

'Was it a rented car?' asks the younger one. 'We noticed the number plate was private.'

'It wasn't an officially rented car. The guy's somewhere here in Scarborough. Island Car Rentals. I have documents.'

Then he says, 'I know who they are. I could identify them in an ID parade tomorrow. That's what we need to have here.'

'Yes, sir.'

They have been briefed; it is obvious by the way they speak to him with a slightly deferential manner.

Deferential is good.

'They looked high, sir?'

He remembers the boy's face when he realised Georgia was there. Excited, yes, not high. They knew exactly what they were doing.

'Their eyes were normal, no sign of dilation.'

He gives a thorough description of each of them, and they scribble away on their notepads.

'My wife must have told you, one of them came to the house the night before it happened. We'd seen them before. You'll probably find them on the beach tomorrow.' Then he says, 'They don't know who they're dealing with.' He sounds arrogant and a little foolish.

The other officer, whose face is also familiar, says, 'Don't worry, sir, we will do all we can to find them.'

'Did you take fingerprints? What about my daughter's dress? There's the sheets in the house. Has anyone taken the sheets?'

He offers them his bag of clothes.

'We have everything we need.'

He is not convinced. He wants to ask why the area wasn't taped. But there is no point. He feels himself getting angry; he must try to contain himself. It will not help the situation. The most important thing is that they have all the relevant information.

He says, 'There'll be CCTV footage at the cashpoint.'

'Yes, sir.'

'I can take you to the town where they live.'

'We don't have a car on the premises.'

He should not be surprised. In Trinidad, police officers are often short of vehicles; they are known to loan their cars to a cousin or an uncle on a Friday night. For a small fee, some rogue officers may hire them out to criminals.

'We could take a taxi,' he says.

The two officers look at one another.

'When will you have a car?'

'Tomorrow, sir.'

In truth, as much as he would like to go now, he is exhausted. It might be better to wait until daylight. He needs to see his daughter. His daughter and his wife need him at the hotel. They should not be alone.

'There was a woman—dressed up, high heels; she came while the boy was getting the cash. She could be a witness.'

He describes the woman and her car.

Then he says, 'It's a good idea to collect the advice slips; there's one with every transaction. You must collect them from the booth and fingerprint them. At the mall, too.'

'A lot of people use these machines.'

'Yes,' he says irritably, 'it might take a couple of hours' work. It could save you time later on.'

He is exhausted and dehydrated.

'Are you staying in Tobago for a few days, sir?'

'I'm not sure. We have this room for a couple nights. I won't be going far, only to Trinidad. You have my mobile number.'

'Yes, sir. We have your number in Trinidad. We explained to your wife and daughter that it would be helpful if they didn't return to England just yet.'

He says, and he sounds angry, 'We have to catch these animals. Do you understand?'

Usaf stares at him for a moment. 'We will do our best, Mr Rawlinson.'

* * *

Their hotel is near the airport. As he limps into the palm-tree-lined entrance, the mosaic tiled floors, the open white reception are familiar; yes, he came here for dinner with Safiya. He remembers the sea, calm like a pond, the tinkling steel pan music at night, the generous buffet. It was romantic, and expensive, one of the better hotels on the island. In the lobby, he halts at the sight of his reflection. His bandage is like a strange half turban; there are several gauze plasters on his face. A graze on his left cheek is a bloody patch. His leg is bandaged, and he hobbles along. People are staring.

Let them look, let them look.

Miriam's face is red and puffy from crying. She looks relieved to see him.

'I thought they might want to keep you overnight.'

The room is cool and pleasant. The curtains are closed and the lamps cast a homely light. It is big enough—a double bed, and a single divan. A tall arrangement of flowers stands on a table along with a bottle of wine and a basket of oranges—gifts of arrival.

'Where's Georgia?'

'She's in the bathroom.'

'How is she?'

'I'm not sure,' she says, her voice hushed. 'I keep expecting her to break down.'

'We'll have to watch her carefully.'

'I know.' Miriam's eyes fill up.

Martin carefully lowers himself into a chair. He is full of

pain—his back, his ribs, his left leg, the back of his head. And he is weak as a lamb; he hasn't eaten since cake at the villa yesterday. A lifetime ago.

'I need to talk to her about what happened.'

'Let her come to you when she's ready.'

She pushes back her hair; it is wispy with heat.

'Has she told you everything?'

'Yes, I think so; mostly.'

'Then why can't she talk to me?'

'Maybe because I was there, or because I'm a woman; her mother. You can't push the river with this, Martin.'

'I want to know.'

She rubs her fingers across her forehead, as if trying to erase something, and he can see that it is difficult for her.

They look at one another.

'I *need* to know, Miriam.'

She walks over to the bathroom and knocks on the door.

'Georgia,' she calls. 'Everything okay?'

Georgia says something he can't quite make out.

'Okay, sweetheart. Take your time, don't rush.'

Now Miriam comes to him; perches on the arm of his chair. He should touch her, he thinks, try to comfort her. But he does not. She speaks softly quickly, as if wanting to get it over with.

'The boy told her that if she didn't do what he wanted,' she stops, 'he'd rape her with his fishing knife and she wouldn't be able to have babies. He said she mustn't scream because it would put him off. At first she tried to get away but then she knew it was pointless. She was calm as if it was happening to someone else. As if her soul had left her body.'

'What about the marks on her neck? He did that?'

Miriam nods.

'Where were the others?'

Martin's voice is steady; inside he is on fire.

'They were waiting for him to finish. When I saw him, I knew what he'd done. It didn't take long. He wanted to let them know. I felt like it was some kind of initiation.'

'Initiation of what?'

'I don't know.'

'Did she stay there in the room?'

'She locked herself in the bathroom and sat under the shower. She thought she was going to die. She was terrified. She thought we were all going to die.'

He cannot bear it.

'Where was I?'

'Lying on the floor.'

The father, the protector, incapacitated.

He remembers the cold tiles, the sight of Miriam on the sofa. By then it must've been over; the boys were in the kitchen celebrating.

'I told them they should make sure you were alive, they'd be done for murder. They weren't bothered.'

'When did you get to her?'

'After they'd gone.'

'What happened to the other one, the one they left behind?'

'He waited for a while and took off. She thought I was one of them. She was screaming.'

'When you came out, he'd gone?'

'Yes. We went inside the TV room and phoned the police.'

Martin gets up and goes to the window. The day is ending; night is starting to fall. His mind is turbulent, as if a grenade has gone off and blown to bits his entire way of thinking. He must gather himself, his scattered, broken parts. He must be strong for Georgia, for Miriam.

'They found the car. It was burnt out. They set fire to it.'

Miriam looks surprised. 'Why would they?'

'Because they can. They've been watching too much TV.'

'Did they find anything else?'

'No.'

She holds up her hands. 'We could've stayed here—we didn't need a villa. There's a swimming pool. Guards.'

They stare at one another. He knows what she is getting at. What can he say? *I wanted a villa so I could keep away from you; so I could have my space, my freedom.*

'But you liked the villa. We all liked it.'

His mind jumps to Safiya. He says, 'Do you have my phone?'

'Yes,' she says.

'I need to call Trinidad.'

'Somebody rang for you. A woman, she rang three times. She was keen to speak to you.'

His heart skips a beat.

'Sapphire. Or something like that. She said she works with you.'

'Okay,' he says, trying to sound casual. 'I'll call her later.'

Miriam says, 'Terence thinks he knows who they are.'

'We know who they are. If we drive through the village where I dropped them the other night, we'll see them sitting by the side of the road. They probably live ten minutes from here.'

She sits down on the bed. 'I don't understand why they let us see them.'

'They expect us to get on a plane and go home. That's what most people do. That's what they count on.'

Miriam says, 'Apparently, just over a year ago, a German couple were murdered. Did you know? They lived five miles away from where we were staying.'

He remembers the incident well. It happened while he was in Tobago running his training course. Both husband and wife, in their fifties, were butchered in their holiday home for no apparent reason. In the pouring rain, the culprit fled, taking off his boots on the way. When Martin arrived at the crime scene, one of the boots, a tan Caterpillar left foot, was floating upright in a puddle. He alerted a police officer, but before he could stop him, the man took up a piece of bamboo and dragged the boot through the water, eliminating all traces of DNA. It had shocked him. He'd wondered if it was deliberate.

'I know about the German couple. They lived in a compound near the beach.'

Miriam says, and her face is contorted, 'So why did you rent a villa if it wasn't safe?'

'Did it seem unsafe to you? If it wasn't for the gate opener, they could never have got into the yard. The place was as secure as it gets. There was even a caretaker on site. This kind of thing doesn't happen often in Tobago. We couldn't have known.'

She puts her fingers into her hair, a sign of frustration.

'Maybe Terence had something to do with it?'

Martin has thought about this. Would Terence have killed

his dog for the sake of a share in a robbery? No, he doesn't think so. No doubt the police will want to question him.

In need of air, he pushes back the glass doors and steps outside.

Miriam says, and it sounds strangely cheerful: 'We even have a patio.'

His heart lurches when he sees Georgia, quiet in her pyjamas. He expects her to come to him, and she does, but only for a moment. *My angel, my poor angel.* A white blanket is wrapped around her shoulders. She puts her hand on his cheek and looks into his eyes.

'You okay, Dad?' She traces her fingers around his bandage.

'Yes,' and he strokes her hair, soft as feathers.

'Good,' she says, vaguely, and she drifts away to the bed and curls up with her blanket. She stares at the television, her expression blank and empty. He wants to say something to reassure her. But he cannot. He is feeble, tongue-tied, useless.

Forgive me. Forgive me.

'I hope you're both hungry,' Miriam says.

She has ordered room service and now it is here she is fretting—Georgia must eat something; they have only had breakfast. There is soup, bread rolls, salad. She arranges plates, napkins; she is trying to make everything as normal as possible. He is grateful.

'Come along,' she says. 'Let's have it while it's hot.'

In silence, they eat and watch the *Oprah Winfrey Show*; an interview with J.K. Rowling. He is struck by the writer's Englishness; her clipped, clear voice. It is somehow reassuring.

He tries to concentrate, but his head feels sore. It is a dull ache at the base of his skull.

'Have you read these books, Georgia?'

'No,' she says, without looking at him.

Miriam says, 'She's more of a *Twilight* girl.'

'*Twilight?*'

'Vampires.'

'Aha. Black nails.'

He did not know this about his daughter; that she likes books about vampires. There are many things he must not know. For a long time she has been a mystery to him. Just as Beth was, only, perhaps, more so. By living here he has lost out on a part of her life. He knew this would happen but the realisation now makes him feel wretched. What kind of a father is he?

There is a clip from the latest *Harry Potter* film. Young spectacled Harry is wielding a sword. Georgia pulls up her blanket and turns on to her side. And he realizes that she is not watching the television; she is looking to the left of the television at a painting. It is a colourful picture of a woman's face. She is Caribbean; her eyes are glittery. It is not a good painting, and yet, there is something about the woman's expression which feels real to him; a confidence, a particular attitude that is exactly right. Whatever the artist has managed to capture in this woman, he would have wished for Georgia to have this same quality, this same poise and confidence. But she will never have it. Or at least, not for a very long time. Enormous sadness rises and swells in him now and he wonders how he will contain it.

* * *

The medication draws him down into deep sleep. Part of him welcomes it, he can slip away from the nightmare. He sleeps heavily; vivid dreams of England and his old life. Twice the boys appear and he is frightened. They are breaking into his childhood home, crashing through the window. His mother is young, and she is screaming. Then again in the woods at the back of his house—with knives and machetes—they wait for him. Above where he stands, Georgia hangs from a tree; Miriam tries to cut her down, stretching up on her tiptoes, her nightdress stained with blood. It is terrifying.

When he wakes, the sheets are soaked; Miriam is there.

'You're okay,' she says, 'you were dreaming.' She gives him water.

'Where is Georgia?'

'She's sleeping right here.'

In the morning, she will call for fresh linen. She strokes his forehead, pushes back his damp hair with her cool hands. 'Try to rest,' she says, and her voice is soft. He doesn't deserve her tenderness, but he will take it, he thinks.

Saint Miriam. My good wife whom I have betrayed. He falls again into his abyss.

It is 5.30; Miriam and Georgia are asleep. He steps outside onto the patio and dials Safiya's number.

'Can you talk?'

She sounds sleepy. 'Give me a moment.'

With his blanket wrapped around him, he walks slowly along the path towards the sea.

'I've been worried sick. I thought you'd call and let me know what's going on. Are you okay?'

'I've been better.'

'We couldn't get much information from the police. Did they hurt you? Did they hurt anyone?'

Her voice is soft; her bedroom voice.

'Martin.'

'We were lucky; no one died.'

There is a breeze coming off the silvery water, it is surprisingly cool. The sky is pale pink like new skin; the moon is still there, its left side eaten away.

'What did they do? Did they take money?'

'Money. Jewellery.'

'Anything else?'

He knows what she is getting at.

He doesn't want to tell her about Georgia on the phone.

He lights a cigarette, blows a cloud of smoke.

She says, and her voice is creaky, 'I can't believe this has happened.'

'I know. I'm okay, sweetheart. We're alive.'

'When tourists stop coming to Tobago they'll want to know why. What's the point of all these international flights and new hotels when no one will want to come. Trinidad is like an animal chewing on its own paw.'

He doesn't know what to say. Safiya is, of course, right.

'We have a donkey running the country.'

'But there are worse places.'

'Trinidad isn't your home; I have nowhere else.'

He finds himself in a curious position of reassuring her. This isn't what he expected or needed.

Then he says, 'You sound angry.'

'Did your wife tell you I rang?'

'Yes.'

'Three times. I hope you had something ready. I didn't know what was going on. I rang the night it happened.'

'You gave your name?'

'Yes. I said I worked with you on the press side. I don't know if she believed me. She seemed a bit hesitant, or maybe suspicious. It's hard to tell with an English accent. It can sound so uptight.'

He lets her keep talking.

'It hit me today when this happened, I can't call you when I want. I can't get on a plane and come find you. I couldn't talk to my mom; in this house we barely mention your name. She says you're having a mid-life crisis.'

He feels himself closing up, shutting down. He doesn't have the energy to tackle this, to reassure. It is unlike Safiya; she has not picked her moment well.

'I'm too old to be having a mid-life crisis. Your mum wants the best for you. She doesn't think I'm good enough. Maybe she's right.'

He doesn't know what else to say.

'Look,' she says, 'I'm going to go. I just wanted to make sure you're alive, and not in the hospital.'

'Well, I was in the hospital but I'm not now.'

'Do you know when you're coming back?'

'We haven't discussed it.'

'Do you think you will?'

How could he not come back? He has an apartment, a car,

a job, responsibilities.

'Of course.'

'Are you coming back alone?'

'I don't know. We have to make plans.'

Below there is a tree and on it, a string of coloured lights. They look like Christmas. He has always liked these trees, their delicate branches, their wide reach.

'How is your dad?'

'He died on Tuesday.'

He should not be shocked, but he is.

'Oh God,' he says, 'I'm so sorry, darling.'

And he is sorry, sorry that she has to experience this loss alone. He'd wanted to help pick up the pieces. Selfishly, he'd thought it might bring them even closer together. It will be more painful than she imagined. It is something he has learned, when someone dies, it is always harder than you think. The dead do not go away for a while. No, they are gone from your life forever. You will never see them again.

'Why didn't you tell me? Why didn't you let me know?'

'I didn't want to tell you in a text message.'

'You could have called. I would've phoned you back.'

Safiya gives a long, slow sigh. He hears the movement of sheets. She is getting up from her bed. He pictures her wild hair, brown muscular legs, her T-shirt, the top of her thighs exposed. To his surprise he feels faintly aroused.

'When is the funeral?'

'Tomorrow.' Then she says, 'I wish you could be here.'

'I know, it's difficult. We'll probably leave in a day or two, but there's a lot to sort out.' Then, 'It's been so traumatic.' His sadness catches in his throat and he chokes a little. 'It's been traumatic for you, too. I'm so sorry.'

The phone call leaves him feeling flat, bothered. Should he ring her back? He must reassure her—her father has gone, and he is there for her. But who's to say it will make either of them feel better. And how can he really be there for her if he's with Miriam and Georgia?

The truth is, they were never good on the telephone; it is always better in the flesh.

Breakfast is served in the restaurant overlooking the bay. They find a quiet spot away from the tourists near the pale, clear water, the floury sand and cabanas. Birds swoop in and flutter onto the white linen cloth—black birds, blue birds, sugar birds—looking for crumbs, scraps of fruit. Bold, erect, alive, he is glad of the distraction.

This morning, Georgia stays close to Miriam. Miriam has applied make-up to her eye and the swelling has gone down; Georgia's bruising is more obvious—the redness has darkened and crept down her neck. He finds it hard to look at. She has borrowed a scarf from Miriam and tied it loosely on one side. Thankfully, no one seems to notice them. It is him they stare at. Today his bruises are starting to bloom. He looks battered, as if he has been in a car accident.

There is a message on his phone from Juliet, telling him how sorry she is. No doubt word is spreading fast in Trinidad. While Miriam selects breakfast from the buffet, and Georgia follows her, he telephones the British High Commission. He explains his situation to the consular officer. A Trinidadian, her voice is high-pitched and thin. He thinks, if a mosquito could speak, it would sound like this.

'Do you have family in England you would like us to inform? We can help with flights, any urgent medical care.'

Apparently, their story is on a BBC news website. A short piece about the robbery; his daughter and wife were mentioned.

'What did it say, exactly?'

'I can send you a link, sir. The report didn't give names, just the fact of holidaying in Tobago. There was no mention of a rape.'

Rape. The word shocks him.

'Unfortunately we can't help with police investigations of any kind. But I imagine you have plenty of support in that regard. Is that so, Mr Rawlinson?'

Georgia picks at her fruit—papaya, oranges, banana.

'Can I get you something else?' he asks. 'There's French toast. Pancakes, your favourite.'

She shakes her head. 'I'm not as hungry as I thought.'

Miriam says. 'Just eat what you can; you need to eat.'

His head is sore, last night the medication was effective, but he is afraid to take it in the day. He will need his wits about him.

'Will you be okay if I go to the station?'

Miriam says. 'We'll stay here and make some calls. I have to ring the airline about our London flights.'

It is hard to believe they were supposed to leave tomorrow.

Miriam says, 'I'll check flights to Trinidad. We only have the room here for one more night; it's booked till the end of the week.' Then, 'I never knew Tobago was such a popular destination.'

She looks upset, and he touches her arm where the skin has peeled and it is dry, flaky, falling away. *Miriam, Miriam.*

She wipes her eyes, and to Georgia, with a half smile. 'Don't worry, I'll be fine. We'll all be fine.'

Georgia looks blank.

Then Miriam says, 'I'm assuming you can travel back with us. They'll give you compassionate leave.'

He says, 'We'll sort something out. The police will want us to stick around. Either here or in Trinidad. They'll have an ID parade. It could take four or five days.'

Georgia says, 'I don't want to go to an ID parade.'

'You don't have to, sweetheart. Your mother and I will go. We just have to wait for them to sort it out—which they will.' He speaks with a surprising confidence. 'Then we can get you home.'

TWELVE

The old, unmarked police car is hot and the air conditioner is not working. With the windows down, the breeze blows in and he is glad of it. He asks if they can drive back towards the villa, it will be easier to direct them from there.

'You want the radio on, sir?'

'No thanks,' he says, trying to sound friendly. 'I came here in the dark; it's not easy to remember. I need to concentrate.'

The dusty road is the colour of old blood and the sunlight is fierce. He tells them to keep driving, and they pass the turning to the village. The grass is tall, and through it he can glimpse the sea, the boats on the horizon. Then the road opens out and, between the trunks of the coconut trees, the sea is there, flat and blue and blurred with the sky. This is where he came with Miriam and Georgia that first day.

'See that boat out there,' Usaf says. 'Morgan Freeman. Every year he come for Carnival.'

He can see the yacht in the distance.

'Princess Margaret spent her honeymoon in Tobago. You know that?'

'No,' he says.

'The Beatles came in 1962.'

Martin says, 'Tobagonians should be careful. If these incidents carry on, no one will want to come here.'

'The problem we have is that these boys have nothing to do. They smoking weed, preying on tourists. They don't realise Tobago needs tourists for the economy.'

Curtis says, 'You didn't find it strange that Mr Monroe was out both times the boys came?'

'No,' Martin says. 'Terence had nothing to do with it. They killed his dog. Let him tell you about that.'

'Yes, sir.'

He remembers a turning on the left. They head up an incline and the road narrows. Despite the lack of rain, the land here is green and lush. They keep driving along the twisting road, and it seems further than he recalls—the car is slow now, and it judders along, straining against the hillside. On the side of the road a woman, plump and young, sits under a pipe and washes herself; she is wearing a red vest and denim shorts. She stares at the car; they slow right down. Usaf calls out and the woman waves.

There is a wooden church, and they drive down the hill which is covered with long bright grass. He runs his eyes over the landscape—the patched-up houses, the gravestones, the big trees. Usaf keeps one hand on the wheel, the other flops out of the car.

'This is where we have our heritage festival—in this little town.' Then he says, 'You ever played Carnival, sir?'

'No,' he says, irritated; he is not interested in making small talk any longer. He is not interested in festivals, or Carnival, or a history of the island and the celebrities who have stayed here. His head is throbbing as if something sharp is lodged inside it.

Now there are shops, a small supermarket. A triangle cross-roads ahead. Yes, he thinks, at last, this is familiar. This looks more like it. He feels his pulse quicken—a new drum beat.

'This could be it,' he says, looking around. A couple are sitting outside a rum shop drinking beers. A man with long dreadlocks strolls by in baggy yellow shorts, thin legs like branches.

On the left, Spiderman crouched, looking up at the sky.

'I dropped them somewhere here,' he says.

On the opposite side, the road forks into a rough trail. He points to the trail and they drive up it and there are two small concrete houses; a cow is tied to a mango tree, its horns white and long, the beige skin stretched over its skeleton. A white bird sits on its head, which is covered with flies.

Martin says, 'Maybe we can drive around this patch for a while.'

Usaf turns the car and accelerates down to the main road.

'Slowly,' Martin says.

For half an hour, they cruise around the area. There is a street market with vegetables and fruit: sweet potatoes, hang-ing bananas, pineapples, papaya, breadfruit, oranges in large baskets; a post office, a hardware store, a small grocery; a rusty sign for Diamond Dental Surgery. It is a poor place; he won-ders how people manage. If this was England, he would send police officers to make house-to-house enquiries.

'You tell them you're asking about a spate of car thefts, find out if they've noticed anything unusual. Take a note of who is in the house, their reactions, descriptions. We can start to build a picture. It's simple.'

'Yes, sir,' Usaf says.

Curtis is leaning back in his seat, mute.

'Circulate an artist's impression of the suspects. Alert other stations on the island. The coastguard. Liaise with the Trinidad coastal authority.'

He feels irritable and weary, but he needs to keep them on side. He must try to be helpful, encouraging.

On the way back, they agree to stop off at the beach. They drive in from a different side, and pull up near the far end of the bay. Coconut trees reach high into the sky, their shaggy heads bob in the warm breeze. In their dark uniforms—knitted sweaters, thick navy trousers, black boots—Usaf and Curtis clomp over the sand. He thinks, they look like they are dressed for winter. How do they work in this heat? They wait for him and he limps along. The sun is burning the top of his head and he feels dizzy with heat as he walks towards the manchineel trees lining the coast. He signals to the rocks, and the sand stretches out like a bolt of white cloth—bare and pure; big waves crash onto the shore. It is rough, this beach, the Atlantic side of the island. Beyond, a turquoise pool of water glistens.

'Nice,' Curtis says, and looks out at the view.

'That's where they were. Fishing with the others. Someone will know them.'

'Yes, sir,' Usaf says.

'Send someone down here first thing. I don't know what time we were here, but it must've been around nine. There were ten or twelve fishermen. Talk to them. Find out everything you can.'

Then, and he almost forgot. 'There's a man known as Tin Man, he's their uncle, I believe. He lives in the village and he owns the boat, *Princess*. Talk to him.'

'I know Tin Man,' Usaf says. 'We pick him up now and then; he smokes plenty weed.'

'You need to speak to him. They borrow his boat to fish.'

Usaf nods, but Martin is not convinced.

He tells them, 'There's no time to waste.'

'Yes, sir. We will do all we can.'

They head back to the hotel. Exhausted, Martin looks out at the empty blue sky. He reminds himself, he is not in charge of this investigation; he can make suggestions all day long, but he has no authority over Usaf and Curtis. No. For the first time in his life he is the victim of a violent crime. Raymond has warned him; he must step back and allow them to get on with their job. He must let go.

They pull up in front of the hotel, and he remembers to thank them, and gets out of the car. He is in pain; his ribs feel as if they are bound with barbed wire; his leg is hot and throbbing. He slowly makes his way along the corridor.

Thirteen

On the way to the airport, they stop off at the villa. Terence is standing at the top of the drive. He's been working out here since early morning; clearing the dead leaves, cutting the edges, watering the ferns and shrubs before the Dials arrive. He is angry about what happened. He has lived here all his life. The police came to see him earlier and quizzed him for over two hours, wasting everybody's time.

'I gave them my ex's number.' Then he says, 'Just yesterday I see Tin Man in the village talking to the fishermen. I almost tell him something.' He wipes his face on his T-shirt. His stomach is muscular, dark as tar. 'Some of your men can't come from Trinidad?'

'And do what? They don't want help.'

Miriam says, 'Martin showed them where they live.'

Terence shakes his head. 'They're young boys. Where the mother? Where the father? Who responsible for them?'

He doesn't mention Conan; Martin hasn't yet told Miriam that Conan is dead.

Martin says, 'It's possible they've gone on the run.'

'Tobago small. Where they running to?'

They look at one another, and Martin realises there is

nothing else to say; he would like to leave. Coming to the villa today was a mistake; it has made him feel anxious—a jittery and unpleasant sensation as if he has drunk too much coffee. In the rear-view mirror, he catches his reflection; his forehead is wet with sweat like butter melting. He wonders if Terence has noticed and dabs it with his handkerchief.

Terence checks Georgia curled up in the back. She is looking out at the golf course—the smooth, shaped mounds.

'Chelsea ask me to tell you goodbye.'

Georgia smiles faintly.

Martin gives Terence his number in Trinidad.

'If you see anything or hear anything, let me know. Anything at all.'

From here, with its immaculate garden, elegant Japanese-style roof, the villa looks impressive. And yet for Martin, it no longer holds any beauty whatsoever.

'Tell the Dials they need new chips in the gate. The boys could come back anytime.'

They land in Trinidad in the middle of the afternoon. He leaves Miriam and Georgia with the luggage and heads off to the car park. He stops for a moment in the shade to get his bearings; he is feeling disoriented. He parked somewhere here. But where? His head feels light, like he is floating.

He finds the car covered in dust: Sahara dust Sherry complains about, blown across the Atlantic from the desert. This morning Sherry will have cleaned the apartment and taken away any evidence of Safiya. When he telephoned, she was surprised to hear about the robbery. She'd heard about an incident in Tobago; she didn't realise he was involved.

'What shall I put away?' she said. 'Safiya has clothes hanging in the spare room. A couple pairs of shoes. But what else?'

'Just use your good sense. Anything that looks like it might belong to her—clothes, make-up, toiletries, pack it away in my suitcase—the one I use when I go to England.'

'How long they coming for?'

'I don't know, Sherry. We don't know.'

As he drives around the front of the airport, he spots Georgia in her white trousers and pale T-shirt; Miriam, with her cowboy hat strung around her neck, is holding it all together. And he is hit by a huge wave of sadness. Miriam is exhausted, her eye is still bloodshot. She told him she cannot sleep for seeing the boy's face.

'It's like a mask stuck on everyone else's face. I try to rip it off but it's always there in front of me. I feel like I'm going mad.'

Miriam has agreed to stay in Trinidad until the boys have been arrested. Their flights to England are on hold. Tomorrow she will telephone Georgia's school and let them know she won't be back for the start of term. Georgia is worried about staying too long; she doesn't want her friends asking questions.

He tells Miriam, 'If the police do their job, it should be a matter of days. Two or three, a week at most.'

'What if they don't find them?'

'It can't be that difficult.'

'Are you going to call Nigel?'

He has thought about this. Nigel Rush could wade in, if necessary. But it would make him unpopular. For the moment he will keep Nigel in his back pocket.

Right now, following his suggestion, Scarborough police are conducting house-to-house enquiries in the town. Despite their laidback approach, today he is feeling more hopeful. He reminds himself, they have enough information; there are three witnesses, and possibly a fourth—if they find the woman at the ATM. His only frustration: Stephen Josephs is in charge of the investigation. But there is nothing he can do about that.

Raymond said, 'The man is competent enough. He might not be your best friend, but he gets results.'

'Results? Since when?'

'Give him a chance.'

Martin said, 'I don't have much choice.'

They drive along the highway in silence. By now the sun is softening, hazy. He looks over at the hills, golden in this afternoon light. Everything feels dry, dusty, baked.

'Is this rush hour?' Miriam says. 'It's awful.'

In fact, the traffic is no worse than usual; fast cars weave in and out ahead.

'It starts anytime after 2.30.'

In front, a pick-up truck rattles along and the tray is jiggling around as if it might come away. Two young men without shirts stand in the back, holding on to the sides. They stare into the car as he overtakes.

'Why do they have to look at us like that?'

'Like what?'

'You know what I mean. There's something lascivious about them.'

'They're just bored, Miriam. And they're probably tired,

going home after a long day's work. They're not staring at us, they're just passing time.'

'They look at us as if they hate us.'

'We mustn't get paranoid.'

Miriam covers her face with her hands, and he is sorry.

'Do you want me to pull over?'

'No, I just want to get there.'

They drive past the big shopping mall with its multi-cinema screens, shopping, food hall. He has been here with Safiya. It was a Saturday and she was feeling sad about her father. They wandered through the mall holding hands; something Safiya was often shy about. *You never know who will see us. What if they tell my mom.* But that day she clung to him. He remembers feeling guilty; he was profiting from her pain. They made love that night in a different, less energetic way. There was a breathy, almost spiritual element to their climax, and afterwards she wept like a child. It was a rare thing to see Safiya cry.

He wonders how the funeral went. Before boarding the plane, he had made an excuse to Miriam, and stepped outside to call her. He left a voicemail message; he wanted to let her know that he was thinking of her. She is young to lose her father, he thinks.

He checks the mirror for Georgia.

She stares at the pile of shabby government houses as they head towards St Augustine. A fire is burning on a patch of nearby wasteland. The leaping flames are a bright and brilliant orange. The kind of fire that could spread out onto the road, into the centre of the highway.

'I used to live near here when I first arrived. It's pretty rough.'

The fire seems to come from a burned-out car. Smoke rises up in dark swirls. It looks like it might have a long life. He thinks, in its own devastating way, it is beautiful.

'Will someone come and put it out?' Georgia asks.

'Yes,' he says, 'eventually.'

Sherry has closed up the shutters; the apartment is hot like a furnace. He opens them quickly; unlocks the wrought-iron gates, drags the plastic chairs into their positions. It is a habit of Sherry's—she cleans the veranda but forgets to put the chairs back. It doesn't matter how many times he tells her.

'So this is it,' Miriam says, and she glances at the pictures on the walls. There is a peculiar wooden shield from Guyana and a wooden dagger, a tribal piece, which he can see she doesn't like.

'Yes,' he says, 'this is it.'

'And these are the famous hills,' and Miriam steps outside onto the veranda. She looks at the yard, the trees.

'It's like a desert.'

'Until the rains come. Right now it's the dry season.'

Fanta springs up from the garden; the cat has spotted him and is making his way through the scorched grass.

'Hey, Fanta,' he says, pleased. 'Come and say hello.'

He strokes his back as he slinks by, and Fanta slows, rubs up against his leg. He squats and the cat rubs against his calf. Yes, Fanta is glad to have him home. He has lost weight, which is no surprise.

'Georgia, do you remember me telling you about him?'

She gently pats the cat and Fanta tips back his head, shows his white throat. She whispers his name, as if trying it out.

Miriam says, 'What will you do with him when you leave?'

This is something he's never considered. Fanta will live with him and Safiya wherever they end up.

'I'll find him a home.'

Fanta lies on the floor and rolls onto his side.

Miriam says, 'Otherwise, he'd have to go into quarantine. There's rabies here, isn't there?'

A beetle is lying on its back, legs wildly kicking. He wondered if Fanta has brought it in. He flips it the right way up. Fanta does not notice; he is lying down enjoying the attention.

'He likes you, Georgia.'

It is the first time he has seen her smile in two days. She pushes back his fur around the mouth, and the cat closes his eyes in a kind of ecstasy. He starts to purr.

'I've never heard him purr so loudly.'

This is true. When he first arrived, Safiya thought Fanta was mute; he had no voice at all.

In the kitchen, he opens the fridge. 'Can I get you a drink?' There is juice, water, beers. Sherry has brought bread.

Fanta wanders away. Georgia follows, drifting off down the passageway.

'Water,' Miriam says, following her. 'Actually, if you have long-life milk, I'll have tea. I don't want that awful powdered stuff.'

'Hang on, and I'll give you a tour.'

But it's too late; he hears the creaky door to his bedroom. And by the time he gets there, Miriam is already examining a stack of books at the side of his bed, some of which belong to Safiya. Sherry could not have known.

'Caribbean poetry,' she says. 'I didn't know you liked poetry.'

She opens the cupboards and peers inside. Then she wanders into the ensuite bathroom. Sherry has put out fresh towels, she has scrubbed the bathroom floor. It feels fresh, clean.

'This isn't so bad, I suppose.'

Georgia stands at the window and looks through the curtains at the yard. The sun ililminates her face.

'Open them,' he says. 'Let the daylight in.'

But she doesn't. She retreats to the bed and flops down; her face is distraught. He doesn't know what to say. He feels useless.

Miriam goes to her. 'It's okay, darling.' She takes up Georgia's hands.

'What if they find out we're here?'

Martin says, 'They have no way of knowing where we are. Remember, we are looking for them—not the other way round.'

Georgia almost whispers—and she sounds defeated, 'I want to go home.'

He sits down beside her. She looks at the floor where the light makes a yellow column.

'We just have to be here for a few days to make sure they catch them. We want them to be caught, don't we?' He strokes her fair hair. 'Then you can go home. Okay?'

With the wrought-iron bars, it is safe enough to leave the French doors open, and yet, before nightfall, he finds himself pulling them to, clicking the locks into place; he double-checks the side windows, switches on the security lamps at the back. In his cupboard, amongst his clothes, he finds his pistol, removes the case, and places it in the drawer of his bedside table. He has been thinking—would it have made a difference if he'd had the gun with him at the villa? The boys might have found it and used it on them. Things might have been worse.

The gates to the driveway are padlocked. For the first time, he uses a chain for the sliding lock—an extra security feature. Through the long sheer drapes, he can see the road, the lights of the house next door—Jeanne and Satnam. They must be back from their Miami trip. He is glad of them.

FOURTEEN

Raymond arrives typically early. He leans against the gate puffing on a cigarette. Martin unlocks the back door, flicks on the kettle. He switches off the outside security lamps. Fanta nips through the open louvers, no doubt ready for his food. Outside the sun is already bright and the ground is warm. Martin hobbles along the concrete, his feet still sore, shading his eyes from the brightness. Raymond's car is running—he likes to keep the air conditioner on. They have spent many hours outside chatting by this gate with the engine running.

'Boy, you look rough.' He offers him a cigarette.

In the last few days, Martin's been smoking heavily. Georgia would usually give him a ticking-off, but she hasn't seemed to notice.

Raymond locks up the car—he won't stay long—and follows Martin through the gates, around the side of the apartment, carrying a sweet scent of aftershave. Whenever Martin is coming from England, Raymond puts in an order for duty-free aftershave and cigarettes.

The girls aren't up yet. He'll make coffee, they can sit outside.

Raymond says, 'Any news? Have they found anyone?'

'No. I'm giving them a couple more days. Then I'll be on their backs.'

'They'll have their ways and methods.' Then he says, 'These boys are so damned bold. There were three of them, right?'

'Yes, exactly.'

Raymond shakes his head.

'It should be straightforward enough; we saw their faces, we know where they live.' Then, 'I keep thinking I'm going to wake up from the nightmare.'

He looks out at the garden, the wilting plants under the trees. Young Vishnu will come soon and water the yard. Everything is crispy. 'I just want them caught as soon as possible.'

Raymond gives Martin an envelope: his new contract.

'If you want to give it some thought, I'll completely understand.' Then he says, 'Remember the British guy from Texaco who was attacked at Mayaro. He took a taxi from the hospital straight to the airport. Left his house, his job, his clothes, his car. Even his dog.'

Martin says quietly, 'I live here.'

'Good. They're taking bets at the office you'll be gone by the end of the month. I told them you were a sticker.'

Miriam appears in the doorway. 'You must be Raymond,' she says. She is wearing her white dressing gown; she looks surprisingly fresh-faced.

Raymond says, 'I'm so sorry for what happened.'

She leans in the doorway, arms loosely folded. 'Have you always lived in Trinidad, Raymond?'

'Yes, ma'am. I'm a Trini through and through.'

'I keep wondering, if we'd stayed in a hotel it might have been different.'

'These things can happen anywhere.' Then he says, 'At the end of the day, you were lucky.'

'Lucky or unlucky? It depends on how you look at it.'

She looks at the yard, at two birds sitting in the birdbath. There is hardly any water, but they are making the most of it.

Raymond says, 'Hopefully it won't be long before they're caught. I'm sure you're keen to get home.'

'Yes,' she says. 'Unlike my husband, I can't say I like your Trinidad. He's obviously fallen in love.'

'Well, Trinidad has a way of getting under your skin. For some people. I can understand why you don't feel that way.'

Martin wonders whether Raymond will say something about his contract. It would be unfortunate timing.

Then Miriam asks, 'Are you married, Raymond?'

'No, ma'am.'

There are rumours that Raymond is gay—a criminal offence in Trinidad. He has talked about a girlfriend, a flight attendant who moved to Miami in the late '90s, but no one else. In Trinidad, if you're not married by a certain age it's often assumed there's something wrong. Gay or straight, Martin couldn't care less, Raymond has been a good friend.

'I like my freedom too much.'

Miriam half smiles; she looks disappointed. She probably thinks Raymond is a bad influence, a ladies' man. It is Raymond who has kept her husband busy and away from his family. She will leave them, she says; she will make breakfast; check on Georgia.

The two men sit for a moment. Next door a radio starts.

Raymond says, quietly, 'You haven't told her?'

'Not yet.'

From inside, he hears the water pump, and he wonders if Georgia is up and having a shower.

'What have they said about your head?'

'Watch for dizziness, the usual things.'

'You should take it easy.'

'I am taking it easy. I just hope they'll crack on.'

He flicks his cigarette into the drain; the orange glow burns.

'I don't want to see you anywhere near the office until you're good and ready.' Raymond gives him a look, gets up and smoothes out his cotton slacks. 'If you want a beer you know where I am.'

Raymond has known about his relationship with Safiya from the start; he had often joked that there's no fool like an old fool. Martin suspects Raymond isn't aware of how serious it is, that they are in love, which is probably just as well. Once when Martin returned from England and was feeling guilty about Miriam, Raymond told him, if you're unfaithful abroad it doesn't count. At the time he'd laughed, though he'd sensed Raymond was, in fact, serious.

They wander out to the gate.

'When does the rainy season start?' Martin asks. 'Is it June?'

'May, June.'

'It feels like it's all about to go up in smoke, the whole island. I don't remember it being like this last year.'

'Well, it was. You've just forgotten.'

There is talk of driving into Port of Spain later that morning. He needs to go to the bank. When he'd called his branch from

Tobago, they said he must come in: there are forms to sign, bring proof of identity; his new cards and chequebook will take a few days. He desperately needs cash. What can they do without cash?

Georgia says that she would rather stay at home with Miriam. She is tired. He tells her they don't have to go for long. He would rather not leave them alone in the apartment on their first day.

'Remember when we were in Tobago, you said you'd like to see some of the island? It's not far into town. We can leave whenever you want.'

From the highway, the hills are brown and burned. The place is singing with heat—the light bouncing off the galvanised roofs, the roads dusty and parched. There are lines of smoke, little fires eat away the hillside. At the port, he slows for the traffic lights; a small crowd of vultures are gathered around a dead dog; like men in cloaks, they stick their heads in the ring where the corpse lies.

He drives slowly along the west side, and the sea is a metallic blue simmering with light and heat, the traffic is building up. Lunchtime. The city feels alive. Safiya is somewhere here. He wonders if he might spot her; she is often on this route. He looks for her car. What would they do? Wave? Toot horns? Right now, she feels faraway from him.

They drift into the cool white shopping mall.

'Would you like to come with me to the bank or would you prefer to have a look around? There's a bookstore upstairs. It's pretty good.'

Miriam checks Georgia who is looking nonplussed.

'We'll come find you in a minute.'

From the bottom of the escalator, he watches them rise—
they look the same, their slim frames, narrow shoulders. And
he thinks, they should not be here, they should be back in
England, feeling rejuvenated, energised by their holiday. It was
not meant to be like this.

The bank is busy; the queue is long and slow-moving. He
notices people staring at him. His leg is sore and he shuffles
along the line; he should probably be at home resting but he
is glad to be out. The apartment—a place where he once felt
free—captain of his soul—is already feeling claustrophobic.

This morning when he woke he did not know where he was,
the light coming through the mustard curtains, the strange yellow
glow, and in Safiya's place was Miriam, her arm looped around
him. He was confused, and then the memory shot like an electric
jolt through his body. He was so angry it frightened him. And
at the same time, he felt an overwhelming sadness. Miriam told
him, 'We'll get through this. We've been through worse.'

And he'd thought, yes, losing Beth was worse, but I could do
nothing about that. This was something I could have avoided.

In the bookstore, Georgia waits near the door. Lost in her own
world, she does not notice when he comes from the bank and
stands beside her. He asks about the game on her mobile. She
hasn't stopped playing since yesterday.

'Word Mole,' she says, without looking up.

'Is it like Scrabble?'

'Sort of. With a stopwatch.'

Then he says—and he is unsure of his timing, 'Are you okay?'

She looks up at him, her grey-blue eyes steady. 'I just want it to be over; I want to go home.'

She lets him put his arm around her. He expected tears, but there are none, and he is relieved, though he knows that they are there and will come later. It is typical, he has seen it many times: in the early days of trauma, a calm, dry-eyed reaction. He has warned Miriam it will not last. And when the tears come, they will arrive like a deluge. If this was England, there would be a family liaison officer, a specialised unit to deal with their case, a twenty-four-hour victim support helpline. She needs to go home soon.

Georgia says, 'I keep remembering how you helped them.'

'I know, darling.'

And I keep thinking of how I failed you.

At the apartment, he telephones Scarborough police station. There is no reply. He tries again. A woman answers. She sounds so vague, he wonders if he has the right number. She tells him, there is no one available to speak to him until tomorrow.

'Isn't there a single officer on site?'

'No,' the woman says. 'They all in a meeting over the road. Try back in the morning.'

The main police station in Tobago and there is no one to speak to. He can hardly believe it. Sherry once told him that she tried to report a stolen handbag at her local station but the police officer didn't have a pen and sent her away. At the time he'd laughed.

'I'd like to leave a message.'

He hears the woman suck her teeth.

'I want to leave a message for Stephen Josephs.'

The sound of paper tearing; a scrap for her to write on. She takes his number and he wonders if she will actually give it to anyone.

He asks for her name, but it is too late, she has already hung up.

Later, when they are asleep, Georgia comes into their room.

'What is it?' He checks the clock, it is 3 a.m.

Miriam says, 'Has something happened?'

Georgia says she heard something. She isn't sure if she was dreaming; it felt real. He hurries down the corridor to her room. The lights are on, and he checks under her bed; he looks behind the curtains, quickly scans the bathroom. He is reminded of when the girls were young and they woke with nightmares. Georgia was always more sensitive than Beth, harder to console, to reassure. This is how it's going to be, he thinks; her world will be full of shadows; it will never be the same again.

When he comes back, she is calmer, lying curled next to Miriam.

'You're safe here, Georgia,' he says, 'nothing is going to happen to you. Do you understand? We have iron bars; burglar-proofing. No one can get through them.'

'They got through electric gates.'

'Only because they managed to steal the gate opener. Otherwise they'd never have got in.'

He looks into her tired eyes. Why should she believe him?

'If someone came to the door now, I wouldn't let them in without checking who they are. In Tobago, I thought we knew them, because they got through the gates. They took my gate opener from the car that night I drove them home. Remember? So I thought it was Terence at the door; I thought it was someone who had an opener. That's not going to happen here.'

'What if they did get in?'

'They won't. No one is coming here.' Then he says, 'I have a gun. Remember that.'

'Where is it?'

He goes to the bedside table and feels inside the drawer; the gun feels cool and hard. He takes it out and holds it flat in the palm of his hand. Like an offering, he brings it to where Georgia is sitting. It is small, neat, no bigger than a bird. Georgia stares at it.

'No one is going to come in here. Do you understand?'

'Why didn't you have the gun in Tobago?'

Miriam looks at him as if to say, yes, why didn't you?

'Because I wasn't on duty. I was on holiday with my family so I didn't take it with me.'

They all go back to Georgia's room. Miriam will sleep in here, she says. They push the twin beds together. He waits until they are both in bed; he turns out the light.

FIFTEEN

The telephone wakes him. It is Usaf. Finally, five days after the attack, there is some news—a shard of hope. Yesterday, during their door-to-door enquiries, the officers spoke with a woman in her seventies, a grandmother. Her grandsons, two brothers, are away fishing for lobster since Friday. They left with a neighbour and are expected to return today or tomorrow. There was a photograph of the boys tacked on her kitchen wall. Usaf thinks it could be them. Something about the eyes.

In his underwear, Martin heads into the living room; the curtains are open, Miriam must be up.

'Where does she live? Did we drive nearby?'

'Right by where the cow was tied. A little blue house.'

He looks out at the sky, littered with shreds of white cloud.

'Did you ask about the boat? Is it the same boat? Was it called *Princess*?'

'She didn't say what the boat was called.'

'Where exactly are they fishing?'

'She said they go all about. We think they might be in Englishman's Bay. It's popular for lobster fishing.'

Martin ought to be encouraging but he can't help himself.

'What are you waiting for? Send a couple of undercover officers down there immediately. Contact the coastguard.'

By now they could be anywhere.

Then, 'Have you spoken to the station down there? Is it in
Moriah?' He remembers the station. A tatty-looking place.

'No, sir. Not yet. I wanted to let you know first.'

He makes a *huh* sound at the back of his throat. He must try
to be patient; Usaf is doing his best.

'The lady indicated they would definitely be back today or
tomorrow, so we will check back this afternoon.'

Indicated?

Miriam is hovering, trying to figure out what is going on.

Martin says, 'Look, you need to search the coast. I've described the boat, you know what it's called. It's simple. When
they hear the police are asking questions, they'll disappear. We
don't have time to waste.' Then he asks, 'What about the advice
slips from the ATM?'

'Sir, we can proceed without them.'

'Fingerprints. They'll be full of fingerprints. You need to
sift through them. Use Ninhydrin solution.' Then, 'You have
the rape kit, right?'

'Yes, sir.'

In Trinidad it is common for evidence to go missing—guns,
knives, machetes.

'What about the woman at the ATM?'

'We haven't yet located the lady, sir. We're still making enquiries.'

He asks to speak to Stephen Josephs. 'Is he there?'

'Yes, sir.' Then, 'Hold a minute.'

He is kept waiting; Miriam is sitting with him now. He puts

the phone on loudspeaker. Eventually, Stephen picks up. He is friendly, as if they are old pals; he is sorry, he says, to hear about their recent trouble.

Martin says, 'When we left it seemed like a matter of course, just a question of locating the boys. We know who they are, we know where they live.'

'We might suspect who they are, but we don't know *where* they are right now. That's our problem, Martin. As you know, Tobago is a small island but there are plenty places to hide.'

Stephen's tone is supercilious. Martin had forgotten how irritating he is. He finds himself trying to get him on side. It is uncomfortable.

'That may be true, but we need to act quickly,' Martin says. 'They could hide out somewhere for days, weeks. They have money. For all we know they might have gone to Venezuela.'

Stephen chuckles. 'Venezuela? Why would they go to Venezuela?'

Martin looks out at the yard; Fanta wanders under the tree, his orange coat foxlike.

'It's only seven miles from here. I told Usaf to contact the coastguard.'

Stephen sighs. 'Come, come, you should try to relax. You need to take care of yourself and your family. Take your wife and daughter to the beach, give them a tour of the north coast, take them to see the pitch lake, the Wild Fowl Trust. Trinidad is a beautiful country. Who knows when they will come back to the islands.'

He is astonished. 'They're not here to sightsee, Stephen. They want to get back home to England.'

* * *

In the early days as a young police officer, he often despaired at the world around him: the woman who held down her five-year-old daughter so her partner could have sex with her. A man who cut off his wife's fingers for coming home late from a party. The family of four who fell from their rowing boat into the river; the father had been made redundant, and, depressed, took them all out in a boat in a storm. The children were missing and presumed dead for hours. It was Martin who saw the nine-year-old girl's body drifting in the ripples of the water. He jumped in and swam to her, dragged her heavy body through the rapids, and hauled her onto the mossy bank. He put his mouth on hers and started to breathe into her. All the time he could hear the rush of the water, feel her wet, cold skin; he tasted her vomit as he started to clear her passageway back to life. When she opened her eyes, and he knew she was alive, that he had saved her, he felt a profound sense of elation.

Yes, he thought, this is why I do what I do. It was a turning point for him. A kind of epiphany. It gave his life a new meaning.

He wonders if Stephen Josephs has ever had an experience like that. He suspects not.

Later, he tells Raymond. 'I want to shake the man.'

'I've known him for years, Stephen has never liked outside pressure. He's always been that way. Try not to take it personally; let them get on with it.'

'They don't have any kind of strategy. He told me to take Miriam and Georgia to the fucking beach.'

Raymond will speak to the Deputy Police Commissioner. He can, at the very least, give Stephen a nudge. Stephen will realise that Martin is not about to sit and wait. If the embassy can also make 'enquiries', it might be helpful. Can Martin speak with them again. The press in England could get hold of the story and make it unpleasant for everyone. The tourist board is keen to avoid any negative publicity involving foreign nationals. It is the last thing Tobago needs; it is the last thing the organisation needs.

'Leave it with me,' Raymond says. 'I'll see what I can do. You're going to need to be a little patient. We can't be seen to be offering special treatment.'

The ceiling fan in the living room is inadequate and the sun blasts through the French doors, making it unbearably hot. Miriam complains—they will die of heat. They leave the air conditioners on in the bedrooms, the doors open, in the hope that the cool air eventually makes its way around the apartment. Miriam is surprised by how shabby the place is. Shabby? It has never occurred to him; he has been happy enough here.

'I never imagined it like this.'

'In what way?'

'I don't know, something more sophisticated; something more homely. It doesn't feel like a home. It feels like a bachelor pad.'

A dig, but he doesn't rise.

Since they arrived in Trinidad he has noticed a change in her, an absence of softness, except when Georgia is around. She is hardening towards him and he suspects that she is blaming him. He is not surprised. It was his choice to stay in the villa rather than a hotel, his idea to drop the boys home, and he—literally—opened the door to them—to their violence and rage.

Yesterday, after they got back from town, and while Georgia

was resting in her room, Miriam broke down and told him that one of them—the one with the cutlass—had urinated on the sofa where she lay. It was warm and pungent like the piss of a dog. He was shocked, dismayed. Why didn't she tell him before?

'What difference would it have made? I told them in my statement.'

'Did he do anything else? What else haven't you told me?'

'He said they never came there to rape. It was only the boy. He wanted Georgia.'

Martin lit a cigarette and looked out at the shadowy hills. He felt sick at the thought of the boy.

'I don't like you smoking,' Miriam said. 'It's making me feel worse. Please don't smoke in front of Georgia; it's sending the wrong message.'

'What kind of message would you like me to send to our daughter?'

'She needs to feel we're in control. When you're smoking it tells her the opposite, that you're anxious, scared.'

'Maybe I am.'

Georgia plays on her phone. It reminds him of when Beth died; she seemed to slip away then too. She disappeared into books. Sometimes she looks vacant, as if she has been emptied. At other times she seems calm and more like herself. There are spots around her mouth, and her eyes are dull as wood. The bruising on her neck is now a purple and yellow stain. She complains about the heat and says that the only way to stay cool is to shower. But he suspects this is not the real reason for the five or six showers she takes every day, he imagines this is the only way she can feel herself clean, fresh, free of the boy. She complains of feeling sick and lightheaded. Miriam has given her travel bands to wear on her wrists; they are, apparently, helping with the dizziness. Miriam is worried about her loss of appetite. She is already too thin; she tells Martin: Georgia is disappearing before their eyes.

He telephones Ali's Drug Store. The pharmacist is sympathetic. He says the sickness should last only a few days. Sometimes the nausea is partly psychological.

'Your daughter must take the medication with her food; even a little bread or rice. Get as much rest as she can. She'll feel tired and achy like she has flu. It's normal. Give it another couple days and it should pass.'

Martin is grateful to Fanta; he seems to be the only thing that makes Georgia feel better. Fanta follows her around the house, as if he knows of her pain; Fanta, his magic cat. Earlier when Fanta wandered outside, Georgia went looking for him. It was good to see her in the garden taking in fresh air, thinking of something else. He knows this much: whatever Georgia is going through, it is the start of a long and excruciating process.

This is just the beginning.

While Miriam and Georgia rest, he calls Scarborough police station. He speaks to the same woman; he finds out her name is Bernadette—the same name as his mother. He decides on a new, friendly approach. Does she know that Bernadette is a name of German origin; that it means brave?

Today she is more co-operative; she makes a note of his questions. He tells her he would like an update on the following: the grandmother, the woman at the ATM, the artists' impressions of the boys.

Calmly, he says, 'Ask either of them—Usaf or Curtis—to call me as soon as they're back.'

'They might not come in this afternoon. We'll most likely see them tomorrow.'

'Do you have a mobile number?'

'No, sir.'

'Perhaps you could alert them on their radios.'

'Yes, sir.'

If this was England, she would pass his call to someone else. Usaf and Curtis's whereabouts would be written on a white board in the office. She could check their electronic diaries; call them on their mobiles.

On the news there are new murders and, near the local pizza bar, an attempted kidnapping of an American tourist. A young woman with a young child is shot. So far the annual murder rate is up to an all-time high.

Miriam makes a face. 'Do we really want to see this?'

Raymond tells Martin that maybe he should stop watching the news; that he is noticing these events more because of his experience. Perhaps he should try to put his attention on other things—recovery, his family.

'I want some information, an update. I feel like I'm being taken for a ride.'

'I've spoken with the Deputy. For the moment, there's not much more I can do.' Then he says, 'It might seem like days are dragging but it hasn't been long.'

'They should've arrested someone by now.'

'Maybe in an ideal world.'

Martin says, 'The point is, I spoke to Usaf this morning; he was supposed to ring me back. I rang this afternoon, and no one has bothered to return my call. I left a bunch of questions. They're fucking useless.'

'Try to keep your perspective. You're looking at things from a British point of view.'

'Exactly, that's the problem; and I know how they operate. They're on a permanent go-slow.' Then he says, 'My daughter needs to go home.'

He keeps thinking about a young woman he once knew in Shrewsbury—Georgina Wilson—who was attacked coming home from a disco with a man she had met that night. On one of his first jobs, he was called to her flat above a florist in the town. He was horrified by her statement, and the medical report that followed describing the brutal, humiliating acts the man put her through. After the man was convicted, Martin took it upon himself to visit her. He liked Georgina—her sense of humour, her bright mind. They talked about music, films, politics. She seemed, to him, to be coping well; getting on with her life. But a year later she drove to the Norfolk Broads, parked her car, and waited for the sun to go down. In the darkness, she walked into the cold, black sea, fully dressed—shoes, coat, skirt and blouse. After a week, her body was washed up five miles along the coast. It had shocked him. He was so certain of a mistaken identity, he went to see her body in the morgue.

Georgia, Georgina.

He tries to put her out of his mind.

Sixteen

Jeanne lets them through their electric gates; she walks out to meet them, barefoot, white tennis shorts, a polo shirt. She has done something to her hair; she appears younger. She looks at his bandage and pulls a face.

'Ouch! We heard there was trouble in paradise.'

Before they came, he'd reassured Georgia: Jeanne and Satnam know only about the robbery, and not what happened to her.

Martin says, 'It looks worse than it is.'

He introduces his wife and daughter. Georgia stands behind Miriam who is dour in her jogging trousers, flip-flops. Miriam apologises for their clothes; when Jeanne called to invite them for drinks there wasn't time to change.

'You're in Trinidad,' Jeanne says. 'You can wear what you like. No one stands on ceremony here.'

They follow her inside to their open-plan kitchen where she opens the fridge and peers inside. She is easy, relaxed. Earlier she made some dips, she says. They are somewhere here.

'What *is* happening in Tobago? You're the second visitors we've heard about this year. Remember the German couple? But they were killed. The police never caught the guys.'

From the living room he can hear music. Spanish, music

usually played at Christmas.

'Go inside and see Satnam, he's hooked his new iPod up to the speakers.'

She rolls her eyes, gives Miriam a look. 'Technology confuses my husband.' Then to Martin, 'See if you can distract him.' She holds up a bottle of wine, and a bottle of Coke for Georgia.

'Great,' he says, and they wander inside following the soft lights into the large American-style living room.

Satnam shakes his hand; he says hello to Miriam and Georgia. 'We heard the news. What the hell is wrong with these people? Did they take much?'

He looks smart, in a long-sleeved, pale blue shirt and chinos. His grey hair is combed back from his smooth brown face. 'There were three of them or four?'

Jeanne carries a tray with drinks, potato chips and dips.

'I'm sure they don't want to talk about it,' she says chirpily.

He is glad of Jeanne's charm, her easy manner. Tonight she exudes a warmth he hasn't witnessed before, as if lit from the inside. Perhaps she is feeling sorry for them. Whatever it is, it is exactly what they need.

To his surprise, she soon has Georgia playing a computer game; Miriam is sipping a glass of white wine by the open patio doors overlooking the L-shaped swimming pool. He feels relieved, grateful. Some normality.

He asks if they often sit here with the doors open.

'Sometimes we pull in the gates, especially if Jeanne is home alone. But we don't want to live in a prison.'

'No one does,' he says. 'That's the trouble.'

'We always feel safer knowing you're next door.' Jeanne grins.

'I'm not a policeman,' he says. 'Not really.'

'But you've been working with them, right?' Satnam asks.

'Yes—it's slow progress. I do my best.'

'They seized a whole pile of stolen ammunition from a station in the East—you remember that? They'd hidden it in the rafters.'

'Yes, some of them rent out their guns. When I first arrived I thought it was a joke.'

'Where do you begin with something like that?'

'Part of the problem is promotion; it comes through years of service. There is little to motivate them. Plus the money is bad. In England it's not much more than a cleaner's salary.'

'So they should be paid more.'

'Rewarded better, I'd say.'

He'd rather not talk about work. He says, 'Have you been to England?'

Jeanne says, 'He's always promising to take me. I want to see the Crown Jewels.'

Satnam and Jeanne exchange a tender look.

They talk about Miriam's job, her excellent Spanish. Jeanne, too, speaks a little Spanish.

'Did you live there for a long time?'

'Five years. I fell in love in Barcelona. You know what it's like when you're young. You think it will last forever.'

Satnam fills their glasses; the wine is surprisingly good. 'Californian,' he says, lighting a cigarette. 'A Chardonnay.'

They bring it in from the States. He has a useful contact in customs. If ever he wants to bring in anything, he should let them know.

Martin is surprised that Satnam could suggest he collude with a corrupt immigration officer.

Jeanne says, 'We kept wondering if you were real, Miriam. Your husband is a busy man.'

He often sees Jeanne driving past the apartment. She must know Safiya's car, the comings and goings, often late at night. She will have made her own assumptions. He is sure that Sherry talks to their housekeeper. But there's nothing he can do about that. This is a place where people talk.

'You're always in Miami,' he says, 'living the high life.'

'Not true!' Jeanne waves her manicured hand. 'He likes to be elusive. We go to the States every couple months. We have an apartment in Orlando. If ever you want to use it, you're welcome. Disney World is right there. Georgia would love it.'

By nine o'clock he is feeling a little drunk; Georgia is sitting on the floor playing with her phone. He is enjoying the music, the wine, the different conversation. Miriam's legs are curled up beneath her. It is the most relaxed he has seen her in days.

Outside, a car alarm goes off and Satnam gets up. He tells Georgia not to look so worried. Apparently, their vehicle alarm is faulty, oversensitive, easily triggered by a bat or a firefly. Satnam apologises. He is surprised they haven't heard it going off at all hours of the night.

'You know the car we rented in Tobago was a Tucson,' Martin says. 'The blacked-out windows didn't do me any favours.'

Miriam narrows her eyes.

Satnam says, 'Sherry said they were young; opportunists, I suppose. They saw tourists and thought cash.'

'I should never have let them in.'

'Any arrests in sight?'

'We're hopeful.'

Jeanne says, pointedly, 'Well, thank God it was only cash they wanted. These days they like to rape.'

'Yes,' Martin says. And Miriam is up, and then everyone is on their feet.

'Come whenever you like,' Jeanne says, and she puts her hand on Georgia's head. 'Don't be a stranger. Come and use the pool. We're here most of the time. If I'm not here the maid will let you in.'

He steps outside to lock the gates. Tonight the sky is dark blue like deep sea. He lights a cigarette and looks down the street. The streetlights are on; the houses are lit.

He is thinking of Safiya, when he last saw her here at these same gates; he wonders where she is. Right now, their relationship seems unreal. There is nothing of her in the apartment, only her few belongings which Sherry has hidden away. He misses her sandals slung on the steps, underwear slipped into his drawer; nail polish on the coffee table, a hair clip discarded in the bathroom. There is no trace of her; it is as if she was imagined.

And yet the consequences of their relationship are there for all to see. They have been in love, yes, but love has made him negligent; and negligence like rust always corrodes. If Miriam had felt more secure, she would have waited until Easter to visit. She was insecure because he had unplugged himself from her, from their life as a family. At Christmas he was not himself; he was preoccupied. Yes, Miriam felt abandoned, bereft. She came to Tobago to bring him back.

He needs to speak with Safiya. He wants to talk to her about her father, to tell her he is sorry not to be with her at such an important time. She, too, must feel let down. She is young enough to forget him; that much he knows. She is probably trying to work herself free of him right now. Why wouldn't she? If he was a better man, he would let her go. But he is not. The thought of letting her go fills him with dread.

Miriam and Georgia don't want to be left for long, and he understands this. His outings are restricted to daylight, an hour here and there; he can make excuses—a meeting, an appointment. The traffic on the roads is often dreadful; almost the moment he reaches the capital, he has to turn around and come back. For now, Safiya is out of reach.

Seventeen

It is another day. He has barely slept. But he is determined to make the most of the morning. He has already called the station and spoken to Usaf, who is on his way to a meeting. Did he see the grandmother yesterday? No, Usaf tells him, he will call in this afternoon.

Martin is irritated; what could possibly be more important? Why doesn't Usaf go there now? He tries to stay calm; he has never been so aware of time passing. But there is no point in getting worked up. He tells himself, he will wait; he must wait.

His ribs are still sore; any sudden movement reminds him of his injuries; his bruises are like watercolours on his body—splodgy shades of tapioca, ochre, pale grey. On his leg the scab is growing thick like bark on a tree. When he woke, he felt dizzy, a sensation almost like travel sickness; he wonders about an aneurysm—it is quite possible—and pictures a balloon of blood floating in his head. He should probably see a doctor, have the scan.

He stands at the kitchen window drinking his third cup of coffee of the morning. Outside in the yard, he can see Georgia; she is looking for Fanta. She is wearing her pyjamas, her hair is loose and wet. She is calling the cat, wandering around the back of the mango tree and peering up into its thick branches. When he first came, it was laden with fruit—hundreds of rosy, sweet mangoes. When the rains come it will bear again. And where will he be? Here? In England?

Martin doesn't hear the clank of the gate when Vishnu arrives. He doesn't see him walk up the drive. No, Vishnu appears in the yard like an apparition; hot from the road, stripped to the waist, his body gleaming with sweat, cutlass hanging from his belt.

He raises his hand to Georgia in a kind of salute. 'Is your father here?'

Georgia doesn't answer. She freezes, paralysed. Then, slowly, while still keeping her eyes on Vishnu, she backs away towards the apartment.

'It's okay,' Vishnu says. 'Don't be afraid, I'm here to work in the yard.' He takes a step towards her.

Georgia screams a loud and terrified scream, and runs inside where Martin catches her—breathless. In the kitchen, she breaks free of him, scrambles into the passageway and runs towards her room. He clambers after her, puts his arms around her and grips her tightly. She pants, struggling for her breath as if she is about to hyperventilate. She kicks at him, and pushes him away.

'Vishnu is our gardener, I told you he was coming this morning. Vishnu's a good person; he planted the lilies you like.' Then, 'Talk to me,' he says, 'let me help you. Tell me what I can do.'

Georgia slumps on the floor.

'Please talk to me, Georgia. It's the only way we'll get through this. It's important.'

Together, he and Miriam lift her up, help her back into her bedroom.

Miriam waves at Martin, Go, leave us alone. He watches from the doorway as she lays down on the bed beside her, and rocks their daughter gently. After a few moments, he comes to her; sits down on the edge of her bed. She is quieter now.

'Why don't we take a drive up to the Benedictine monastery. It's beautiful. You can light a candle in the little chapel.'

Miriam looks surprised. She has not known him go to church since they were first married.

'I went there last year for Beth's birthday. You can see right out to the refinery. We can have tea—the monks make tea, and they sell yoghurt and cheese.'

Georgia shakes her head.

'Tomorrow?'

'Maybe,' she says. Then, 'I'd rather stay here.'

'You can't stay here all the time.'

'Why not?'

'Georgia, you have to talk to us so we can help you.'

'Martin,' Miriam says.

Georgia says, 'I want to go home. Please let me go home.'

He tells himself, as bad as things are, it could have been worse. He remembers Asif Mercano, a respectable man in his sixties, whom he met at a neighbourhood watch meeting in 2007. Asif raised funds for security street lights, a patrol car. He said Trinidad was going down the drain. He called it a 'beautiful, ruined country'. Decorators were working on Asif's family home—a modest house with a small swimming pool—in time for Christmas. A week after they were paid, they came back, four of them; they tied him up, robbed him, then cut off his head with a machete. Right there on the driveway in front of his wife.

He telephones the station. He speaks to a male officer. Neither Usaf or Curtis are in the office.

'Can you tell me where they are? I'm calling from Superintendent Raymond Marchant's office in Trinidad.'

'I'm not sure, sir. They were here earlier and now they're not here.'

'I'd like to speak with Stephen Josephs.'

'He's away for the rest of the day.'

The officer takes a message. Somebody will call him back. He waits.

Nigel Rush is glad to hear from him. Sympathetic, he is horrified by Martin's news; he is not surprised that there are no forensic facilities on the island.

'A banana republic—my worst nightmare.'

Martin pictures Nigel in his Shrewsbury office, the view from the window of the busy high street; a framed photograph on the wall of Nigel collecting a medal from the queen. Yes, Nigel has done well for himself; he is now a Chief Officer, leader of the West Mercia Police Force. It was expected that Martin would have followed a similar career trajectory if Beth hadn't died. Yes, he'd lost his way for a while.

'What would you like me to do? Should I call the station in Tobago? Do you want me to complain to someone? The High

Commission? Put some dynamite up their backsides.'

Martin says, 'What about Scotland Yard?'

'In my experience, they don't like to interfere unless the Foreign Office or the government want them involved for political reasons. Remember the case of the student murdered in Tokyo? It's a delicate area. Everyone's wary of treading on toes.'

'I know.'

'It sounds like you're caught between a rock and a hard place. If you complain, they drag their feet. If I do nothing they still drag their feet.'

Then Nigel says, 'Maybe you need some press. What about the *Daily Mail*? They'd love a story like this. Of course, you'd have to deal with the fallout. But it might get them moving. You can speak to our media department. They'll know what to do.'

He asks about Miriam. When is he coming back? They must get together. It's been a long time. His new wife, Marilyn, is pregnant. Life has never been busier, he says.

'How is Georgia? Is she coping?'

'Not really. She needs to go home.'

'Let me see what I can do.'

Eighteen

At the Hilton Hotel, the car park is jammed. He drives around for a while. From the signage, he guesses that there is more than one conference. The place will be swarming, which is no bad thing.

The receptionist is familiar. She gives him a key and wishes him a pleasant stay. Does he have any luggage? He shows her his briefcase, and makes his way to the bar. And he is reminded of the early days with Safiya, when he picked her up from Woodbrook and brought her here for cocktails before heading out for dinner. He'd guessed that she wasn't used to restaurants. She saw friends in their homes, drank at the odd sports bar, and mostly ate takeaways. Restaurants gave their meetings a certain romance and sophistication. From the beginning, he'd wanted to give her a different kind of experience; he was clear about that. It also allowed them privacy, and it suited her. It was unlikely Safiya would bump into anyone she knew.

He picks up today's paper and glances through it; he looks up now and then at the entrance. A large arrangement of tropical lilies reminds him he'd meant to buy flowers. He checks himself in the mirror above the bar. The bruising on his face has faded: more yellow than blue; yes, he is on the mend.

Earlier, after his shower, he removed the hospital bandage.
Miriam cleaned around the wound, and covered it with a large
padded plaster.

'Isn't it better to let it breathe?'

'You should keep it protected. Who's going to see it? We
don't care what you look like.'

He'd told Miriam that he had to go to the office: a final ap-
praisal for a team of officers he'd been training since last year.
There was no one else who could do it. He didn't know how
long the meeting would last.

'At the station?'

'No, at head office downtown.' Then he said, 'You can come
if you like. I can drop you off at the mall or the cinema.'

'There's no point in us hanging around in town. I have
washing to do; I'm sure Georgia would rather stay here. As
long as you're back before dark.'

'Call my mobile if you need me. I'll keep it switched on.'

At the gate, he quickly kissed her goodbye; her lips were dry
and dead as leaves. He thought how pale she looked standing
in her dressing gown, her eyes blinking in the sun. At the junction, he felt so guilty he almost turned around. But the closer
he got to Port of Spain the less guilty he'd felt.

Safiya strides into reception—yes, she has seen him—her
hair is clipped back, its wildness contained. She is wearing
jeans, a black cotton top, sandals. She offers her cheek, and
kisses him lightly. She looks tired. He tries to read her, but it
is difficult.

She says, 'Shall we go somewhere quiet?'

'I don't want you to be annoyed, I booked a room. I thought

it would give us privacy and save time.'

'We could sit by the pool.'

'There's a conference on; when they break in about half an hour, which they will, the place will be heaving.'

'My car's outside.'

'It's too hot for the car. Don't you think?'

She looks at him blankly.

'Come,' he says, and walks towards the elevators.

She will feel awkward in front of the receptionist. She will imagine that the girl is thinking the worst of her. But if his instincts are right, Safiya is here today to give him a goodbye speech. Let her give it to him in private.

The room is on the fifth floor. A tired-looking room with a king-sized bed; small desk, ensuite. Safiya drops her bag and disappears into the bathroom. Down below, the sprawling Savannah is hazy with heat. He checks his mobile phone; there is nothing. A good sign. From the minibar, he takes out a half bottle of Chardonnay. It is ridiculously expensive.

There is something about hotel rooms that unnerves him; their multiple use—affairs, suicides, misdemeanours; they are soulless, nowhere places. But where else could they go?

'Look,' Safiya says, in the bathroom doorway. 'I don't want to drag this out: I just can't do this anymore.'

He opens the wine, begins to pour; his heart is in his mouth.

'By *this* do you mean us?'

'I don't want wine. I have to go back to work.'

She fishes in her bag and pulls out her car keys.

'Can you tell me why? I mean, apart from the obvious reasons.'

She looks away at the painting above the bed—a turquoise tie-dye butterfly. It reminds him of the '70s, before Safiya was born.

'It feels different with them here. You never mentioned any-thing about Trinidad.'

'We didn't plan on getting robbed.'

Then she says, 'It's not only about Trinidad. I've got to look at the facts. You don't sound like someone who's going to be free anytime soon. I'm tired of being on my own.'

Her voice wavers; he is glad to see that she is finding this hard. She should find it hard.

'Does this have anything to do with your father?'

'It has nothing to do with him.'

He stares at the Savannah as if it will somehow give him strength. He says—and it is patronising, 'Sometimes I forget how young you are.'

'It's not about age, Martin. This would be hard on anyone. Do you know how you sound?'

Her face looks different. From grief, perhaps. Yes, he thinks, grief can change a face.

'I'm sorry I wasn't there for the funeral. I wanted to come.'

She glances down at her hands; he has always liked them; square, thin fingers. The convent ring, the short nails.

'I don't want to talk about the funeral.'

She stands up straight, her bag on her shoulder. Soon she will be gone and that will be that.

He says, 'What I meant about being young—I've been in the world longer than you. In all these years, I've been faithful to Miriam.'

He rarely uses Miriam's name. It has felt wrong, a kind of blasphemy. But now it feels necessary.

'I would never have fallen in love with you if I didn't think there was a future in it. I'm not a fan of self-sabotage, Safiya. I wasn't looking for a quick fling. Quite honestly, I could do without the drama just as much as you. You would prefer if I was younger; I would prefer if you were older. So what. Nothing is perfect.'

Next door, a television starts up, a theme tune: 'The Young and the Restless'.

She says, 'Nothing is perfect. But some things are less complicated. I don't want complications in my life now. I want to give myself a chance; I don't want to be at war with my mother.'

So Marjorie is behind this. Now her father is gone, Safiya is feeling responsible for her mother.

'The point is, you need a man to take care of you. Not just a playmate, you'll need someone who will love you well. If you're happy, your mother will be glad.'

He knows this is not necessarily true. Life doesn't always work that way. Marjorie will probably never like him even if they marry—he will have robbed her daughter of a normal life. He is old, he has done it all before—children, a home of his own, his career. One day, in twenty-five years or so, he will make her a widow.

Fuck Marjorie Williams.

'Pete loved me; he was young.'

He wondered if she would bring him into this.

'Maybe you missed the boat. We only get so many chances and when they're gone they're gone.'

'Maybe I didn't know what was good for me. Maybe I still don't know what's good for me.'

'Hindsight is a wonderful thing.'

He gives her a long look. Then he starts to fold himself up, pull his energy back inside. He must not let her see him so exposed. 'The point is this, I know the world a little better because I have been in it longer; I know its hard edges and sharp corners. And I say these things because I love you. I want the best for you. I would say this to my own daughter.'

He sits down on the bed, suddenly weary, unable to keep up a show. Georgia. Georgia. His beloved Georgia. He feels himself welling up with it all, with the pain of the last few days. Safiya walks slowly over to the bed and sits down. Her eyes are wet and river green. She sighs, a long, heavy sigh. They sit there for a moment. He can feel her heat. The idea that he will not see her again is terrifying and real.

She says, quietly, 'I'm sorry.'

He feels for her soft springy hair; it smells of her, his beautiful Safiya. She touches the side of his head.

'Does it hurt?'

'It's getting better.'

'They hit you with a cutlass?'

'Yes,' he says.

Then she asks—and she is tentative, 'Is it true that one of them raped Georgia?'

'Yes.'

She looks appalled.

'Why didn't you tell me?'

'I didn't want to tell you on the phone.'

They look at one another.

Then Safiya says, 'So you *have* to go back to England.'

'We're talking about it. Nothing is certain.'

Safiya leans into him—it is all too much—and he lies back on the bed and he pulls her close. She does not resist. Their heads rest together. It is a tender moment. *Safiya. Safiya.* He thinks, if he really loved her he would let her go, cut her loose. She is too young and beautiful to be unhappy. Safiya could have anyone she wants. Marjorie Williams is right, he should know better; he has had his life. He could set her free and go back to England with his wife and daughter. Yes, he should do the right thing.

He puts his lips on hers—her soft pillow lips, and Safiya opens her mouth and lets him in with small biting kisses. He feels her tongue, her strong neck, the hungry push of her head.

Now he works his way down her warm, sticky neck and into her shirt, beneath the collar, peeling back the cotton and probing his mouth into her breasts. They have always been a joy to him, their size, their firmness, her big, dark nipples. She shifts back on the bed, drawing up her legs, unfastening her jeans, pulling them down, and he can see the net of her crotch. He crawls on top of her, slowly now, and with pain.

Safiya says, 'Are you okay?'

'Yes.'

And so it goes, as they have done many times before, not as urgently as this, and he wonders if she is surrendering to him for today or for longer. He mustn't think about it. It does not matter. What matters is now. He has her now and he wants to fuck her until he can't fuck her any longer because life is over in a moment, in the blink of an eye. There is only one life, there is no room for compromise. Naked, he stands to draw the curtains, his cock pointing to the sky, and he catches sight of his mobile phone blinking on the windowsill. It is probably Miriam. He should check it. But he does not.

Safiya is lying with her head on his chest; he can smell her hair, feel her stickiness. His eyes are heavy, sleepy; he must shower and leave before it is too late; the traffic will be appalling. Miriam will be fretting. In the bathroom he checks his phone. In the message from Miriam she sounds anxious; she is wondering where he is; she has made soup. He will call her from the car, he thinks. Right now he must say his goodbyes.

Safiya is turned towards the window. There is a gap where the outside light comes in. She looks so young, her hair tossed to the side in an '80s way. He reminds himself, she was born in the '80s.

'What are you up to tonight?' he says, reaching for his clothes.

She pulls up the sheet. 'Nothing much. There's talk of a beach trip tomorrow.'

She seems sad and withdrawn. Is she sad because of him, or is she thinking about her father? He should ask but he'd rather not know. He'd rather quit while he's ahead, even though he suspects he isn't ahead at all.

As he leaves Port of Spain, the sky is soft pink with strips of dark blue smudged over the sea like charcoal. He drives along the hillside, and looks down at the city, glittering, humming with lights, cars, music. He imagines Safiya making her way home to her mother's house. He thinks, whatever they did today is a bandage, it will hold for a while. But not for long. In a couple of days, she will reconsider their relationship; she will return, in her mind, to the same place she started at today. And there is nothing he can do about it.

Before he reaches the highway, he calls Miriam. He tells her the meeting went on longer than he expected. He is sorry.

'We missed you,' she says. 'I don't like being here alone in the dark. Georgia says it's creepy.'

'Turn on the lights, Miriam. The outside security lights. I won't be long.'

Nineteen

It is Thursday morning; they have been in Trinidad for almost a week. Stephen Josephs telephones. At first he doesn't recognise his voice; it is clipped, less friendly than before. He tells Martin there is good news. Two boys fitting their descriptions have been found in Plymouth, and brought to the police station for questioning.

Martin takes the phone outside; his heart is hammering.

'How do you know it's them?'

'They were down that side of the island fishing. Someone heard them talking about buying a boat and flashing money around.'

Martin feels his blood rise. 'What about the third one?'

'We don't know yet. They were high like kites when they got here. We'll leave them in the cell for a while, let them come down.'

He pictures the boy, his lumpy hair, bug eyes.

'How were they when you brought them in?'

'The usual way; they had no idea why we were arresting them. We took them by surprise.'

Above, in the blue sky, there is a long white line, an aircraft flying high.

'Any news on the woman at the cash machine? She's another witness.'

'One thing at a time,' he says. 'I thought you'd want to know.'

Martin says, 'We need to have a line-up.'

'We'll set something up.'

'When?'

'Within twenty-four hours. Hopefully in Port of Spain.'

'I thought we might have to fly back to Tobago.'

'No, apparently these are *exceptional* circumstances. We will come to you. When Mohammed can't come to the mountain, the mountain must come to Mohammed.'

Martin is irritated. He would like to tell Stephen to fuck off. No doubt, there's been pressure from somewhere. Raymond, perhaps, or the High Commission. Has Nigel been in touch? Who cares. The most important thing is that they have a result.

Miriam is surprised, pleased.

'Do we know anything about them? What they were doing when they picked them up? Have they found any of my jewellery?'

'We don't know very much yet. We only know they've got two of them.'

'Why are they bringing them here?'

'Sometimes they do. It's not unheard of.'

He is relieved; the thought of flying back to Tobago to identify the boys was bothering him. Georgia would not have wanted to go. Yes, for them to come here, this is better all round. He assumes they will gather up fillers from Port of Spain and bring the two boys by boat.

For the first time in days, he feels hopeful. He telephones

Safiya and leaves a message, letting her know that there's been some progress; good news might be on its way.

He feels more like himself, less adrift. In his raised spirits, he takes Miriam and Georgia to lunch at the Indian restaurant on the other side of the highway. And he senses that something has lifted for all of them. Georgia, too, seems brighter. She has washed her hair, changed her clothes. Miriam suggests that now they can start to make their plans to go home.

The restaurant is cold; Georgia makes a joke about it feeling like winter and how they all better get used to it because they'll soon be back and spring will not have yet arrived.

'I don't care if I never come back to the Caribbean again,' she says. 'It's overrated.'

Miriam says, 'I was thinking next summer, we could go to Aix. Or stay somewhere near Cannes. The Cote d'Azur.'

He tries to imagine driving their Volvo Estate through France; Trinidad far behind him; Safiya gone from his life, no more than a fading memory. His heart plummets at the thought.

'Georgia could bring Harriet.'

She looks pleased at the mention of Harriet. 'Will you come, Dad?'

'Yes, darling,' he says. 'Unless I have to work.'

On the way back, they stop off at the supermarket. Within walking distance of his apartment, it is part of a bigger shopping complex with a chemist—Ali's Pharmacy, The Royal Bank, The Golden Palace—a Chinese takeaway, and a pirate DVD rental shop. When he arrived, he was surprised by the colourful exterior—orange, purple and yellow walls; it reminded him of a theme park. He is used to it now. Once a week he comes here to buy groceries, and rent a couple of DVDs, which he'll usually watch with Safiya on the weekend. Yes, it is familiar.

Miriam is not impressed. He pushes the old trolley while she wanders the aisles and Georgia trails behind. There's a smell he recognises, a mixture of bleach and spices. They buy meat, a few imported vegetables, some tired-looking fruit. Enough for a couple of days. He picks up ice cream for Georgia.

'You never know,' he says. 'You might like it.'

It is Safiya's favourite, a local coconut flavour.

The boy at the checkout loads up their trolley and wheels it out to the car park. A plus here in Trinidad, he tells Miriam. Someone packs your groceries and carries them to your car.

He tells Georgia he found Fanta here when he was tiny.

'How did you get him home?'

'In my car.'

Georgia says, '*Please* can we take him back to England?'

He had a feeling she would ask this.

'Let's see how long he'd have to stay in quarantine. But in theory, yes. I don't see why not.'

He puts his arm around her back and she nuzzles into him. He feels momentarily reassured. He was concerned that Georgia would be distressed by news of the boys' arrest. But she seems more like herself. It bodes well, he thinks.

They are driving out when he realises there is a roadblock of some kind. He winds down the window. Cars are backed up by the exit barrier. Someone sounds a horn, then another;

a symphony of horns. The sun pours in and the car feels hot. They crawl along.

'What's going on?' Miriam says, adjusting the visor.

At the crossroads there is a small crowd. There has been an accident: a white Mitsubishi Lancer has gone into the back of a Land Rover; the cars have been moved to the side of the road. But that's not all. Something else has happened here.

Martin winds down his window. A man is selling oranges. He tells Martin, the driver of the white car got out to speak to the other driver and one of the stray dogs went for him.

'The dog is a maniac,' the man says, shaking his head, looking ahead. 'Somebody needs to shoot it.'

Further along the road, a young man is cradling his arm and bawling. 'Oh God, oh God.' The skin of his forearm is torn; the flesh is exposed and bleeding. His shirt is soaked with blood.

Nearby, the dog has turned on a security guard, who is backing away now towards the middle of the road. The dog's teeth are bared as if grinning, ears back and flat. It looks like a small pit bull. The guard is holding up a cardboard box as a shield. Two more security guards are trying to hit the dog from behind with sticks. The crowd stands back, afraid and transfixed. Three or four other dogs are yapping on the side of the road.

At one time Martin would have stopped to see if he could help in any way. But he keeps on driving, slowly at first, then speeding up when the road clears until they are out of sight.

Miriam says, craning her neck, 'Did you see his arm? Were they stray dogs? What are they doing there?'

Georgia says, 'Don't they belong to anyone?'

He remembers Safiya's ex-boyfriend, Pete Blanc, picking up strays. He was obsessed, Safiya said.

Martin feels shaky, the sight of the young bleeding man, the gawping crowd—a circus of horror. It could have been him, he thinks; he has come here on foot often enough.

The good feeling he had earlier has vanished.

TWENTY

At the front office of the station, he gives his name, and they are told to take a seat. He thought they would be invited to wait in the offices, but it seems that no one was briefed. They must wait there with everyone else. The waiting room is packed; the benches are full; people are up against the walls. Martin and Miriam stand near the open doorway; Miriam fans herself with a magazine. Apparently, the electricity stopped working an hour ago; it has slowed everything down; the computers are not working, nor the air conditioning. Outside, garbage bags are piled up waiting for collection; a rotten smell drifts in.

Miriam is dressed in trousers, a plain shirt. Her hair is pinned back, and she is wearing little make-up. She looks at her watch, checks her mobile phone. He can see that she is nervous.

Miriam says, 'I want to call Georgia, make sure she's okay.'

He'd asked Jeanne if she could spend the afternoon at their house. Jeanne was happy to help.

'She can swim, play on the computer; whatever she likes.'

He is grateful to Jeanne. It is strange to think she has been there all along. He admits to himself that in some ways his relationship with Safiya has held him back. He would have seen more of Jeanne and Satnam; he might have made other friends. He hasn't heard from her since he saw her at the Hilton. He's tried calling, but she doesn't answer her phone. Right now, he thinks, there are other things to think about.

'She'll be okay. Let's ring when we're finished.'

After fifteen minutes, a police officer appears at the counter and calls them over. Martin feels the eyes of the crowd and the officer leads them through a door marked Private. They follow him down a narrow corridor, to a concrete bunker attached to the main building. The room is tatty, the yellow paint of the walls peeling; it has a ceiling fan, and two cubicles. Miriam and Martin will be held in these separate 'waiting' areas. Then, individually, they will be taken to view the suspects.

The officer explains that each person will have a number written on the ground in front of them. They must give him the number of any individual they recognise or are able to identify. He apologises for the heat; for some reason the generator still hasn't kicked in. Martin is impressed; the young man must be no more than twenty years old; he is articulate, polite, immaculately dressed.

Miriam looks out at the courtyard. The sun is a fierce white light. Yesterday she told him she was sick of the sun; something he has never heard her say. While the officer talks, she presses her fingertips together—a new habit, she tells him, it stops her hands from shaking. Since they spoke about going back to England, she has been quiet. On the way here, he explained to Miriam that she and Georgia should fly back without him, he will need to stay on, to ensure the boys are charged.

'Travel back on our own?'

'If I take my eyes off them, they'll do nothing. Can't you see that? Just for two or three weeks. We want the boys charged.'

'And what about us? Who'll be keeping an eye on us?'

'You'll be okay, Miriam. You said it yourself, Georgia needs to talk to someone professional.' Then he said, 'I have things to sort out. The apartment, the car, Fanta, work. I have a whole life here.'

'I can see that. But you have a life in England. Or have you forgotten?'

They agree that Martin will go first. Miriam waits in her cubicle, and the young officer leads him into a narrow room where the men are in a line of eight. His body is tense, stiff; he braces himself. The air is thick and hot; sunlight pours in from behind, and he is glad of it. He will be hard to make out. He stands back, away from the men, and runs his eyes quickly over them, scanning, looking for similarities, and he is struck by a mixture of different heights and physiques. And he knows—at once—the boys are not here.

The first man has a round, fleshy face with short black dreads; another is a bearded light-skinned man in his forties; a half-Chinese youth, one has a bleached goatee, light eyes. There are two black men in their mid-twenties, perhaps, and one of them is obese. They look nothing like the boys. There are no teenagers. Most of the suspects look old enough to have children of their own. He wonders, which of these men came from Tobago? What were they thinking? What is Stephen Josephs trying to do?

He says, 'They're not here. There's no one here that looks

remotely like either of them. It's a fucking joke.'

The police officer says, and his tone is polite, 'Sometimes it's difficult to remember; would you like to take a break and come back?'

He says, 'Tell my wife I will wait for her outside.'

He leaves the room, feeling as if his head is about to explode.

In the car park, he telephones Stephen Josephs. Miriam sits beside him; her face is long with worry.

Stephen is cheerful, upbeat. 'We brought them on the boat last night. It was quite a feat.'

Martin says, trying to control his voice, 'I told you they were younger. These guys were in their twenties, thirties.'

'Not all of them.'

His voice is rising. 'The boys who came to the villa were teenagers.'

Stephen says, 'It was nighttime and you were distressed; you also sustained a head injury.'

'I saw them three times. Once on the beach fishing in broad daylight. The night they came with the boat. The second night they came back and attacked my family. I drove the boy in my fucking car. I know what he looks like.' Martin lights a cigarette. 'Three times.' He can feel Stephen bristling. 'My wife is very upset. Do you know how harrowing it is to prepare yourself emotionally for something like this?'

'We tried to get a cross-section; we felt the line-up was representative of the people in your statements.'

Miriam is staring at him.

He asks, 'The ones you picked up, where do they live?'

'They live in Scarborough.'

'But that isn't where the boys lived. I could take you to their fucking village. Usaf spoke with their grandmother. The last I heard they'd gone fishing. What happened?'

Miriam shakes her head; he is losing it.

Stephen says, 'Just because you dropped them off in the village, it doesn't mean they haven't come from somewhere else. You come from England, but you are living in Trinidad. I come from Trinidad but I am living in Tobago.' Then Stephen says, and his voice is grave, 'This is disappointing; one of them already confessed.'

Martin makes a strange *ha* sound, a kind of laugh. 'Well, he was fucking lying. Or someone beat it out of him. That's what you all do, isn't it? Beat them until they admit to something they never did. You must think I'm a fucking idiot.'

Silence.

Miriam covers her face with her hands.

'For fuck's sake,' he says. 'This is like the Dark Ages. You people need to pull your fucking fingers out.'

In the background, he can hear birdsong. Tobago birds. He pictures Stephen's office: from the window a postcard view of the Caribbean Sea.

'We've been making good progress; it would be a pity to start from scratch.'

'Can't you see, this is not fucking progress. There was never any progress. You should be ashamed.'

'Martin,' Miriam says, glaring at him. 'Enough.'

Then Stephen says, 'If you wish, you can speak to Raymond, or the deputy commissioner and he will explain this to you.

You are not in England now.'

So he is being punished. For being English? Retribution for his behaviour when he first arrived? For putting on some pressure? For wanting his perpetrators caught and justice for his daughter and his wife? This is insane.

'Fuck you,' he says, and snaps his phone shut; his heart is thumping and sweat trickles down his face. There is no air in the car; there is no air. This heat is insufferable. He has come to loathe this heat.

They drive home in silence. Miriam stares at the passing hills, the sprawling slums below. The light is starting to fade. Ahead, cars fly along the highway, randomly switching lanes. They have escaped before the worst of the traffic, which is a relief. They should talk about their plans. But he cannot bring himself to speak to her.

As they approach the traffic lights, he spots a vagrant sprinting along the hard shoulder, coming towards them. He is wearing tattered shorts, his shirt is open showing an emaciated body like someone from a concentration camp; he is running fast, barefoot, his eyes are big and glaring. He is running as if he is on fire. Like something from a nightmare.

'What kind of a place is this!' Miriam's face is filled with horror. 'How can you stand it?'

By the time they collect Georgia from Jeanne's house, it is almost dark. They explain to her what happened at the station. She is agitated; does this mean they have to stay longer? She doesn't want to stay another day. Please say they can go back.

'Yes, darling; you and your mother are going back just as we discussed.'

'When?'

'As soon as you can get flights.'

'What about you?'

'There's still some things to do here.'

'What about Fanta? Can he come back with you? Will he have to go into quarantine?'

'We'll see.'

'Please don't worry.'

He needs to reassure her, but he is finding it difficult; he, too, needs reassurance—from where and whom, he does not know. Everything feels shaky, hopeless. He would like to speak to Safiya; she has yet to reply to his message letting her know that the boys had been caught.

He senses in Miriam a heaviness; returning alone with Georgia is not what she wanted. She tells him she will never come back here. This is not paradise; this is hell.

It is late; Miriam and Georgia are in bed. He has been drinking steadily from a bottle of sipping rum given to him by the Training Department when he first arrived. He never realised how good it tasted—the slightly sweet, smoky flavour is smooth and easy to drink. He pours it into a small glass: straight, no ice, no mixer. Just pure undoctored rum—as it's meant to be drunk.

And while he drinks, he watches television with the sound low: a BBC documentary on British coastal birds. At first the pictures calm him: the white cliffs, the sheep, the black and white cattle, the English countryside with its hedgerows, woods and wild flowers. But then he starts thinking about the day. Playing it over in his mind—the line-up, the conversation with Stephen Josephs, Georgia's pain, Miriam's despair. He wants to speak to Raymond but it is probably too late. When he tried to call him earlier, he did not answer.

He feels a sense of doom, as if he is a tiny island in a state of erosion, splitting off, separating from its continent. It frightens him. His powerlessness frightens him.

TWENTY-ONE

The car park is mostly empty and in darkness. It is 5.30 and the sun is rising slowly. He climbs the stairs to the second floor and enters the open-plan office where the strip lights are still on; two or three people are sitting at their desks. They don't seem to notice him. It is familiar, the light green walls, the modern windows, beige vertical blinds. At the far end, he can see Raymond in his office.

Martin makes his way.

'Hi,' Raymond says, surprised. 'What's happening?'

Martin is wearing the T-shirt he slept in, his jeans, flip-flops. He is unshaven; there is a faint smell of alcohol.

'Did you hear about the line-up?'

Raymond closes the door behind him.

'Stephen Josephs is a fucking idiot. We have to do something. Get someone else on board.' He sits down and checks his pocket for cigarettes; the packet is empty. Raymond offers him a Du Maurier. He fumbles with the lighter. 'Don't they know I'm not going anywhere? Do they think I'm an idiot?'

Raymond says, and his voice is serious, 'I had a phone call from Stephen; he's made a formal complaint. He said you were abusive yesterday; you accused him of beating one of the boys into a confession. He said you've been interfering and if you hadn't been so pushy, they might have been more productive. Now they have to go back to the drawing board. He thinks your head injury might be affecting your judgement.'

'Well if that's my excuse, what's his.'

'He had a call from a Chief Officer in England. Nigel somebody. You know anything about that?'

'Not really. Nigel is my friend. I've known him for years.' Then Martin says, 'Can't you see what's going on here?'

Raymond gets up. 'They might be inefficient, but I hate to tell you, you're sounding a little paranoid.'

'I might well be paranoid but it doesn't mean it's not true.'

'There'll be more line-ups. You know how it is. We keep going until we find them. We work together as a team. We don't need help from anyone in England. You hear what I'm saying?'

For the first time, he feels that Raymond is not entirely on his side. Or is this part of his paranoia?

Martin feels weak, as if he has suddenly had a drop in blood pressure. He remembers he didn't eat anything last night; he barely slept.

'I gave them everything they needed to find the boys.'

'They'll find them. Just let them get on with it.'

'My daughter needs to go home.'

'Then go home with her; take two weeks. You'll have my blessing.'

'I don't want to leave and it all fall apart.'

'It's not going to fall apart.' Then, 'It might not be a bad thing to take some time off. There's some rumours around the place.'

Rumours? What rumours?

Raymond half smiles; his tone is light-hearted. 'Oh, you wanted your wife out of the way because of some Trini girl—Safiya, I'm assuming—and you paid the boys to break in.'

Martin stares at him.

'Young and Restless. Romance. Drama. It makes it all more interesting. You know how people like to talk.'

Martin looks out of the window at the boulevard, the old-fashioned street lamps, cars lining up at the traffic lights. From here he can see the sea, the Tobago ship in the port. He feels like screaming.

'Look, I want you on our team, and the contract still stands. But I think you need a break. Go back to England; settle your daughter and wife. Speak to Miriam about your contract. Does she know yet?'

What he tells Miriam is none of Raymond's business.

He says, and his voice is hard, 'I want them caught.'

Raymond looks at Martin, his eyes steady. 'This is not your investigation. You need to back off.'

He asks, if, on their last day, Miriam and Georgia would like to go anywhere, or see anything in particular. But they are not interested and he cannot blame them.

Georgia says that she would like to swim next door in Jeanne and Satnam's pool. Jeanne tells Miriam to come too. They can have lunch, sit in the sun and chat while Georgia swims. Take it easy. When they're ready to leave, Martin will escort them back to the apartment.

Through the fence, he watches Georgia dive under the water,

her shape run along the bottom of the pool, then break through the surface; hair smooth and slicked back from her face. She looks free, without troubles, without pain. He watches her swim; a strong breaststroke. He'd meant to tell her how much her swimming has improved. Yes, she is a fine swimmer. The truth is he has never praised her enough. Why? When Beth died, he promised himself he would do things differently. He would seek to appreciate, encourage, applaud. But he hasn't done any of it. He hasn't even been there to praise his daughter. Yes, he has failed on this, too.

Life is a series of natural changes. It is only resisting them that causes pain. He learned this well enough with Beth. The more he fought the reality of her dying, the more pain he felt. There was relief in accepting his dreadful lot and navigating his way to a place of recovery. But this feels different.

Yes, what the boy did to Georgia has been done—there is nothing he can do about it, but he finds himself unable to accept it. Every time he thinks of it, he is horrified all over again; inside himself, at his centre, he feels as if he is burning up, raging, insatiable. And he finds himself thinking about how much he wants to make the boy pay for what he's done. He has never felt like this before.

Georgia climbs out of the pool, her body lean in her navy swimsuit; she wraps her towel around her. The late afternoon sun casts a silvery light. She is lit from behind. She is looking up at the fence where he is standing, cigarette in his hand.

'Dad,' she says. 'We're ready to go.'

TWENTY-TWO

It is 10 p.m. Georgia is in bed; Miriam and Martin sit in the veranda. For some time, they have been watching fireflies glow in the darkness. Their little lights flit on and off. Safiya said once they were a symbol of hope. Something he could do with right now; something they could all do with. The air is hot and sticky; there is no breeze.

This afternoon, he had left Miriam and Georgia to drive over to the mall where he filled up with petrol and checked his tyres. When he got back, Miriam was packing. He asked if he could help, if there was anything he could do. There was something about her manner that bothered him—a certain aloofness, a distance. Tonight, when she asked him to join her, he assumed she wanted to talk; a final conversation before they leave. It is likely to be heavy; so be it. He would like to get an early night. Tomorrow will be a long and difficult day; they will all need their rest.

Miriam says, 'They are probably females, they use their lights to attract a mate and then they eat him.'

'Really?' He has never heard this before. 'That's rather depressing. I thought they were a symbol of hope.'

'Life is depressing. I'm surprised you haven't noticed.'

He says, trying to brighten her, 'The thing is, we never know what's round the corner.'

Miriam looks at him. 'Isn't it funny how things turn out? You never liked change much. It was always me who liked it. I had to push you into doing anything new. You wanted everything to be familiar.'

This is true; for years he followed the same routine. He had no interest in travelling, or reading about other countries, or eating in foreign restaurants.

'Now you don't want to come home to the familiar. You only want the adventures.'

He wants to ask what she is getting at, but he senses something. She is looking out, her legs crossed. The sky is clear and bright with the moon; it spills a milky light on the hills. It is astonishing to him, he has never grown tired of this view.

'I was always optimistic, and you were the pessimist. Now we've swapped. Since you've been living here, I've never known you so glass-half-full.'

It hadn't occurred to him that he could be an optimist. A new thought.

Then Miriam says, 'I'm guessing she is young. Is she young?'

He says, 'Who?'

'Who?' she says, and smiles: a fake smile.

Then he says, 'What are you talking about?'

Miriam looks at him. 'Don't argue or deny it. I don't really want to know the details. I thought it might be Jeanne but I realise she's not interested in you. There was a woman who phoned when you were in hospital; I'm guessing it's her. She sounded keen.'

'I don't know what you're talking about.' His face flushes with heat.

Her foot ticks quickly back and forth. 'I can't imagine you'd risk losing everything for someone you didn't love. So I'm guessing you are in love. Is that right?'

'Miriam.'

Then she says, almost casually, 'Georgia will never forgive you.'

He wants to say something; and he would like to stand up but he doesn't feel as if he can.

Her voice is strained. 'It makes sense. At Christmas, you came for five days; you barely talked to me. In fact, you've been distant for a while. Whenever I say we'll visit, you tell me you'll come there instead. It all adds up.'

She smacks her hand against her head. 'I can't believe I didn't see it before. What a bloody idiot.'

Miriam gets up and goes inside. From the passageway he hears the bedroom door slam shut. His mind quickly sifts through the last few days. Has she looked at his phone? He has been careful. Did Raymond say something? Jeanne? Sherry?

After a few minutes, he follows her to the bedroom; he stands in the doorway. She is sitting on the bed, quieter now. Her suitcase is open on the floor, everything neatly folded. She has always been tidy, organised.

They look at one another. Her face is pale with bewilderment and exhaustion. There are dark shadows around her eyes; she looks as if she is about to collapse. He feels sad; overwhelmed. Miriam, Miriam, his good wife.

He has thought about this moment for so long, and now it

is here, it feels unreal. He didn't want it to be like this.

She is glaring at him.

He says, 'I've wanted to tell you.'

Her face crumples, and he knows—at once; she was hoping he would deny it; that it might be a lie, after all.

'Then why didn't you?'

'I could never find the right moment.'

It sounds pathetic and yet, it's true. He says, and he means it wholeheartedly, 'You've been so unhappy. I didn't want to add to it.'

'But you've been adding to it for months, you just didn't tell me.' Then she asks, 'How long? A year?'

'No,' he says, 'not so long.'

It all sounds false. His tone is wrong. He doesn't feel like himself. He feels like someone—an actor, an impersonator, pretending to be Martin Rawlinson.

Miriam says, 'I've been *unhappy* because our eldest daughter died, in case you'd forgotten.'

He looks at his hands, they are shaking. 'You're not the only one who's been unhappy.'

'Fuck you.'

Outside, a car alarm goes off. He wonders if it is Satnam, but it is coming from the other side of the road.

Miriam stands up. 'I found her things. At first I thought they were Sherry's. Then Georgia said they must belong to someone younger. I'm assuming she likes poetry.'

'What did you say to Georgia?'

Miriam watches him coldly. 'Nothing. If I'd told her, she'd probably hate you. Georgia has enough on her plate.' Then she asks, 'Does she live here with you?'

'No, of course not.'

The questions come quickly now, and he would like to be somewhere else, anywhere. Her voice is rising.

'Is she black?'

'Why does that matter?'

'It doesn't. I just want to know. I have a right. I want to be able to picture her.' Then, 'How old is she?'

He lies. 'Thirty-two.' If Miriam knew Safiya was twenty-eight, she would be appalled. 'Her name is Safiya. She works for a newspaper.'

Miriam sits on the bed. She sighs and draws her feet up to her chest. A sound comes out of her like a kind of groan. He wants to tell her how very sorry he is. For everything. But his breath is shallow, his tongue thick in his mouth.

'So you're a father figure. How clichéd. She wants a father, you need a daughter.'

He gets up and walks over to the window. Outside the night is still, the orange glow of the streetlight falls by the gate. He thinks how many times he has stood here waiting for Safiya to arrive, checking the gate, looking at his watch. It is a fact, for the last fifteen months, she has been his happiness. He has been deeply in love.

Miriam says, 'Before I came here I hated my life. Now I hate it even more. I didn't think that was possible.'

On the bedside table is a copy of *Time* magazine. He picks it up and flicks through it. He does not know why.

'Even now, with all this. You don't want to be near me. You'd rather look at a magazine.'

Her feet are bare, her toenails unpolished. Georgia has her same feet, the same high arch, the large big toe. Miriam once told him it was a sign of fortune, a happy life.

'It's not true, Miriam.'

Her eyes are red and so very sad. He wants to comfort her, but he cannot bring himself to. Whatever is between them feels dense and hard as concrete.

Outside, he can hear rain starting up, like maracas gently shaking.

Miriam says, 'Why didn't you talk to me? We could've stopped it from happening. We could've avoided it—all this, everything that's happened here. Georgia, everything.'

He looks at her deep frown lines, as if carved.

'Can you see? It didn't have to be like this.' She starts to cry. 'It didn't have to be like this, Martin.'

Is Miriam right? He has made his choices; all his little decisions have brought him to this place, here, now. Yes, in a way, he is responsible.

He rubs his eyes. He would like to rub it all away, all this pain. Start again.

She says, 'What do you want to do?'

'I don't know.'

She looks down at her bare hands; he remembers her rings. They are somewhere out there.

TWENTY-THREE

All day, Miriam is busy getting ready. There isn't time to talk or to go over things. She tells him, she has said all she needed to say. Her manner is cool, detached. He is surprised by his reaction, he'd expected to feel relieved, liberated. But he doesn't, he feels debilitated, morose.

Last night, he'd stayed up late thinking about his life—about Miriam, Safiya, his life here, and mostly he thought about Georgia. For the first time since that night, wandering in the dark garden, he cried. He has failed his daughter in every way he can think of. He has failed his wife. Perhaps they are better off without him. Everything seemed stark, real; the black hills seemed to be watching him, and he felt afraid; of what he doesn't know. Miriam was right; he used to want the ordinary. Now he wants adventures. Is this what comes with adventure—loss, pain, confusion? By the time he went to bed, the sun was coming up.

They leave for the airport around three p.m. It is just starting to cool down. Georgia sits in front. He talks about the cold weather waiting for them at Heathrow, the Tupperware English skies, the long journey home on the M40. Tomorrow they will unpack, buy groceries, settle in. Miriam has arranged an appointment with their doctor on the afternoon they get back. He wants Georgia to call him as soon as the appointment is over. He tells her Fanta will miss her. He will miss her. Georgia is wearing jeans, a T-shirt, and tied around her waist is her hooded top. She looks more like herself.

'What's the best thing about getting home?'

'I don't know,' Georgia says. 'There's loads of things.'

'Call me as soon as you're in the house. Tell me if the roses have made it through the winter.'

At the airport, they check in quickly and easily; it is quiet, he is surprised. Only the Tobago check-in desk is busy; the line weaves around the pillar towards the arrivals.

Tobago, for newlyweds and nearly deads.

They have a drink in the food hall. He can see Miriam flinching at the dirty tables, the flies, the trays piled high, a dustbin overflowing with food cartons. 'Someone needs to clean this place up. It's a mess.'

Georgia is cheerful, and he can see—really see—her relief that she is leaving. She has Jeanne's email address, they will keep in touch. She tells her mother not to fuss. Soon they will be home.

Around five p.m. Miriam says, 'I think we should go through.'

He hates this last part, the goodbyes. He has dreaded saying goodbye to Georgia since she arrived.

They stand at the passport checkpoint. He hugs Georgia tightly; he smells her hair. She is thinner than when she came. Yes, there is less of her now.

'Don't forget to wave. I'll be watching from the gallery.'

Miriam is determined not to cry. When he kisses her, he

feels ashamed. He wants to say that he will be back soon, that she mustn't worry, and that he is sorry; and he would like to thank her for keeping his affair with Safiya from Georgia. But he doesn't; he cannot find it in himself to reassure her, to thank her. He has nothing left in him. Last night she called him a small man.

He watches them walk through the double doors, off into the bright lounge where the shop fronts shine. They both look back, and he sees that Georgia is upset; Miriam puts her arm around her.

Outside the sun is dipping. It is a good time of day to fly, he thinks; by the time they reach Barbados, the sun will have set and the skies will be glorious. He buys a cold beer and makes his way to the waving gallery. On the balcony, the breeze is warm and he is hit by the smell of fumes. The hills are bronze in the late afternon light. He waits. It is almost an hour later when they appear. Ground staff are gathered now at the bottom of the aircraft steps. He watches Miriam and Georgia walk across the tarmac to the rear of the plane.

At the top of the steps, Georgia turns and waves.

TWENTY-FOUR

It is just after six when he pulls up outside Safiya's Woodbrook house; he rings the bell on the metal gate. The roads here are badly in need of repair, the pavement is high and uneven. Where the roots of a tree have burst through, the tarmac is split and raised. And yet, he likes this street; it feels like an old part of Trinidad, a part where community still exists. If he were going to buy a house in town, he would like it to be here.

It is Marjorie who comes out to greet him. She wears a polka-dot dress; her hair is plaited and tied. She does not look surprised or angry. If anything, he catches in her a look of pity; something he could do without, and a sure sign that his instincts are right and his relationship with Safiya is in trouble. Yes, he would prefer if she was angry.

'Marjorie,' he says. 'how are you?'

She calls out behind her, unlocks the gate and stands to one side to let him in. He glances around the yard; along the path are blue glass bottles. It is orderly and simple: the potted plants, the hanging baskets, a bicycle leans against the wall. They have a visitor. He has not been here much in the day-time—just briefly, when dropping Safiya off after the beach in the early days. Back then, she didn't have a car. She took taxis everywhere. He never liked the idea of her in a shared cab, bunched up with people she did not know. It was Martin who encouraged her to learn to drive, and went with her to buy her first car, the Mazda 626. The seller had thought Martin was her father. He'd felt awkward, embarrassed.

Safiya appears in the doorway, her hair is wet; she is wearing shorts, a vest top. Her home clothes.

'Martin,' she says, and to her mother, 'Go inside, I'll talk to him out here.'

She walks quickly down the path towards him, and leads him just beyond the gate. She's taken aback, he thinks; she doesn't want him in the house. The sky is pale blue. Gold falls on the pavement; there is a lick of gold on the wall. She leaves the gate open, and they stand together, awkwardly.

Safiya says, 'Don't worry, no one can hear us.'

He says, 'I want to know what's going on.'

'There's nothing going on, Martin.'

'You haven't replied to my message since I saw you at the Hilton.'

She stares at him; her green eyes are lighter in the sun, with tiny copper flecks. She looks about eighteen years old; a college girl, barely out of school.

'Well?'

She says, 'I'm sorry. I told you how I felt at the Hilton. I'm sorry.'

He leans heavily against his car, feels its heat. He takes out a cigarette.

'Are you, really?' he says, lighting up. 'You don't seem sorry— you seem quite jolly.'

'That's such an English thing to say.'

She has her thumbs hooked in the loops on her shorts, her head is cocked to one side, and he knows with every fibre of his being that he has lost her; her mind is made up. There is no point in trying to persuade her. Their relationship is over. Like the ground below, the sky above, it is a fact. He looks away at the road where two young boys are playing cricket at the far end. The batsman hits the ball down the street towards them. It rolls along the centre of the road, drops down towards the drain.

Safiya says, and he can see that she is uncomfortable, 'I just can't do it anymore. I think you need to be with your family. They need you. Your daughter needs you. We both need to be free now. It's gone on too long.'

'I am free,' he says. 'Since yesterday. I told Miriam everything. She's gone back to England; she left this afternoon.'

Safiya looks surprised.

He says, 'She knows your name, she knows what you do. I've told her all about you.'

He pulls hard on his cigarette, puffs the smoke out of the corner of his mouth.

Safiya says, 'Why did you tell her when you knew it was over? I told you at the Hilton how I felt.'

He stares at her mouth; her beautiful *rude* mouth.

Then she says, 'We can't build a relationship on someone else's pain.'

For some reason, perhaps because it sounds like it came straight out of a self-help book, this makes him laugh.

He says, 'It's not like we're starting from scratch. We've

already built a lot. Now you want to knock it down. Why?'

'It's not about knocking anything down, it's about moving on.'

'I've moved on. I'm a free man.'

Safiya stares at him. Then she says, 'What about Georgia? Is she okay with it?'

Georgia. She shouldn't bring Georgia into this.

There is a voice from the house. A male voice. And a young blond man appears at the gate. He is handsome, sun-kissed, an Adonis.

The visitor.

He says, 'Is everything okay, Safi?'

Safi? Safi?

'Yes,' Safiya says, her face is flushed; she is embarrassed, and he realises without a doubt that this man with a Canadian accent is Pete Blanc. He stands in front of Martin.

'Pete's here for a few days from Vancouver. He got in on the weekend. He's here for a wedding.'

'Okay,' Martin says. 'I see.'

He is nodding, and he can't help himself. Everything is coming together in his mind. It is forming a shape. A shape he doesn't like.

Pete Blanc is standing with his arms folded, his head upright, back straight.

'I think you should probably leave,' Pete Blanc says. His teeth are even and white. 'Safiya doesn't want to see you again. You should get the message.'

'Fuck you,' Martin says, and he waves his hand as if shooing Pete Blanc away, as if he wants to hit him. 'Fuck you both.'

Pete Blanc takes a step towards him.

Suddenly Martin rushes at him, his hands open to grab him around the throat. Safiya tries to stop him but Pete Blanc pushes him back, and then he punches him. It is not a good hit—though the knuckles strike Martin's cheekbone where the flesh is still tender, and he falls back against the wall. He is like an old man, stumbling and falling on the ground.

To Pete Blanc, Safiya says, 'Just give me a minute with him.'

Pete Blanc looks at his hand and waves it in the air; then he looks at Martin. 'Loser,' he says, half-smiling. 'You're a fucking loser.'

He trots up the steps to the house.

Safiya helps Martin stand, and she pats his clothes where the wall has marked them with white paint. At the window, he sees Marjorie.

'Don't bother,' Martin says, checking himself for blood, and he backs away towards his car. It all seems bizarre, childish.

Safiya says, 'Please, Martin; it's not how it looks.'

TWENTY-FIVE

He decides that he will get there by boat; that way he can take his car. No need for a taxi at the other end. It is an eight-hour journey, and he will travel overnight. He can rest, arrive at sunrise unnoticed when it is quiet. He packs a small bag; he does not need much. Just the essentials. He has arranged it well. Sherry will come tomorrow; she has her keys, she can let herself in. Before he leaves, he will take Fanta to the TSPCA in Port of Spain. Fanta needs his rabies injection; there is a thirty-day wait before he can be shipped to England.

He spoke briefly to Jeanne and said that he might go up to Blanchieusse, to stay at the German hotel. He doesn't know why he lied but he found himself doing so, and it felt okay. She had brought him a pot of lasagne, garlic bread. 'We're here if you need company,' she said. 'You look tired, you should get some rest.' She didn't know that he had just come from Safiya's house, that he was in a kind of shock.

Before he left, Georgia called to say they had got home safely. The weather is spring-like, primroses and daffodils are out in the garden; there is a fox nesting in the hedge at the back. There are baby foxes, Georgia said.

'Mum says we have to call environmental health but I don't want them to take them away.'

He imagined it all, the little creamy flowers, the bright daffodils, the clear spring skies, and it looked in his mind like heaven. She tells him the roses made it through the snow.

Georgia will be feeling better for a day or so, but then she will hit a wall. Miriam needs to keep an eye. He wanted to talk to Miriam, but Georgia insisted her mother was busy. For the first time since they were married, he senses Miriam's absence. He feels exposed, vulnerable.

Miriam, his good wife.

It is dark when he gets to the port. There is a long line of cars, large crates stacked, small trucks, lorries, people on foot, and he remembers, there is a public holiday tomorrow. By the time he drives on board, parks up, it is almost ten and the boat is heaving. He leaves his car, and makes his way up the narrow metal stairs to the air-conditioned bar. It is lively, the television is on showing CNN news, and the volume is turned up loud. People sit around the bar, mostly men, smoking. He buys a beer, and takes it upstairs to the top deck. He steps out into the warm night air and the wind is blowing hard, flattening his hair, his shirt. He finds a seat on a bench near the front of the boat. The sea is black, the sky is black. There are lights behind him, but ahead there are no lights.

Up here, he feels alone; as if he is the only person on the boat. Today he has hardly spoken to anyone, and he feels disconnected from the world around him. He feels as if he is invisible. How is it that, one day, he can have so much, and on another day, nothing. Safiya, Miriam, Georgia, Beth—they have all gone. Strangely, last night, for the first time, he dreamt of Beth; she was riding her horse along the road to the villa in Tobago. Seeing her like this, somehow, gave him strength to do what he needed to do.

This morning when he woke, he erased Safiya's messages and contact details from his phone. Then he built a fire in the far corner of the yard; onto it he threw her clothes, books, sandals, make-up; anything he could find that reminded him of her. He stood and watched the little flames flutter about and clouds of smoke drift into the sky. Fanta sat on the veranda wall, mesmerised. At one point Jeanne came outside, and he waved as if to say, everything is okay. Yes, he'd thought, this is a season for fires.

He has had his life; he has been lucky. Twice he had found love. Safiya didn't know what they had. She is too young to realise. One day she will look back on her life, as he is doing now, and she will remember him. With regrets? He hopes not. Today he is full of regret. It is pointless, he knows; as pointless as digging up old bones.

The boat arrives into Scarborough just after sunrise. The delicate light is pale and the sky is clear. The atmosphere is subdued, everyone starts getting ready to make their way from the boat. He is surprised by the number of passengers spilling out onto the walkway. Where are they going? Who have they come to see?

He takes a slow drive along the sea front, looking at the waves unfolding on the beach. This is where he came with Stephen Josephs that night. He no longer feels angry towards Stephen. He feels only pity. He is living a life without meaning. What is the point in that?

The night he came back from Safiya's, his life had felt utterly meaningless. He had wondered if he was better off dead, if the boys had killed him. Better for him, better for everyone.

There is a broken-down bus on the side of the road, the wheels have gone, the body of the bus is rusting. He seems to remember this from before. They should take it away, not leave it to rot. But this is typical, he thinks. He keeps driving, heading along the highway now, until he reaches the turning which leads to the ATM machine.

It looks different; the blue front, the yellow lettering, its glass door. A safe, harmless place. He wonders about the woman he saw that night. Did she see him? Did she mention it to her friends, 'There was something not right about that boy.' We all have instincts and hunches about things. Quite often, he would hear from a victim: *there was something about X that didn't seem right. I didn't get a good feeling. I sensed someone behind me.* And so it goes. If people followed their gut, there would be a lot less crime to report. At La Vie de France café, he orders a white coffee and scrambled eggs; he finds a table near the back. He is hungry; the eggs are cooked with pepper; they are delicious. The café starts to fill up; airport staff, children on their way home from school. No one seems to notice him. He sits and watches. In his mind, he feels a strange sense of calm. It is the first time he has felt like this in a long while. He doesn't understand it; only that perhaps he has discovered his decision, and there is peace in that.

Along the golf course, the light is silvery, the grass is dewy, the trees are still. He wonders about Terence; Terence is a good man. He wishes him well. 'Good luck,' he says, aloud.

He drives down the path to the beach with the manchineel

trees. It is empty. Not a soul in sight. Under the trees he takes off his shirt and trousers; he folds them and leaves them on the black rocks. Then he walks across the warm sand. In the distance, the village houses look as if, with a gust of wind, they could fall away.

The sea is cool, and it rushes around his feet. He walks in up to his waist, feeling the water lick around his calves, thighs, groin, belly, and then he dives down to the sand bed. The blast of water on his face and the pressure against his chest is exhilarating. He holds his breath, pushes out his arms and presses the water back, kicks out his legs.

There is nothing you can't do.

He swims along the bay, stopping to look out at the beach, and take a breath. He feels like the only man on earth. A castaway. Yes, he has had his life. But he wants more of it. He knows that now. It is not over yet. Perhaps he can love again. Yes, the only remedy for love is to love more. He has been a fool.

Now he drives through the village where the man in a pork-pie hat sits outside his little hut, selling fruit which hangs from the eaves. The man waves at him, as if they are friends. A witness, he thinks. But he doesn't care. He has it all worked out. *Get in, get it done, get out.* He heads past the hotel where the turtles lay their eggs; the '70s hotel is tatty and in need of paint. Safiya once told him that she stayed here when she was a child; when it was glamorous. Safiya, he thinks. Safiya. He mustn't think of her again. Safiya is dead, dead, dead. He will never see her again.

He remembers it now, the curve of the road, the rise of the

hill, the place where the woman was bathing. He keeps driving until he reaches the church, and he drives slowly down the hill, looking around the open grass, the tall trees, the graveyard. He sees the Spiderman figure, and takes the turning on the right. He pulls in, puts his car into neutral and switches off the engine.

He gets out of the car, walks slowly up the muddy path. Rain must have fallen last night. When he reaches the top of the road, he sees the second house and a pink curtain blows in the doorway. The cow is tied to the mango tree, its rope stretched, and it is sleeping in the grass. From inside the house he can hear a radio. There are two steps, and under the house, he can see chickens running around. An old fridge is propped up, its door swung open, the wires exposed. Frigidaire. There are empty tins of powdered milk stacked; he wonders what they are used for.

The grandmother's round face appears in the doorway. She peeks around the curtain, checks him, and then looks again. She has grey hair scraped back in small plaits, held at the back in a small bun. Her big face is open, her dark eyes bulge; her lips are blueish, thick. She pulls the curtain back and he can see her nightdress. It is pink, knee-length. She does not wear a bra, and her breasts are big and heavy like bells. He has caught her by surprise, unprepared. She draws the curtain over her body.

She tips her head, 'Yes, mister. Wha' happen? Who you lookin' for?'

Martin does not speak to her. He walks with certainty towards the steps, and he pushes past her, into the little shabby house, the sitting room which has two chairs, a painting on the wall, a view onto the open space behind the house where sheets are hanging on a line. He looks quickly around.

The woman says, 'What is this? What happen here.' And he knows that she is about to scream, and he shows her, without trouble, without effort, the 9mm Glock in his hand, and her eyes are bigger now.

'Edward,' she says, and he thinks: so that is his name. That's his name. Then louder, 'Edward. Good God. Get up now. Please.'

She puts her hands up to her face and Martin steps quickly into the next room. There is a mattress on the floor and a long figure wrapped up in a sheet. The boy, suddenly awake, sits up. His bug eyes are frightened. Yes, he has seen the gun.

'Get up,' Martin says, his voice calm. 'Get up now.'

The woman says, 'Oh God, no, please don't hurt my baby.' And her voice is high, like a little squeal. 'He is a good boy.'

The boy is on his feet, his Y-fronts big and floppy, his skinny legs like two sticks. His hair is matted, lumpy.

'Come,' Martin says, 'put up your hands.'

He feels his power; his desire to bring terror.

The boy raises his hands; Martin points the gun to the living room.

'Move it, he says, and he pushes the barrel of the gun into the boy's back; it is moist with sweat. 'Move now.'

They shuffle into the small living room. Martin tells the woman to sit on the floor. She slumps down, puts her big legs in front of her, her droopy breasts rest on her waist. She looks terrified.

'I don't want to hurt you,' he says, and his voice is not unkind. 'I just don't want you to make a noise or go anywhere. You understand. I won't hurt you.'

The boy is looking around; he is thinking of making a run

for it, Martin is sure of it. If it were him, he would do the same. Martin keeps the gun pointed directly at him. His hands are steady, he is calm. He has never felt calmer in his life. He knows what to do, the two-step catch. He has opened the first safety catch. A solid click.

'I want you to tell your grandmother why I'm here.'

The boy is looking at the woman, looking at Martin. He might go for the window, more of a hole in the wall, it is right there.

'Tell your grandmother, how you came to our house and stole our money. Tell her what you did to my daughter.'

The boy is silent. He stares at Martin; his grandmother shakes her head, confused.

'Tell her,' Martin shouts now.

The radio plays a song from the '90s, an old song he recognises. 'Savage Garden'; yes, he remembers this.

'You did something to this man?' The woman's eyes are moist. 'What you did? You bring trouble here to us?' She starts to cry. 'What you did. Tell me. You were a good boy. I tell everybody you are a good boy.'

The boy is fidgeting; he looks around.

Martin fires the gun once, an astonishing explosion booms through the galvanise ceiling, and the grandmother screams; the boy is startled. Martin too is startled.

'Tell her what you did.'

Frightened now, the boy says, 'I rape she.'

'Say it again.'

He says, 'I rape she.'

To the grandmother, Martin says, 'When the police come, you will tell them what he said; that he raped my daughter.'

The woman says, 'Oh, God.' Then, 'It's true?'

The boy suddenly turns and hurls himself at the window and he tries to leap out into the yard. Without thinking too hard, Martin fires again, this time he hits the boy in the back of his leg, the slim, young upper thigh. And he falls back onto the floor, his head cracks against the side of the wall; he lands half-slumped, his face blank with terror and surprise. Mouth open, panting.

'Fock,' he says, 'fock yuh mudder cunt.'

Martin is shaking now, he knows what he has done. Blood spurts bright and fast from the hole in the boy's leg. And the boy is clutching it, rolling over now, his face twisted with pain, disbelief. Blood pours through his fingers and drips onto the floor.

Martin stands back, looking on at the scene as if it is nothing to do with him. The woman watches him with terror, then she looks at her grandson. Tears pour down her fat cheeks.

'Doh kill mah baby,' she says. 'Doh kill him.'

But Martin is not listening. He has already walked down the steps of the house, out into the yard, past the cow now standing up, and back into his car. A few people have come out into the street, and they are looking at him. He drives away towards the main road as if nothing has happened. *Don't sweat the small stuff. It's all small stuff.*

By the time he reaches the airport, he is calm, though he is also hot, and his clothes are wet with sweat. He leaves his car in the airport car park; the key out of sight on the wheel. In the bar, he buys cigarettes, a cold beer, and he waits. If the boy does as he expects, he will go with his grandmother to the hospital and have his wound dressed. The police will come and ask about the man from England who shot him. And the grandmother will deter them, just in case—*just in case*—it is true that Edward, her grandson, raped the Englishman's daughter.

The flight from London is due in early this afternoon. He tells the reservations clerk that he is travelling light. The departure lounge is full with in-transit passengers, waiting for the plane to be cleaned: Tobago passengers, sunburnt holiday makers with their bags of duty-free. He stands at the small bar. He is sweating, he has changed his shirt; he feels as if he has been on the road for days; it has been less than twenty-four hours. He needs to take a shower, eat something, rest.

The flight is called and the doors open. He sets off along the tarmac, the hot breeze blows and he makes his way to the tall steps of the aircraft. Two baggage handlers in orange boiler suits laugh about something as they drive under the wing. They are having a good time. Young men, enjoying themselves. At the top of the steps he looks back at the car park; he can see his car on the other side of the fence. Someone will notice it tomorrow or the next day. It is not his problem now.

He is immediately reassured by the air stewardess—her red uniform, the south London accent. The engine starts up and he is glad. Cool air pours down from above.

When they cruise to the end of the runway, he looks at the little houses, the trees, the tall grass, the beach at the other side, the water sparkling in the early evening light. Then the engine gets stronger, and the plane turns around. He leans back into the chair, feels the touch of the patterned fabric on his neck. It is all familiar. Then the sudden acceleration along the runway, and finally, lift off, the nose tilts to the sky.

He is going home.